The Dark Side of Destiny

A Collection of Thirteen Tales of Terror

By

April Campbell

INFINITY
PUBLISHING

Copyright © 2013 by April Campbell

ISBN 978-0-7414-9688-1

Printed in the United States of America

Published July 2013

INFINITY PUBLISHING
1094 New DeHaven Street, Suite 100
West Conshohocken, PA 19428-2713
Toll-free (877) BUY BOOK
Local Phone (610) 941-9999
Fax (610) 941-9959
Info@buybooksontheweb.com
www.buybooksontheweb.com

Dedication

Heavenly Father for giving me the talent to write.

Michael, David, and Kevin Veselsky, Georgeanne Grey, Luke Colehower, Tashianna, Juanita Campbell, Tiffany Campbell, and Grandmom Grey for the all the love and support any one person could ask for.

Meghan N. Lustica, Lena Mayer, Xavier Cotto-Rodriguez, Lauren Wall, and Katrina Green, for being yourself and being supportive.

In the loving Memory of

Evelyn Campbell

Papeh "Pete" Campbell

Willie Freeman

Justin Matthews and Hunter Straub

Thank You and I Love You All!

About the Warning Labels

This book contents disturbing sex scenes, pervasive language, strong graphic crude and very in depth violent, torture, sex events and other extreme topics because some topics offend people.

Destiny

Foreword

Destiny is defined as something that is to occur which is the powered and determined by the cause of events. People utter that we cannot choose our fate but we can choose our destiny but nothing cannot stop what is meant to be.

Ever wonder what your future may hold. Do you sit around thinking of the decisions that you made in your life. Do you wonder where your decisions will take you to and where you're going to end up at.

One night as you are walking home, a fog fills the street. Into the night a dark shadow lurks around the corner; waiting for his moment to take your soul. The midnight cold air is creeping in. The frozen darkness pricks your skin. The lights around you grow dim. The fog thickens as you continue to head home. It will be hours before dawn to come and rescues you. He is the Grim Reaper.

He is capable of very little emotion, only the brief pride and enjoyment of the lives lost by his hand. He was cursed to do this kind of work until the end of time. Most of the time, he enjoys his work, and thinks of clever and crafty ways to carry it out his task. He will track down all those that he must seek out and find.

He is the personification of death. He is a cloaked skeleton holding his scythe; a flash of silver under the black emptiness is ready and waiting for you to take your last breath. He is silently moving through the night. He glides by night, his destined victims for which he will seek. The Grim Reaper is on the loose and he is on the lookout for someone like you.

You duck into a dark alley and hide behind a dumpster. He is getting closer to you as his scythe scrapes the ground as he draws near. The echoes of his footsteps fall nearby your blood starts to freeze and tears run down your face. You try to stop the tears from falling hoping he won't hear them.

Deep inside your head your pleas for mercy will not keep him from doing what he needs to do. His ghostly shadows before you; only brings on misery your screams are echoing inside for help that only you can hear. Your eyes are closed hoping and wishing he would pass by you; all you can do is stand there and cry. The grim reaper is a heartless, emotionless spirit that has no pity for you. Your chest is quickly pounding. The air is calmer and you freeze with fright.

You are starting to get that weird feeling in the pit of your stomach wondering if the grim reaper is around the corner and is waiting for that moment to take you to your final destination. Thinking about what you have done in the past, is now beginning to haunt you. Oh, how one little decision can have drastic effects! Some by choice, some by force and some by reflex, even though some go unnoticed and some can lead to sorrow.

Now you cannot move. No one to warn or help you, it is already too late. You cannot resist him. He will steal your soul within a wink of an eye. His presence burns your heart and even through your bones. There isn't much time before he finds you. Your soul starts to burn. No one can save you, now. You cannot hide from the grim reaper because when your time is up, it's up! There are the dirty streets your bones shall lay there turning to dust.

Death is waiting for you. He is around every corner waiting to take your soul. When it is your time, how will the Grim Reaper take you? Will he takes your soul out in a very peaceful calmly matter or rip your soul out of your body by sweeping it up leaving you in excruciating pain as you slowly see your life slowly drifting away to hell.

Off to hell you go to be casted into a fiery oven, or a great furnace, where your pain would be much greater than that occasioned by accidentally touching a coal of fire, as the heat is greater. Your body will be laying there for a quarter of an hour. The pity are lying in is filled with fire, and what horror would you feel at the entrance of such a furnace!

How long would that quarter of an hour seem to you! After you had endured it for one minute, how overbearing would it be for you to think that you had to endure the other fourteen! What would be the effect on your soul, if you knew you must lie there enduring that torment to the full for twenty-four hours or how much greater would be the effect be? If you knew you must endure it for a whole year; and how vastly greater still, if you knew you must endure it for a thousand years!

Oh, then how would your hearts sink, if you knew that you must bear it forever and ever! That there would be no end to your misery! That after millions of years, your torment would be no nearer to an end, and that you will never see the end of your torment! Your torment in hell will be immensely greater than this illustration represents.

Tales from *The Dark Side of Destiny* will have you thinking about your own choices. Life is full of surprises and it can be a bitch that way!

The Dark Side of Destiny, I present to you this collective and ambitious work. Therefore, have a seat turn down the lights, and make yourself a cup of hot chocolate as you allow, "*The Dark Side of Destiny* take a hold of you.

The Dark Side of Destiny

A Collection of Thirteen Tales of Terror

Evil Within

In The Beginning, April 29, 1998

When, I saw him for the first time, I was amazed. I walked up to him; he looked at me into my eyes. He even pulled out my chair for me. I would love to get to know him better as I just smiled at him. I wanted to look deeper into his eyes and get lost in them. As I sat in front Ridley at the dinner table. I stared deep into his big blue eyes; I was hoping that he would be the one.

He wanted to know who exactly who I was, so I started to tell him. I am Nalia Franklin who is a brainy girl who is searching for love. I can charm you with my wit. I want to see if your intelligence can meet mine. My voice was soothing calm; it making him feel relax and all warm inside.

My syllables of words unspoken carriage of believing carousel of rainbows painted upon my heart become the seal of my energy. I am irresistible that's because I am able to manage looking pretty. I am a strong woman who is both soft and powerful.

I am a strong enough woman that he can see the fire burning in my eyes. It's not the strength of a powered muscle, but the fire that burns within my soul. The hand is feeding my soul. I am a strong woman that sees beyond the veil. This was place over my eyes when I was a child. I walk on clouds as a virtue they have become my cushion.

I stand between the two poles of darkness and the light I don't rely on the potency of the flesh that weakens me with every pore the power within my only authority so vivid and immense remains. I am a woman who is one who feels deeply and loves fiercely.

My tears flow just as abundantly as my laughter. I am not afraid to be afraid. I will take the compliments to heart and treat myself like the queen that I am. I am a woman who is equally visionary and decisive. I am able to hope when things look hopeless. I am both practical and spiritual. He seemed excited by who I was, that by the end of the night he had asked me out again.

● ● ●

July 1998

We were now dating for three months now. He was so perfect. I've never been the one to feel protective but he makes me feel that way. He is all I ever wanted. He is now a part of my heart and for us to be together, to never be apart. No one in the world can ever compare. We have so much more than I ever thought we would. I love him so much more than I ever thought I could. I promise to give him all I have to give. I'll do anything for him as long as I live.

In his eyes, I see our present and our future. I could tell just by the way, he looks at me I know that we will last. I hope that someday he will come to realize, how perfect we are together and ask me to marry him. A new love affair this was the first of many I have only dreamed about. Oh how I yearn for his warm embrace. I think about him all the time. I always wanted to be with him and do the things that lovers do together. Dreaming of him is all I do.

The fire I was feeling burned inside of me for his everlasting love. My feelings for him I just cannot hide it. I am always wishing, hoping, yearning, wanting, and needing him near me. Oh God, can you tell me why I want him so much. I can't pretend anymore.

I just want to give him all my love. I hope will never apart. Only time will tell how long this journey will go. I hope it lasts forever. When I haven't heard from him I start to have a panic attack. He always calls me at a perfect just when I need him the most. I hope that when he does calls me just to let me know that he was thinking about me. I always am thinking about him in the morning until I got to bed at night.

● ● ●

I had decided that he would be the one I wanted to lose my virginity too. Tonight was going to be the night. I was going to give myself to him. I knew that Ridley wanted to lie down with me just as bad as I wanted too. We met up for a late movie and we went back to my house.

There we stood in my living room. I was so afraid of being near him so close, but deep inside I yearned to feel his body pressed against me. When he came close to me and, made me unveil my hair. My long brown hair dropped from underneath the hat I was wearing, I was gazing into the floor. I was embarrassed to look up at him. When his exploring hands, tried to undo my bra, I began to shiver with an inexperience fear.

Within moments, his hands glided further down my skin. He pulled my arms into his and held on them tightly. My head lay against his head this felt so right. He slowly moved to the back of my neck with a soft touch. His breath on my neck had sent a chill down my spine. We were in unbreakable bond. Then he moved his lips to mine. Just kissing was getting me excited that I wanted to jump him now, but I was patient. His lips were soft and sweet. Now my heart commenced to skip a beat. My teeth press down and I lightly moan.

He whispered, "I love you" in the softest tone in my ear. He then took off my shirt while asking me if it was ok. I just nod lightly not knowing what to say. His body was pressed against mine; it was so hot and muscular. It felt wonderful. Then he slowly pulled down my pants, which he threw them on the floor. I could feel the love burning inside of me all the way down to my bones. He moved slowly making sure not to scare me and he kissed me some more while I stood there naked.

He touched me everywhere and I did the same. As he kissed me, I was getting wet. I couldn't help it, but to adore every inch of him. This was perfect! He held my body tighter. His touch was the sweetest thing that I have ever felt in my life.

I've loved him ever since we met. There was nothing, anyone could to do to ruin this moment. I can do. He means the world to me. I don't want to get rid of this love and feeling that we shared. He stretched me out on the couch beneath him. He climbed on top of me and went back to kissing me. After a while of us kissing and touching each other, I pushed him onto the floor.

I sat up atop his thighs, he didn't like that. Ridley grew wroth and sought to lay me again the ground beneath him. I wrestled with Ridley and sought to lay with him side by side, as equals. Then Ridley grew very wroth.

"This is bullshit," he yelled at me.

"Excuse me…what is wrong?"

"You belong on your back. If I wanted you to be on top I would have told you to!"

"What is wrong with me being on top?"

"You don't need to control everything!" Hell you like to remind me how you are such a strong person. I don't need you trying to fight me to be in control especially during sex." He said as he got up and put on his clothes.

"What's the big deal?"

"In my world, you belong either on your back or face down and ass up."

"Oh hell no...that is some bullshit! I wanted my first time having sex on top. You are full of shit if you think that I should be on my back! You are a fucking joke!"

"Fuck this...I'm out of here!"

I could hear my heart breaking. I wrapped a towel around and ran to the door as he jumped in his car. I yelled at him, "No, please don't leave." I was shock about the way he reacted when I climbed on top. I really didn't think it was a big deal.

●●●

A few days later

Ridley showed up at my house. He wanted to talk. He asked me to go for a ride. I agreed to go with him. I missed him so much. He didn't seem the same. Something about him was cold. He didn't even have the nerve to even open, the door for me like he used to. Well I guess chivalry had died a glorious death. It was slain in battle for the honor of some distressed damsel. Just because I wouldn't lie on my back. Well good riddance of a device created to control women under the guise of courtly grace and manners.

He wanted me back but he pushed me into a corner with ultimatums of loyalty and silence coupled with monogamy or else in exchange for lifestyle maintenance and random rendezvous. He wanted me to stop being independent and controlling and kiss his ass as if he was my God. I refused. He wanted me to offer up bits of myself to him when he felt the need to be in control. Of course, I couldn't have control over everything but the ultimatums he was giving me wasn't leaving me any choose but to tell him the fuck off. He wasn't trying to hear that. Boy was he piss. He ended up dropped me back off at my house.

My refusal sparked our goodbyes especially after I felt my morals were being compromised as my self-esteem was being demolished. Anything that was self-worth measured with a price tag attached, bartered and sold. I was done with him, so I thought.

Ridley, distraught and with no doubt he was angered by my insolent behavior. He still wanted me back. As much as I wanted him back, I had to stand my ground. At Ridley's request, his sister came over to my house "to talk". They pulled me outside and threatened me to see listen to Ridley and be his girl. They were going to kick my ass and make my life a living hell. I knew better than to trust anyone ever again, but his sisters were a bunch of thugs. I was scared to death of them. I held back from saying anything to them. In the way, I really wanted to do anything to get him back. Now I just need to try talk to him.

● ● ●

Two days later

Before I knew it, his sister started to spread lies across the town. The rumors were not true. Some were about me being a cold-hearted bitch and then some. I tried to hide from the rumors but both of my secrets and lies were being spread. The rumors were finally getting to me. I was tired of the rumors. Ridley's sister were having fun lying about me and putting my business out in the world for all to know.

People would see me out on the street and would ask me all kinds of questions about my life. I wished that people would respect my privacy. Why can't they just let me be and leave me alone? I just wanted to go on with my life. People were wondering why I had trust issues. They were all because of Ridley and his sisters. I gave up. I wanted to try to work things out with Ridley.

● ● ●

I had called his house to talk to Ridley but his sisters answered the phone laughing. They told me were I could find him. I put on my Sunday best and drove to get him back. Ridley was at a Drive-In movie in Burlington. I didn't care were I parked my car. I walked around the Drive-In to find him. When I find Ridley seating his car, he already had a new girl in his life. I was heart-broken even more.

Ridley's new girl Emily was not as some wicked femme fatale but as a naive and largely sexless as Eve from the Bible. Emily was a very obedient to ever Ridley's commands. She was such a good girl. I became the other woman, the one that never gets the guy. I am all his lustful thoughts dreamed up in one.

●●●

The Rage

I was Emily's nightmare in a can. She will never give him all the needs I can. I could love him better than she can. He will never leave her and that was a fact. She had his family and his past. I am the woman who keeps coming in last. I know I am not everyone's biggest fan but I loved him the way he really wanted me to and she can never truly do for him.

I missed the way he looked at me with love in his blue eyes. I love the way he touched me and hold me when I cried. I missed the way he kissed my hair or when he kissed me just right unexpectedly and the look that showed me that he cared about me.

I can only dream about the way he touched my hand or how I suddenly I felt like all the love in the world was next to me. I thought of someone this wonderful can't be real. Was it was too good to be true? I guess it was. Sitting around my house all I could think about how he would hug me, I fit perfectly in his arms. I could feel my love for him was turning into hate, now.

I remember the way, he would call me, his snuggle bunny, and enchant me with his charm. I loved the way his adoring hands touch my heart so intimately. I knew most of his hidden secrets and his holiest dreams. I hated thought about his strong legs, arms and rosy face. I miss him so much that it hurts. It hurts so much that I scream and cry for hours.

My heart just aches for him for his touch, his warmth, his love. I miss him more than he could ever imagine. Right from the very start, I keep forcing myself to think that this was just a dream.

●●●

Now I keep asking myself why we were apart. Why I wasn't I good enough for him? Why wasn't I enough for him? Maybe I should've changed just for him. Why couldn't he be who I thought he was? I tried to tell myself that I had no problem making that call to let him go. I had to deal with the fact that he wasn't mine anymore. I have to deal with the fact that I couldn't see him all the time.

The reason doesn't seem good enough I guess, or maybe it seems like there should be more to it. The days grow longer and my heart grows colder. I am becoming more evil and seductress person. Much more so than Emily will ever be with him, I was becoming the personification of female sexuality and didn't give two shits what people thought about me.

My mind has become more unstable than before. I guess once again, I'm on my own. Normally that doesn't bother me, but now it does. I guess because I feel as though, in some way, I lost the closest person to me. I lost so much. I have so little now. With each passing day, I miss him more and more. I have lost more than I can explain, but I guess it's good to know that at least one person has gotten all of my love.

The love we had for each other, others will not feel completely in a lifetime. Just to clear the thoughts in my head I started to sleep with any type of man I could sink my teeth into. I was becoming more and more angry at Ridley with each passing day. Everyday a thought of Ridley would ran though my head or an imaged would pop up in my head about him like a bad movie. Every man I met was not even close to him.

I'm jealous of his friends because they talk to him every day. They get to hear his voice. I am so jealous he moved on with his life and pushed me in the back of his head as a faded memory. Sometimes I wish I could be his bed. I will always be jealous because I love him. He was mine and I wanted him back. Being jealous just means I cared about him and I didn't want anyone to take my place but of course, he found someone else.

●●●

Six months later

When I look back, I saw a wise and cool person. I would gaze with silly sickness on that fool. I gave him all my love I was the fool. I have a big bag of jealousy sitting on my shoulders. Anyone can see what it does to me every day. I have never been the jealous type until I saw Ridley with her. Jealousy has taken over me.

Jealousy made me into a completely different person I thought I would never become. I just don't trust anyone around him because I know how special he is to me. At the same time, I don't want anyone else to discover how much I still love and care about him. I won't stop until I have him back in my life. I would do anything to get Ridley back in my life.

All I wanted was a second chance. I understood that's wasn't going to be easy to do. I couldn't even get him to give me a glance when he I saw him on the street. I wanted him to know, that will always love him. I see what I did wrong. I wanted to take back everything that went wrong between us. I loved him too much to lose him to Emily. He was the best thing in my life and he made my life come alive. Every time I think of him, tears just come rolling down my face and I can't stop them either.

●●●

That Christmas Eve

I was lonely. A good friend of his and mine had invited me to an all-adult Christmas party in the mountains. Since I had no one in my life, I decided to go. When I arrived, I headed straight for the kitchen to get me a few shots of whiskey. Just then, I heard the news that Ridley was coming without Emily. I ran to my car to get a few things to make myself more noticeable. I had a few tricks up my sleeve. I became the wolf in sheep's clothing.

I dazzled up my smile. My teeth were whiter than snow. I had the latest hairstyle. I stood in the kitchen with a drink in my hand. I tried to not show excited I was. I waited patiently for his arrival. Twenty minutes later, the door rang. I jumped up little a fat kid in a candy store. Someone answered the door wide enough for me to see who it was. Of course, it was Ridley. He walked in and greeted everyone as he headed to the kitchen.

There he stood in front of me; his blue eyes had a glow. As he stared at me, my heart started skip. Then as if on cue, he commenced to talk to me in his sweet voice. I almost forgot how sexy he was. With a flirting wink charmingly he said, "Can I get you a drink?" Without giving it much thought I nodded my head yes. After a few rounds, we started to get cozy. My heart gently pounded.

"You're the sweetest girl I have ever met. A gem and a pearl that I deeply respect, I miss you."

It was music to my ears. I was floating on air. It felt like we were picking up from where we left off at, but I had other plans. I knew that once this night was over I was just going to be a one-night fling that he finally got to fuck. Leaving me would be his fatal flaw.

He was underestimating the seething rage that swept through my heart. It was being erased by all the rationale and calm eradicating logic I once had.

The rage that fueled me was the reason that was driving me to plot against him. He had pushed me to that breaking point of no return.

"Excuse me I have to go to the men's room don't move," he says as he tried to get up out of the chair.

●●●

I almost felt bad for what was about happen to him tonight. Now it was time to put my plans into motion. While he was in the bathroom, I slipped a Roofie it into his drink. It contained half a dose of GBH and the other was a dose of Ecstasy. Together, the dosages would not knock Ridley out; just give him a mellow buzz, a feeling of being disconnected from what was going on. I was hoping it would also make him horny and make him highly suggestible.

I will wonder one day whether if I would serious doubt my intents. This ruthless inclination of my revengeful desire to destroy what I couldn't have. I'm twisted its true, and it's all because of him. All the hateful things you said, and what you've put me through, fucking asshole. I'm evil indeed, and it's all because of me.

I wanted to just to be loved, why couldn't he just understood that. If I started a new relationship then I know for a fact I would have taken out my pain on someone else. It would be pointless to do so. Ridley is the only thing I know but for tonight, I will give him back all my pain. These twisted evil ways of mine, are all I have to show. I'm twisted and evil, through my flesh down to the bone and I do twisted evil things.

I headed upstairs and waited for him to come out of the bathroom. As soon as he came out of the bathroom, I give him his spiked drink. He had drunk it down in one sip. I began to kiss him. He didn't fight back either. I pushed him into the closed bedroom. My wicked passion bursting with love and hate, this will be my last action with Ridley.

● ● ●

The Dis-advancement

I closed the door behind me. He had laid back onto the bed. We began to undress each other. Then Ridley tried to stand up and suddenly he fell back down onto the bed. He commenced to complain about his head began to swim as the drugs took effect. I just gave him a devilish grin. I wasn't going to tell him about what was going to happen. His legs were wobbly. The started to tell me his tongue was thick in his mouth and that his whole body was tingling in a strange way. He quickly sat back down on the bed.

"I don't feel good," he said pitifully.

"Oh you're fine, Ridley, just fine," as I reassured him.

"I feel hot," he told me.

"Let me see, do you have a fever?" I put my palm on his forehead and applied a little pressure. Ridley leaned back and rested his head against the pillows while shutting his eyes.

"Yeah, you're really feel warm, sweetheart. Is your heart beating fast?"

"Oooh, God yes," he said.

"Do you want me to stop?" As we were making out, I dig my fingernails into his chest.

"No"

"We'd better cool you down. Let's get you out of those clothes."

Just as I pulled off his pants with one swift movement exposing his erected penis, he passed out. That wasn't going to stop me. As he was passed out, I started to take advantage of him. I bent my legs and knelt on the floor, taking Ridley's hard cock between my lips for the very first time. He waked up and moaned a little bit.

He never said anything. He just laid there looking down at my head bobbed back and forth. I guess the feeling of my tongue sliding along his cock was making him excited. Reaching down, Ridley stopped me, and asked me to stand up. He didn't want to cum just yet. He was still having trouble standing but he gathered himself.

He then picked me up in both arms and placed me gently onto the bed. He then removed what little clothing he still had on, and climbed onto the bed next to me. We kissed as he positioned himself between my legs, and I closed my eyes as I felt his hard body pressed against my delicate skin.

He started to slide cock into my pussy, I held my breath, and only letting out the air once more as Ridley picked up the pace. Then we kissed passionately. We made love for another hour, before Ridley finally passed out again. I left him on the bed. I got dress. I slipped out of the back door without anyone seeing me. I headed home and went to bed with biggest grin on my face.

● ● ●

The Next Morning

Yes, I did it and there wasn't a damn thing he was going to do about it. I enjoyed having sex with him while was he all drugged up, passed in and out.

I will be one whore in a billion that he has fucked. I was fine with that. What had happened last night, it all wasn't just a dream, had nothing to do with love.

It was strictly sex and getting mine. I did know one thing. I would never tell anyone what had happened, because even if I did, who would believe me anyway. Yeah, I wanted to let Emily know that every taste of me has a lingering residue on him. Every technique I performed yesterday, it was learning in my secret sanctuary.

●●●

Three month later

I was happy and I knew all the time I kept dreaming it would come true. An answer to a prayer that was sent from above. I find out I was pregnant. I spent my days dreaming of what Ridley's and my baby was going to look like. As I wait to see its face. I dreamed of a better future for the baby and myself. I didn't know if it would be a girl or boy. I knew it would be my dearest joy. A bundle of joy to relieve worries and strife, a breath of heaven's blessing was knocking on my door.

A completely new meaning of love to explore for even in the womb, our hearts will learned to kept and cherish. The bond that sways to it, I promised of joy of caring for a little angel and a lifetime to enjoy. I promised and prayed to do my best for the child. As much as I wanted to tell Ridley and others about my secret, I couldn't.

What a miracle it was, though it was not here yet. The thought of having Ridley's baby wiped every hurtful thing I had about Ridley at this time. The bliss that comes with the idea of having his baby filled my mind every day. Indeed the baby was a miracle, a spark of God's enduring love.

● ● ●

Friday the 13th at 3:15 AM

A storm was raging that night, when I had to give birth. I was going to give birth in my house. My mother and few of her midwife friends were all gathered in my room to help me with the delivery of my baby. They were there out of curiosity than good will.

They had all heard the rumors that I was involved in witchcraft, and had sworn I would give birth to a little devil. They were all trying to figure out who was the father. I didn't dare tell them who he was, not even my mother.

Tension mounted when at last the baby arrived. It was a relief. It was a surprise when the baby was born completely normal. What a tiny little miracle he was. It all started the moment he opened his eyes, I was in shock, a boy, what a surprise.

His two little feet wiggle, just as with every tender giggle. I counted his ten little fingers, ten little toes. He was something so new to me, but I was so proud to have a piece of Ridley and me in one that I now I could hold him forever in our child. He would always be mine. I named him Ryder Franklin.

● ● ●

From Ryder's Birth

I listened to his heartbeats when he was sleeping. It was my goal to make Ryder happy and good person. He had the rose-red cheeks I have ever seen. His adorable blue eyes and a button nose resembled his father's! I gave him so many hugs and kisses with love to wrap Ryder with. He had the sweetest smile that filled my heart with so much delight.

I loved to watch him sleep at night, in my arms. He was my little angel, who had came into my life for me to love. He was always by my side as he grew up. He filled my life with so much pride.

● ● ●

13 years later

However, an over a few years later, before the public eyes, he began to slowly go through changes but the funny part he only went through these changes at night. By the age, thirteen he grew at an enormous rate, becoming taller than a man and changing into a beast, which resembled a dragon, with a head like a horse, a snakelike body and bat's wings.

By day, he resembled a 13 year old boy and at night this creature. He was still handsome no matter what he looked like. I still loved him even more.

● ● ●

Revenge

As soon as he was full-grown and old enough, I decided to tell Ryder the truth about his father and his family. Ryder didn't want to have anything to do with his father. He hated his father dearly and wanted to seek some kind of revenge on Ridley and his family. We put together our heads together and thought of a plan.

So together, we brought a wrath down on Ridley's family. We went around killing any children that were connected to Ridley. I took advantage of any of the men in his family while they were a sleep. There were some I didn't have sex with I just killed them. With those I liked, I had sex with them and used their semen to replenish my own offspring.

My son would sneak into the woman's homes and beat on every woman who was connected to Ridley with his thick, forked tail and with a harsh cry; he would fly through the chimney and vanished into the night. Once Ryder and I was finished killing everyone in Ridley's family we moved.

In the end, I gave both to three more children that was from Ridley's family. Ridley and I settled with my children in New Jersey. I knew my son would be unique. He has made me proud. Well now, I'm glad I didn't end up with Ridley. He was a jerk; at least him and family made beautiful children together. I guess I can say I had the last laugh…ha-ha.

A Dark Secret

In Bensalem, Pennsylvania

Life isn't always what it seems anymore. My name is Raven Penton. I am a 25-year-old biracial have African American and half-Italian woman living in Pennsylvania. I am up here because of my dad. My father lives with a biker gang and was known as the "Preacher."

He had personality but the minute someone would cross him, that was the end of Mr. Nice Guy. He was well respected and at the same time, people were terrified of him. He was not the type of man you wanted to piss off.

He was a paranoid schizophrenic in a drug user. Heroin was his staff of life. My father died on his couch, a gun in his hand. The body lay undiscovered in his house for at least a week. The cause of his death was a drug overdose. I really do not know my father that well, only from what people tell me about him and what I can remember about him. He left me the house. I ended up moving into the house. There were so many bullet holes in the walls. The floors were covered with old newspapers and syringes. This house was a mess.

● ● ●

Since I have lived in the house, strange things have happened to me. I have had hallucinations of women coming through the wall, blood pouring out their necks. There are times I think I see my father in the house talking to me. I can even go shopping without getting paranoid that people are out to get me. I wear my MP3 player just to drown out the voices I keep hearing. Before I stop socializing with my friends, they had encouraged me to seek medical treatment.

My nightmares are so bad, I'm afraid to go to sleep at night. I dream I killed people and then eat their body parts. When I wake up, I'm sweating so badly my sheets and bedclothes are soaked. The taste of the victim's blood is on my lips. I hunger to kill. Something is wrong, locked in the deepest abyss of my soul. I'm spinning out of control like a train about to derail. I know that if I do not get the help I need, I would end up like my father.

● ● ●

After some searching, I finally found a doctor in Bensalem, named Michael Jones. I gathered my courage and called his office to make an appointment. That day I was very nervous. I felt that what I would learn was not going to be good. I open the office door in there, behind a wooden desk sat a man with dark wavy hair.

He wore glasses over his hazel blue eyes and had a goatee. His figure was trim and firm. He got up from is that as I close the door, walked toward me and extended his hand. "Hello, Raven." His hands were hard and calloused, like the laborer's hands and he didn't wear wedding rings. "Come over here and have a seat. Tell me what brings you here today."

He put me at ease with his nice smile and kind eyes. Before I knew it, the hour was up and I had made an appointment to come back next week. On the way out, I try to think of what we had talked about, but for the life of me, I couldn't remember. All I could think about was what I wanted to do with his body enfolded in mine.

● ● ●

One week later

The week flew by quickly. I dressed in a sexy, but casual outfit. He greeted me, saying, and "Welcome, Raven, I am glad you have decided to come back." I thought to myself, me too, and I smiled.

All business, he walked towards the couch. "Raven, come sit down on the couch. I want to try something to see if you can find out why you are having these dreams. We are going to try hypnosis. Maybe we can get to the root of your problems."

"Will you be able to tell me what's going on?" I asked.

"I can try," he said. "Are you ready, Raven?"

"I nodded. As ready as I'm going to get."

"Good. Let me get my notebook and turn my phone. Then we can start."

He said the chair. "Please lie down the couch and close your eyes. Clear your mind and relax while you listen to me. Now imagine a relaxing sensation in your feet." His soft voice described the relaxation of every part of my body until he reached my head.

He continued. "With each breath, you become more relaxed. The sensation is running through your entire body. Every muscle and nerve are relaxed. As I count down from ten, your body will become light and your mind will empty of all thoughts. You will drift into soothing tranquility."

As he counted down, I felt myself slipping away. "Raven, can you hear me?"

"Yes", I answered.

"Very good, he said. Now I need you to go back to the earliest time that you can remember your dreams. Can you recall your first dream? Tell me everything you see."

● ● ●

"I'm in the house," I said.

"Raven, I need to look at the house and tell me what else you see."

"I'm in a beautiful house. To floors cover with a nice, expensive carpet, faded. There's a border of polished floorboards around the edge of the carpet. The walls are papered with an elaborate total pattern. The background is red, blue, and green, overprinted with colors of cream and tan. Their stylized leaf and floral patterns was amazing to look at. Paintings by James Baker Pyne hang on the walls. The sitting room is crowded with furniture. There's a beautiful fireplace off to the side, but there's some kind of fabric that drakes dangerously from the mantle."

"Raven, go look in a mirror. I want you to look at yourself and tell me what you look like. What do you see it?"

"There is a full size matter. I look at myself. I'm a white middle age man with a black mustache. I'm wearing a black silk top hat on my head, a black coat, and speckled trousers. There is a long black cape draped over my arms."

"How tall are you?"

"I am about 5 feet 6 inches."

"Tell me more, Raven."

"I have a doctor's black leather bag in my hand."

"Raven, can you tell me about the bag and what's in it?" Doctor John asked.

I kneel down to open the bag and see a gold plate with the initials "JW, MD." Inside, there is a mahogany brass bound case. I open the case. It is lined with blood red velvet. The case holds scalpels, tenaculum, aneurism needles on a wire tie with an ivory handled Mott's aneurism suture set, a painted brass bone brush, and other cranial surgery (trepanning) instruments, including a Hey saw and raspatory.

The elevator contents of the upper tray include olive forceps, trephine, elevator, scalpel, spare saw blade, scissors, and chisels. There is a set of Liston's amputation knives, including Carlin and metacarpal saw. I list all these for Doctor Jones.

"Raven, how come you know these insurance so well?" he asked.

"I don't know."

"Is there windows near you? If so, look outside and tell me if you see anything familiar."

"I see a tall clock tower and it looks very familiar."

"What do you think it looks like, Raven?"

"Big Ben. I'm in London."

"Now Raven, is there anyone there with you?" Doctor Jones asked.

"Yes."

"Do you know this person?"

"It's J W." As I make a statement, I see myself transforming into a completely different person. I am no longer Raven Penton. Doctor Jones looked up at the change in Raven's voice. It had deepened.

"What is your full name?"

"If I tell you I would have to slit your throat."

"What do you do for a living?" Doctor Jones asked.

"I'm a doctor. Who am I talking to?" Raven asked.

"I am Doctor Michael Jones."

"Why am I here talking to you?"

"Do you know Raven?"

"No and yes…maybe, why…should I really I know this person?"

"Raven is a patient of mine. Raven is here to seek some help because she is having bad dreams. I am trying to find out what is going on in her head."

"Can I tell you a secret, Doctor?"

"Yes, JW."

"I know who Raven is because I live within her."

"What do you mean?" Doctor Jones asked.

"I'm a part of Raven."

I would like to know how about you, JW. We'll find out if you're just a bad dream or character Raven may have created and brought into her world.

Raven stirred. "I may have to kill you, if I tell you everything." Even if you try, they will find you. This is a different era and things have changed, Doctor Jones said.

"Well that's a chance I'm willing to take."

"Where do you work, JW?"

"I operated in the East End, White Chapel, for a variety reasons. The smoke and the stinking gas fumes choke the streets so badly that at times it is not even possible to see your hands your own hands in front of your face. They call this smog, pea soupers, because of the greenish color. They're so many ill people and the East End. This is a poor area and many people need my help."

"JW, can you tell me what day it is and about the weather?"

"It's a Friday, and there is a thunderstorm. I can see a quarter of the moon as it rises to the dark sky."

"So, what are you up to today?" Doctor Jones asked.

●●●

Re-calling a Memory

"I am working. I see my first patient. She is of short stature and average weight, with dark eyes and hair. She is perfect. No one will miss her. As I approach her, I offer her money for sex. We are walking into the back alley. She thinks we are going to engage in sex. As she turns away, I pull out Liston knife. I raise my hand with the knife to her throat and with a precise of a surgeon. I cut her throat. I tried to cut off her head, but it doesn't happen.

I placed her body on the ground. I left her skirt. I am surprised the rotten parts and very clean. Her soft white skin becomes translucent. I can see her blue veins as her pulse fades away. I cut out pieces of her bladder and her fanny and pull down her skirt to cover what I did.

Putting on my gloves, I leave her lifeless is a body is a front of the gate stable entrance in Buck's Row on that back street of Whitechapel, two hundred yards from the London hospital. I am not satisfied. I enter my carriage and go home for the night."

"Tell me JW, how did the killing make you feel?" Doctor Jones asked.

"It felt...thrilling! It is a rush unlike any other."

"Unlike any other?" Doctor Jones reported. Tell me more.

"This wasn't the first whore I slashed."

"Tell me more about the others."

"My first whore didn't mean anything to me. She was a practice run. I even tried to cut her in a different direction, but I had a hard time cutting straight through. Besides, she was too easy to catch."

"What made this one different from the first one?"

"I was asked to take care of some business from a "higher power."

"Higher power?" Dr. Jones looked puzzled.

"None of your business."

"I apologize, were there others?"

"Yes."

"Tell me more about them," Dr. Jones said.

"Damn drunken whore. This one should be good. I make her a glass of absinthe that was laced. I have my driver pull up to her and put my head out the window just a little bit. Do you fancy a drink miss? How much money do you charge for a moment with you?" I asked.

She turns around and stumbles towards me. "Yes Sir, I would like a drink. If you want to get a quick shaggy, it will be one pound.

High priced, I thought, but one pound it is. I stepped out of my carriage and hand her a drink. We walk arm in arm to a more secluded area. When am I going to get my money?" she asked. As you give me what I asked for I said softly in her ear.

She leads me to the backyard of 29 Hamburg Street, Spitafields. This one is about five feet tall. She has a pallid complexion with blue eyes and dark wavy hair. She was coughing a lot. I think that she is suffering from chronic disease of the lungs, perhaps, tuberculosis.

I move swiftly, forcing her back against the fence. Wrapping my hands around her neck, I strangle her. The word, murder, slips out of her mouth. I hope no one hears her. I fear that I will be disturbed or caught in the act, as I hurriedly lay her on the ground and cut her throat. She dies, finally, and the blood runs red in the filth-filled gutter. I cut her abdomen, but that doesn't satisfy my lust

I continue to cut and remove her intestines, throwing them from the body. I reach in and grasp the first thing my hand touches, her liver. It is still warm and I know I am going to enjoy this for supper. I place it in my bag. I take time to search her. I remove certain articles from her and position them in a ritualistic manner at her feet to send a message. I love the pretty necklace I have given her, the red ring of blood that begins on the left and ends on the right side of her neck.

The whore has bled like a pig all over my leather apron. Unfortunately, I have no choice but to take it off and leave it there. I can't be seen walking back to the street with blood dripping down into my favorite shoes. After all, I am a respectable doctor." He paused.

"What did you do then?" Dr. Jones asked.

"I went back home and decided to write a letter to the newspaper. I think this is going to be fun."

"What does the letter say?"

"It says,

17th September 1888

Dear Boss,

Now they say I am a Lid. When will they learn Dear Old Boss! You and me know the truth *don't we. Lusitania can look forever he'll never find me but I am rite under his nose all the time. I watch them looking for me and it gives me fits ha ha. I love my work and I shouldn't stop until I get buckled <u>and even then</u> watch out for your old pal Jacky.*

Catch me, if you can!

<u>*Jack the Ripper*</u>

Sorry about the blood still messy from the last one. What a pretty necklace I gave her."

"Why did you write the letter?" Dr. Jones asked.

"For fun"

"Aren't you afraid of them?"

"No, they couldn't catch me."

"Why are you not afraid of them catching you?"

"I am just too good for them. I am like a ghost. I slip by them to do my deed. They act as if they are going to miss them. I am doing them a favor, cleaning up the filth the runs up and down our street and alleys."

Dr. Jones thought for a minute. "So, what are you up to next?"

"I think I want to send them another letter to give them a clue. Would you like to hear it?

Doctor Jones nodded.

25th of September 1888

Dear Boss,

I keep hearing the police have caught me but they won't fix me just yet. I have laughed when they clever and talk about being on the right track. That joke about Leather Apron gave me real fits. I am down on whores and I shouldn't quit ripping them until I do get buckled. Grand work the last job was. I gave the woman no time to squeal. How can they catch me now? I love my work and want to start again.

You will soon hear of me with my funny little games. I saved some of the proper red stuff in a Ginger beer bottle over the last job to write with but it went thick like glue and I can't use it. Red ink is fit enough I hope. Ha. Ha. The next job I do I shall clip the lady's ears off and send to the police officers just for jolly wouldn't you. Keep this letter back till I do a bit more work, and then give it out straight. My knife's so nice and sharp and I want to get to work right away if I get a chance. Good luck.

Yours truly,

Jack the Ripper

Don't mind me giving the trade name.

P.S. It wasn't good enough to post this before I got all the red ink off my hands curse it. No luck yet. They say I'm a doctor now. Ha. Ha.

"Would you like me to call you Jack?" Dr. Jones asked.

"Yes."

"Well, Jack, I have to let you go. I need for you to let Raven come back to me."

"Ahhhhhhhhhh, don't you want to hear more?"

'Yes, I do, but I need to talk to Raven."

"Well, see you later."

●●●

"Raven, Can you hear me?"

"Yes"

'Good, is Jack there with you?"

"No, she answered"

"Now, Raven, I'm going to bring you out of hypnosis. I am going to count down from one to three. When I get to three, you will wake up feeling refreshed. You won't remember anything that Jack and I talked about."

"One...becoming more alert."

"Two...getting ready wake up."

"Three...wake up."

"Wow!" I looked up at Doctor Jones. His face was flushed and sweat was poured downhill his face. He looked nervous or scared to death. I was afraid to find out what had scared him so bad.

"How do you feel, Raven"

"I feel more relaxed. You don't look so good, though. Did you find out anything?" I asked.

"Yes, I did, he said. "You sound like you're having some past-life recalls. What I have done for you a Past Life Therapy is utilized clinical Hypnotherapy de-hypnosis. It allows the unconscious to experience past-life traumas or emotionally charged events, in order to resolve any unconscious survival-based scripts that could be negatively affecting your present health, behaviors, or quality of life."

"Survival-based scripts?" I was puzzled.

"I'm sorry. It means that you. May have developed ways of coping with traumas or bad events in your early life that are not the best choices to use now." he said.

"Is there anything else?" I asked anxiously

"You do have some signs of paranoid schizophrenia. We can get you back on the right track and help with you and your hallucinations. I am going to give you a prescription called Aripipzrazole. You are to take this pill once a day. It may take a few days to a week for them to fully kick in, so give it some time."

"What kind of decals am I having?" I asked

He didn't answer the question. "The medicine may cause some side effects, so if you feel lighthearted, dizzy, experience blurred vision or vomiting, and call me. I can prescribe something else. I need to get more details in order for me to understand what is going on. I want to analyze my notes, so when you come back I can tell you what I have gathered so far. We need to make another appointment. I want to see you again in a week."

Great, I thought. He's acting a little strange. It sounded far-fetched that he couldn't tell me all the details of my hypnosis. I left it alone for now. The next time I saw him, I'd raise hell if he didn't tell me. We settled on following Wednesday. As I walked out of his office, I didn't feel right I felt like part of me was missing.

● ● ●

Later that evening

I drove to the pharmacy. Waiting for my prescription, I heard a faint voice. I looked around, but nobody was in sight. Finally, the pharmacist called my name. As soon as I left, I took one of the pills.

● ● ●

Monday morning

In spite of the pills, I keep hearing the voice in my head. Monday came and I had to go to work. I put music on the CD while I got ready for work. At work, the voice was still haunting me, teasing me, begging me to.

Today was the day I had decided to ask my boss for a promotion to manager. I figured that after all this time busting my ass I should get the position. Instead, she said. Oh, I'm sorry. I have enough people in the manager's position but it's good that you learned so many managerial skills.

I have learned through times more than most of the managers here. I'm the only one she calls a floater, bouncing between different departments in this damn store without complaining. I felt very small. I actually thought about how it would feel to cut the bitch from throttle and groin. Just the idea of cutting her up was arousing.

It would be very refreshing. I fought the urge during my shift. When I left, I was still pissed off and at the same time very aroused. I felt like every video I watched and not every book I read on management mattered. I had done more than my share when others didn't even finish. I felt like I wasted those ten months trying to get something that she will never give me.

●●●

After work

The conversation replayed in my head like a bad movie I couldn't stop. I went home and tried to relax, but the more I tried, the more I deliver the day. The voice was getting louder and louder. I tugged on my hair and screamed at the top of my lungs as loud as I could hope it would go away.

I picked up the pill bottle; bur threw it across the room. They weren't helping me. The walls were closing in on me. I called Dr. Jones to tell him what was going on, but the voice in my head was so loud I could barely make out what he was saying. I had to get out.

I got in my car and drove to a liquor store for some vodka to wash away my thoughts. The voices were louder. I drove out of the parking lot, not knowing where I was going or what I was doing. I thought I was on the wrong side of the road and the car was heading straight towards me. I couldn't story the car. I closed my eyes and held tightly to the steering wheel. All I could hear was the breaking the glass and metal crackling around me.

People were talking as they gathered around my car. Someone yelled into the window that no longer had any glass in it. "Miss, are you okay? Can you hear me?

I didn't answer. I was in a daze, barely able to open my eyes. I heard the sound of sirens. Someone reached in and put a brace around my neck. Then I heard a saw whining. They were cutting me out of my car. The last thing I remembered was being slowly pulled out of the car.

● ● ●

Flashback

I couldn't wake up. I am in London walking in the back streets. I have no control over my body. I am no longer Raven. I have become a faint voice in my own head, as someone else takes over my mind.

I search the streets and alleyways to find myself a whore. Then I take her where the lights are low. I strangle her and push her to the ground. I slash her throat before she loses consciousness. I am interrupted when a carriage goes by. It stops and the driver looked towards me. I feel his eyes penetrating the darkness. I know he sees me and that adds to thrill of the kill.

The lust is stronger. How satisfying! The carriage moves quickly forward. I assume he is going to get the police, but I won't be here. I gather my things, leaving her corpse on the ground in Dutfield's Yard, while I slip quietly into the dark alleys off Berber Street. I make my way back to my carriage.

My lust is not yet satisfied. I need more.

In the distance, I see my next victim. I have my driver stop the carriage far from her. I slip out and into the darkness. The driver moves the carriage down the streets and waits. The squared area is dark, ill lit surrounded by houses and shops.

There is hardly any movement on the street. It is still too early for people to be about. She walks right by me. I jump out of the dark and force the white's head back in an effort to expose the throat. She has no time to react to the feel of the knife as it slits her throat from left to right.

The air is like a cool summer breeze, as I breathe the scent of a newly bloomed rose from the blood flowing out of the wound. I hold her head away from my body. Laying her gently on the ground, I am finally satisfied.

Her body lies on pavement in full view of all the businesses and residences. I have ripped this one apart. I have satisfied the lust of frustration. She was perfect. I take some of her organs for sovereign. My hands are soiled with mud and her filthy blood.

I rip off her apron to wipe my hands, but the smell is heavenly and I want it to last. After I am done, I walk halfway up the road from her lifeless body in Mitre Square in the City of London. I write a note for the police on the wall.

"The Juwes are not the men to be blamed for nothing."

I write in chalk, not the bitch's blood, and leave her bloody apron there.

In October, I decided to write the Boss another letter

I was not coddling dear Boss when I gave you the tip, you'll hear about Saucy Jack's work tomorrow double event this time number one squealed a bit couldn't finish straight off. Ha not the time to get ears for the police. Thanks for keeping last letter back till, I get to work again.

Jack the Ripper.

I sit at the table, ink up my pen, in the gathering dark I write from the hottest hell. I write just to tell the police to stay awake.

I'll be out tonight

I love writing letters to the stupid police. This letter should be good. Of course, George Lusitania may not like this one, but I do. On October 14th I send a letter to George with half a kidney. I hope he enjoys it I think. I will address this one a little different. "From Hell." That has a nice ring.

Mr. Lusk,

Sorry I send you half the Kidney I took from one woman and preserved it for you the other piece I fried and ate it was very nice. I may send you the bloody knife that I took it out with if you only wait a while longer signed

Catch me when you can Mister Lusk.

● ● ●

I open my eyes and look around. Everything looks so different. There's a clipboard at the end of my bed. I reach for it and through the notes. My name is Raven Penton, and it is October 31, 2007. I am in a hospital. It has been over a hundred years since I committed my last murder.

I am wearing a weird white dress with the back open. I look at my body. I have breast. Well, at least they are nice. Now I am in a woman's body. How ironic that I have been reincarnated as a woman. It will take some time to get used to living my life as a woman. Even though I am no longer "Raven", I am still Jack and I am not planning to tell anyone. This may actually be fun.

I lie back down on the bed with a devilish grin on my face as a doctor and nurse walk into my room. They start to check my vital signs and tell what has happened. I don't hear them.

I am amazed how different this hospital is compared to London's hospital in the 1800's. The police and even the person who was involved in the accident come visit me. I learn that it was the other driver's fault. We decide that once I get home and feel up to it, we are all going to meet and straighten things out.

After everything calms down and the doctor is sure I am well enough to be released, I call my new mother. She picks me up from the hospital later that night. She is very kind to me. I glimpse myself in the mirror. I can see how I look like her. She makes sure I have settled for the night.

●●●

Back at the house that night

Then she goes to sleep in one of the bedrooms. I sit by the window with a cup of tea and watch the rain. I look through my stuff, or shall I say Raven's stuff to learn about her, so I can become her. I even find a Dr. Jones number so I can make an appointment with him.

The storm finally abates and fog rolls in it reminds me of my last kill. It was the best and last. One they will always remember. I remember wanting to be patient with this one. I have to make sure this the most gruesome and perfect murder I have ever committed.

I see the door. On the left side there are two windows perfectly angled and broken. I reach through and unbolted the door. I slip into her room as sleeps. I try to strangle her, but she puts up a fight. I muffle her and slit her throat down to the spiral column. I was nice enough to leave her attached.

I remove my clothing before the mutilation to avoid soiling them. She is looking at me despite the fact that she is dead, so I slash her face. I start cutting and work my way down to her breasts, completely cutting them away from her body. The blood smell is like perfume to my senses. I place them on the table next to the bed. I rip the whore's body open and remove the kidneys, heart, and liver and laid them beside her thigh.

I even cut into one of her thighs. I peeled off some skin. It is very soft and supple. It feels like silk in my hand. I take her uterus and place it very gently in my case. I have a lot of time with her. I feel so powerful. It is the best satisfaction I have ever had. Cutting this one sends chills through my body, better than an orgasm.

After the murder, I walk up to a woman in the street and asked her, "I suppose you have heard about the murder in Dorset Street?"

She nods, whereupon I grin and say, "I know more about it than you." I walk away and disappear up the street. Fine memories. I slept well that night.

●●●

At Dr. Jones's Office

The next day I called Raven's, or shall I say my doctor. He wanted to see me as soon as possible that day. I have nothing. I am a God and will always be. I will be remembered until the end of time. Now I get the chance to meet this Dr. Jones face to face. My new world is exciting.

Should I live in my secret world or tell others about it? I could live as every person's nightmare, while feeding off my prey like little ants roasting in the sun. I am powerful. I want to go back to work as soon as possible. If they only knew, but if they did…could they really catch me……

Devil's Fortress

Correction

ℑ sit here alone in this prison as I write down my thoughts as a historical record. This is where I will live for the next 40 years. Let me start from the beginning when I was in court. I stood there in front of the judge hopefully for the last time. The judge gave me my sentence 5 -10 years in maximum security as he slammed down that gavel. I rushed to a located prison and was told by the guards that I was going living in my cage for 23-hours a day.

When I got booked, into jail, they take your clothes away and strip search me, making me bend over and cough. Then they gave me one of their old over washed orange outfits to put on, to match the rest of the prisoners. As they put in my cell, I eyed the thin, plastic-covered mattress sitting up on the metal frame bed bolted to the wall. I lay down and stared the four walls.

• • •

A short time later, a correctional officer brought me a blanket and some toiletries. I turned myself into a human burrito and tried to sleep. I no longer look like an individual; I was now part of a herd. I swear the prison try to steal your individualism in here.

I become institutionalized, just another number, last name, and an orange uniform. Perhaps it's easier for them to dehumanize if one does not look like them. Anyhow, I was huddled in some urine smelling cement room with small bloodstained on the wall with two other people to share this damn cell with.

A guy in my cell, and another person I liked in the whole hellhole. One of the guys had zipper pouches in the tongues of his shoes that the guards didn't even notice or check when the booked him in. He also had a pipe inside one of the pants pockets the whole time, until he got paranoid and flushed it down the cold dingy toilet. He failed to mention what kind of pipe it was because before we knew it water flooded our cell.

The guy I liked and became good friends with had somehow managed to smuggle in a bag of about forty ten-dollar crack rocks in his mouth. I don't know how he managed to do that. They search your mouth. They look all through your mouth. They make you lift up your tongue as they run their finger around your gums. They searched me so many times. It was becoming an everyday routine.

● ● ●

Reality Check

The first few weeks of incarceration are the most difficult for an inmate. I had to learn to deal with the loss of loved ones, loneliness, sleep deprivation, hunger, and the gnawing uncertainty of the future. In some way, I had to learn to live in this very unfriendly place.

I don't know my neighbors, although I realize some are very dangerous people. I realize that extortionists, gang recruiters, gangsters, murderers, and rapists are watching my every move, looking for the opportunity to take advantage of me. They will test me to see how far they can push me and if I have the "heart" to fight back.

• • •

Prison is a cesspool where usually only the worst scum floats to the top. Many inmates seek protection from the predators of other stronger inmates or just check into protective custody. I've seen many inmates who are unable to mentally handle prison life. Suicide and attempted suicides are common methods of escape.

Prison is designed to keep you constantly uncomfortable. What exactly does comfort mean? Freedom from pain, trouble, or anxiety; feeling at ease? It's easy to take all the little things that make you comfortable for granted when you are in the "free world".

That said, "Sometimes you don't realize what you have until it's gone", this is so true. Have you ever been for days without seeing any type of sunlight or the sky? Can you even fathom what it would be like to spend years with no type of affectionate, physical contact? Not even a hug!

Try to picture a colorless home of concrete and steel, every seat, table, and even toilet nothing but cold, hard steel, no cushions, pillows, or back rest. This is a harsh reality for many people. A comfort was being able to eat when and what you want; not being told when and what to eat. You never have the option for seconds regardless of how horrible the food tastes. Privacy was another comfort most people don't think about. Who doesn't enjoy and need some peace and quiet occasionally?

What do you think it would be like to not have even one second of alone time? Literally, always having eyes on you especially when you are sitting on the toilet, or shower in an open room with 30-50 other men, no stalls? Can you imagine how humiliating it was getting caught on the toilet by a female officer during count time? What about the daily, repeated strip-searches, got to love them?

A comfort was 6 to 8 hours of undisturbed sleep in a nice, soft bed with fluffy pillows, a heavy blanket and someone to cuddle with. Instead, it was uncomfortable steel bunk with a thin mat, waking up every 15 or 20 minutes because some part of your body is aching or asleep.

Try having a loudspeaker next to your bed with someone constantly yelling: pill call, kitchen workers turns out, chow time, count time, In and out, and so on, repeatedly every day. Waking up at 6AM and having to walk a few hundred yards to eat breakfast.

● ● ●

I am trapped in a nightmare I cannot wake up from. A past that I can't be rewritten or mistakes undone. No, matter what I do or how hard I try to fight. My regrets wrap themselves around me every night. This pain surrounds me like an iron cage. I weep, I scream, and I fill with rage. A helpless feeling keeps coming over me. As I search in vain for a way to be, free. I cannot escape the hell I have created, although I tried.

● ● ●

At Night

Sitting alone in the dark corner with my knees against my chest, my head in my hands as the tears run from my eyes to the floor. The happiness has left my soul, now it was so dark and cold. Life in my eye was no longer shown. My eyes are black. Black tears was all I cried anymore. If only I could escape these chains, cuffs, and once again run from my thoughts. At times, my hands are bound and my legs are shackled.

I am only wearing these chains with the hatred in my heart, which was evident in my actions. I am a prisoner of life and contaminated by this strife. This cell was filthy and it stinks of sweat and desperation. The rats are out playing along the walls.

Now I can do was sit in my tiny room for hours on end with nothing, but the light from the screen as the warmth of the monitor to keep me company. There are times when I am invited to a movie or a game of basketball. My heart pulls me back to the quietness of my room. The serenity that it bears what was little of my soul.

I long for kinship to be included in my loneliness but I also long for solidarity for the warmth of my bed and a moment alone with my thoughts. My mouth was dry and sour. The taste of blood was what I tasted every night. My ribs are cracked. My head was throbbing.

My face was purple from all the fights I have been in. Many of my thoughts were to "sleep" but my anger cuts right through the pain. Being locked up in here was becoming devastating, emotionally, physically, and mentally draining on me. It was taking its toll.

With death hanging by my side as the anger has built up in my blood. All the revenge was creating a flood. These chains will one-day break. Look at me now try to read my heart. All my love and joy was forever departed.

They shouldn't have locked me away. To think I was once a little boy but he died with my mother. At night, when I am fast asleep in my bed, the words echoing in my head of the judge as he tells me my sentence.

•••

Flashback

When I was a child, I was something of a misfit. I use to get A's and B's in school but once I hit 15 years old I went down the wrong road and started doing drugs. I quit school when I was 16. I came from a strict religious family.

My mother died young and my grandmother raised me. My grandmom would reminded me every day that sin was a wicked act and that God punished sinners. I left school and for a short time, I was unemployed.

I was the type of boy that was quick to hate people. I always mad at the world. Therefore, when I started to do drugs, drinking it would take all the anger out, and I would feel a lot of relief. I wouldn't be mad. I felt like myself a normal person but I was doing drugs so much that I would go out, steal cars, and take from others because I didn't give a damn about shit.

I had to do what I had to do to survive on the streets and just to have money. By doing all that shit, stealing and taking from others, it didn't do anything for me. The thrill was gone.

The first time I ever was locked up was when I was 14. I was all tweaked out on speed and I pulled a knife on my own grandmom. I spent 3 weeks there until I was released on juvenile probation but those 3 weeks were fucking miserable.

• • •

Then I joined the army and learned to kill. I knew I killed people but I was driven to it. I guess you might call it killing for company. Killing was easy as breathing to me. I was able to deal with the sight of blood without being squeamish. After a few years of that, I left the army and became a civil servant. I worked for the local government in a job center, helping people to find work and sort out their benefits.

I decided I didn't want to do the human thing and be a good little boy anymore. I became an active gang member in a motorcycle club. I became a gang member because I liked the way it felt to fit in with dangerous guys. I didn't feel so alone when I was with them. I felt like I mattered.

As cool as I thought it was, the truth was that it was a weakness I had. I thought my new friends gave a fuck about me. When in fact they didn't care about me at all. Sure, at the time, they played the part very well, but they only did that because there was no risk in that, and a whole lot of profit. I was a moneymaker. I would do the shit no one else would, so they pretended to care.

Let me tell you how it turned out in the end. When I was busted, none of the fake fuckers weren't around for long. The only time I heard from them was when someone was coming to the pen. Then it was all about brother this and brother that. Even in the prison, I had to play a role as if I am this badass gang member.

I was representing a gang that didn't give a fuck about me. Especially now that I couldn't make them any money. Every time I went to the hole, and I went a lot, my so-called brothers weren't doing shit for me. The crazy thing was that it was my grandmom, who stepped up and cared. I have been transfer to Alcatraz so it is harder for her to come and visit me.

● ● ●

**Alcatraz Island,
In San Francisco Bay**

Now my new home was Alcatraz. Many of these guys were in my wing were in serving life sentences or just came off death row. Some of them were here for killing people. They were murderers and rapists in my wing. They were also a few gang members. I don't know what I was doing in this wing. I think they put me here as punishment and wanted to see how long I would last.

I was in jail for stealing cars and assault on the man whom I was stealing the car from. If I get one thing on my adult record, I will permanently stay here, based on the "Third Strike Rule".

● ● ●

Lesson

Alcatraz Federal Penitentiary was a maximum high security Federal prison on Alcatraz Island off the coast of San Francisco, California. Given this high security and the location of Alcatraz in the cold waters and strong currents of San Francisco Bay, the prison operators believed Alcatraz to be inescapable and America's strongest prison.

Alcatraz was designed to hold prisoners who continuously caused trouble at other federal prisons. Over the years, Alcatraz housed some 1576 of America's most ruthless criminals including Al Capone, Robert Franklin Stroud the "Birdman of Alcatraz", George "Machine Gun" Kelly, Bumpy

Johnson, Rafael Cancel Miranda, Mickey Cohen, Arthur R. "Doc" Barker, James "Whitey" Bulger, and Alvin "Creepy" Karpis. It also provided housing for the Bureau of Prisons staff and their families.

Black people were segregated from the rest in cell designation due to racial abuse that became prevalent. D-Block housed the worst inmates and five cells at the end of it were designated as "The Hole", were badly behaving prisoners would be sent for periods of punishment, often brutally so.

The corridors of the prison was named after major American streets such as Broadway and Michigan Avenue. Working at the prison was considered a privilege for inmates. Many of the better inmates were employed in the Model Industries Building and New Industries Building during the day, actively involved in providing for the military in jobs such as a sewing and woodwork and performing various maintenance and laundry chores.

It was believed that 36 prisoners made 14 escape attempts during the 29 years of the prison's existence. The most notable of which were the violent escape attempt of May 1946 known as the "Battle of Alcatraz".

The arguably successful "Escape from Alcatraz" by Frank Morris, John Anglin, and

Clarence Anglin on June 1962 in one of the most intricate escapes ever devised. Faced with high running and maintenance costs and a poor reputation, Alcatraz closed on March 21, 1963 but has been reopened just for people like me.

This three-story cell house included the main four blocks of the jail, A-Block, B-Block, C-Block, and D-Block, the warden's office, visitation room, the library, and the barber shop. The prison cells typically measured 9 feet by 5 feet and 7 feet high.

The cells were primitive and lacked privacy, with a bed, a desk, a washbasin, and toilet on the back wall and few furnishings except a blanket. The dining hall, kitchen and lay off the main building in an extended part where both prisoners and staff would eat three meals a day together.

● ● ●

Back to Now
August 7, 2007

I am hated all over the jail. I was now known as a snitch. As part of the snitch ring, prisoners such as me were buying and selling information about pending cases to offer to prosecutors in order to reduce our own sentences. The heart of snitching was the deal between the government and the criminal suspect, in which the government permits the suspect to avoid potential criminal liability or punishment in exchange for information.

Occasionally I would hear "Death to the snitches", as some of the inmates acted as if they were slicing their throats open as I walked by them. I will dead one day lying in ditch probably. I don't want the money the inmates offer me to keep my mouth shut, I just want to kill them. Killing was always my second favorite thrill besides sex. I heard about guys getting raped in the shower, guys getting "shanked" in the mess hall by some guy that looked at him the wrong way.

I had heard the rumors about prisoners being savagely beaten by guards and other inmates. There was even a rumor, about the warden having a "special" room. In his special room he would tortured the inmates.

After snitching on so many inmates, I was on everyone's shit list. I now had the Thug Nation, KKK, and Aryans to watch out for. Aryan gang members resided in this 16-man pod; two of them were top member enforcers.

The Thug Nation was about to make me look like a bitch, always reminding me every day. Their reign was ruthless and straight vicious. They will turn me red even when it snows. They are about to bring the heat on me. Not everyone knew or understood why I had to die. All it took was one person to tell others who I was. All they needed to know that I was a snitch and that was all that needed to be said.

● ● ●

I knew my death wasn't going to be neat and quick, it was going to be slow and painful. Thug Nation was about being wise and trying to find all types of ways to limit problems that affected the gang.

Forget the KKK and Aryan nation the vengeance they had was aimed directly at me, now they all was working together and was plotting. Their plan was to finally defeat me and shut me up. It was bad when Thug Nation joined with the KKK and Aryans to cut me down to size.

I didn't want them to beat my ass with some switches. They kept telling me I better shut the fuck up and stop telling the guards and warden secrets about the inmates, before I ended up sleeping with the fishes. I didn't want to lose my life to any of them because I was snitching but at the same time I guess I deserved it. The warden was all about getting information through snitches and spies within the prison walls. I wanted to get the hell out of here.

●●●

The more information and secrets I shared; the more time off my sentence I got. It would be easier for the police to do their own work and try to take our riches but why not get a little happiness from an inside source. I started being attacked almost every night.

Hell, I have had a knife pulled on me. It seemed that once the rumors spread through the jail about me being a snitch. I was jumped and beaten on in the prison to the point I had to be baby sat by the guards when I wasn't in my cell.

I had put in another set transform papers to get out of Alcatraz but I still haven't heard anything. In the meantime, I was going to stay quiet like a good obedient soldier, who's not allowed to show any emotions.

The sun's rays seemed but a fairy tale as I am a trapped soul and mind that was craving nothing but to escape. I wanted to get away from all of this confusion. Everything I thought I knew was only an illusion. Nothing about any of this seemed fair. I just cannot believed I fell into this snare.

I guess this gives me time to dwell on my crime. I just walk around like a demon with little glitches. Soon it will be time for me to burn like some black magic witches. They believe that all snitches can't fight that is why they stab a man in his back. Some of the inmates have been in longer than me. They are looking at me as if I am fresh meat.

• • •

Ass on the Menu

They knew there was nothing like booty to kill a man's need. They would do anything to just to get their dicks wet. To them looking at my ass was delicious to them. It has been known that they really love snitches.

• • •

Now it seemed like all the horny inmates wanted to screw me and make me into their bitch. Just for some of them looking at ass made their dicks rise, too. You are labeled as a faggot if you are raped.

Once it gets out that you took it up the ass, well that opens the door for many other predators to come hunt you down. Anywhere throughout the jail I was, everybody would look at me as if I was a target, a juicy steak. It appeared funny nowadays before they acted as if they never knew me, until I told the warden one of the biggest secrets about one of the inmates.

●●●

There was a few inmates who would treat their cellmate like a drug store; as if it was opened like a *7-11*. A number of them would pimp out his cellmate to get something they needed. An inmate had prescription pills, illegal drugs; he was selling them throughout the prison. There was methamphetamine and heroin distributed among the jail as well. The money was stacked on the walls for all to see. Hell, they sold a pill $5 or $50 for the fish scale cocaine.

A couple of the inmates even find a way to make the best moonshine. Some of the workers would get a chance to try the moonshine. When they tried it, they let off some sexy sighs, as if they just had the best sex of their lives. At trouble times, if they didn't work together then the person causing trouble had die and was replaced by another inmate that is willing to work together.

There were inmates walking around like zombies on pills and drugs. This was making me sick to see. Other inmates were selling so much powder and crack out in the opening for all to see and they didn't care who was watching. I was surprised the warden had so many problems trying to find the main source to this problem. It didn't help that some of the guards were in on it.

Hell even family members were smuggled cocaine and marijuana to the inmates. If you paid off the right prison guard, he or she won't even bother checking your visitors especially if they knew they were going to get something out of it.

There were even cell phones being smuggled in by the guards to help run the drug ring. They even got the nurses to help sell some of the drugs. The nurse would usually sell the drugs to other inmates during their routine checkups.

It was easy for the nurses to get the drugs into the prison, because it was quite normal for a nurse to carry different kinds of drugs. The more honest guards were not suspicious, because they thought the drugs were medicinal, for the inmates.

●●●

Giving In

After a while, the drugs became a viable option inside. There was a lot of drugs being offer. If you could get it out in the world, you could get it inside for a better price strangely enough, considering the difficulty of getting it in. I decided to get into the group after a few months, mostly as something to do.

I'd tried heroin outside, but hadn't liked it. Since getting on the nod seemed like a waste of time, but inside, it was a great shot in solitary could make a week pass in no time at all.

The problem was that the fucking drugs were being cut with flour, baking soda, Jell-O crystals. Not all that shit should be in your vein. After a while, I just end up doing things that I would have never dreamed of. I was paranoid about getting AIDS, so I kept one needle the whole time.

The needle ended up getting rusty. I landed a month in sickbay with tetanus. When I couldn't score for junk, I scored for codeine tablets. I grew my thumbnail long and wrecked it on the concrete so it was sharp enough to cut open my thigh, so could stick the crushed up tablet inside.

I got a tiny allowance from my grandmom, but I tried to spend it on food and junk. The best and most effective way to score was to have someone on the outside pay your person on the outside. My preferred method was to get a bank account and deposit on using phone banking.

●●●

At my worst, I was using my monthly phone call to transfer cash to my dealer's mom instead of calling my own grandmom. He was actually a cool person, apart from being an AIDs infected drug dealer inside for a double rape.

I could trade for candy meaning a candy bar would get me an eight ball. I wrote everything down and documented it. Despite that I was using while snitching on the drug dealers and guards to the warden, eventually, the warden put me in protective custody for a little bit. After I got the last require due for the warden. I put together my last piece of evidence and details dropped off to the warden.

● ● ●

Later That Night

My cellmate had already left the cell and I was about to make my bed, when two people entered my cell. "Look what we have here, Mr. Adolf Crawford. You are fresh meat!" One of the guys said as they entered into my cell. Some of us have been dying to tear that ass up."

● ● ●

This horrible feeling of dread came over me. "I'm done" was all I could think about. I tried screaming for the guard but no one came to my aid. Both of them were big guys, especially compared to me. They were huge. They both knew exactly who I was. One was a white male I knew him. It was Scott. He was an Aryan brother. He was about an inch or two taller than I was. He had to weigh about 220 or 230 pounds. Scott was the biggest drug dealers and gang leaders up in here.

The other one was a black man. His name was Regis. He stood around 6' 3" tall and weighed around 250 lbs. He was a muscle-built guy who was doing a life sentence for aggravated rape. He was a member of the Thug Nation.

As for me, well, I was 5' 4", white man who weighed about 130lbs. These men were hard-core. They would cut your throat and watch you bleed while sitting there eating a sandwich.

Before I could run out of my cell, Scott pushed me to the ground. He flipped me onto my back, and straddled my chest. Scott was kneeling on both of my wrists, I was pinned to the ground and I couldn't break free. My legs were free. Regis ripped off my pants. He then spread opened my legs and held them down.

Scott then opened his pants, and tried to put his cock into my mouth. I refused to open my mouth. He started slapping my face with it and became more aggressive with his verbal instructions. "Come on and open up for daddy. You are going to be my bitch tonight." As he said this with a devilish grin on his face.

Regis then took a hairbrush with hard bristles and told me if I didn't open up my mouth, and let Scott face fuck me, that the hairbrush was going to rip open my intestines. I refused to. I wasn't going let anyone put their fucking cock in me.

Regis shoved the hairbrush into my rectum and forcefully pushed it in further, losing the entire hairbrush and his fingertips inside me. It hurt so badly. I felt myself screaming inside but the sound wasn't making it out of my throat.

Regis left it in there for what seemed like hours but was probably only seconds and then he finally pulled it out. He then repeated to yell at me to open my mouth. This time, I complied. I sucked off Scott.

Just then a deputy walked by. He saw me fighting and struggling with them, but he didn't do anything. He just started laughing. After Scott was done cumming on my face, he then urinated on my face, and afterwards he punched me in the face. The two got off of me. I was bleeding from my rectum, but it wasn't too bad. I expected there to be more blood.

Before I could get up and ran out my cell. They went back to raping and beating on me. This went on for hours. They finally stopped when I vomited after Regis ejaculated and urinated in my mouth. They walked out of my cell I thought everything was done. I noticed that my eyes and lips were swollen. Just then, a deputy ordered me to follow him to the shower to clean up. I did so, I was so embarrassed and ashamed, I wanted to die.

●●●

About Two in the Morning

As I walked into the shower, Scott, Regis and a few others of the Thug Nation and Aryan were in there waiting for me. I tried to run for the door but I was pulled back before I could run out. The guard stood outside the shower to make sure the coast was clear. Another guard who loved to watch inmates being raped was sitting in a corner watching everything. I was alone. I had no one to help me.

One of the Thug Nation members hit me four or five times in my sternum, ribs, and kidneys. He threw a right cross that hit me in my right eye. He repeatedly to hit me in the face until I had two gashes under my eyes and a crushed eye socket. He had hit me so hard in the face that it sounded like a gun was going off. He gave me body blows that literally put me to the ground.

He then grabbed me and put his arms around me. He commenced to slam me up against the walls and forced me down. Another inmate forced my pants off of me. Unlike Regis, he had a toilet brush in his hand. He beat my penis and testicles with the bristle end of the toilet brush and then tried ramming the handle in my ass.

Once he was done, he raped me with his hard cock. Then other guys to rape me too. I swear they started off with the smallest cock and worked all the way up the biggest cock in the room. The pain of having my ass being raped repeatedly was so bad at one point that I passed out. Enough was enough I was then coherent and tried to fight back.

● ● ●

At this point, my sternum was cracked and my ribs were bruised, I could barely breath. I felt like there was a possibility that these guys might kill me if I tried to resist I didn't care anymore. I wasn't going to take it anymore. My bones were crashed together blood spills, they using their fighting skills to break me. Anger began to rise up in me as I look at my opponents who despise for this was the end for either one of us, who was going to survive?

As I clenched my bloody fist, I started to lose my breath as blood dripped down. Soon it would be certain death for one of us. I thought to myself to calm down. I looked inside my heart, my soul and I ask myself, "What power do I hold?" I tried to call for help. Repeatedly I had my breath beaten from my lungs. Curled up on the floor, my arms protected my head, as they kept throwing blows at me.

● ● ●

My breathing was slowing down I opened my eyes. My life flashed before my eyes. My focus began to zero in, as I tried to focus harder while my head was spinning. Pictures of the past of love one's family member, and friends were flashing before my eyes. I began to draw strength for my defeat was within arm's length.

They hit my body with all their power. This was the way everything was going to end. I gather the last bit of strength I had and retained my focus. My punches were coming in so fast like a million of locus.

As my attackers drew near to me, I began to realize, that I won't kill them. I can't do that for who would I fight next? I sat back down on the floor and I began to cry and laugh at them. I have damaged their fighting pride. They looked even more piss than there were before they started. I was hoping that they would spare me my life but to them I was a pathetic piece of shit.

The blood washed away my pain. It had melted away all my fears I was ready to die. My wounds were deep. I chocked back all my tears. The hurt inside my darkest dreams, had showed through my stone cold eyes. They stopped just for a moment to let me forget my past and gather my thoughts. I did not ask for much from them but just to make this quick.

I begged and asking "God why?"

One of the inmates replied, "You should have just shut the fuck up! So now you are going to get what you deserve!"

I closed my eyes; it was about that time for me to dead. I gave out my final sigh. Let me live forever in this world. I wanted to leave this world in a silent way. I don't want anyone to cry for me. I was ready to meet my loved ones in the other world. Trapped in my own little world of despair, the feeling of the warmth in my body started to fade, my body started to shiver.

Every bone in my body was aching. I was laying on the cold cement floor steady and weak. I inhaled my last breath. My heart stopped pounding.

My brain had stopped functioning. My pulse had no beat. My last breath was now gone. Life seemed rough but God knows; now Satan and the snitches such as I will soon get to take that long walk together. My fate was truly sealed. I am and will be a legend here at Alcatraz that it will make the Pope kneel.

Hellish Sanatorium

Jefferson, Kentucky

Waverly Hills Sanatorium was a two-story frame building, with a hipped roof and half timbering. The massive, collegiate, gothic style sanatorium was designed to safely accommodate 40-50 tuberculosis patients. Tuberculosis was a very serious disease. People who were afflicted with tuberculosis were isolated from the public and placed in an area where they could rest, stay calm, and have plenty of fresh air.

Tuberculosis became an epidemic in Valley Station, Pleasure Ridge Park, and other parts of Jefferson County in Kentucky. It was because tuberculosis was so extremely contagious and at epidemic proportions, those living with it could not be allowed to live and exist among the general population.

It was so bad that the government gave Waverly, its own post office, water treatment facility, so they could grew their own fruits and vegetables. They would raise their own meat for slaughter and maintained many of the other necessities of everyday life.

Tuberculosis attacked the lungs, but can also affected other parts of the body. It would spread through the air when people who had been an active tuberculosis infection cough, sneeze, or otherwise transmit their saliva through the air. Most infections were asymptomatic and latent, but about one in ten latent infections eventually progresses to active disease, which, if lefted untreated, killed more than 50% of those who were infected.

●●●

The classic symptoms of active tuberculosis infection are a chronic cough with blood-tinged sputum, fever, night sweats, and weight loss. Infection of other organs caused a wide range of symptoms.

Diagnosis of active tuberculosis relied on chest X-rays, as well as microscopic examination and microbiological culture of body fluids.

Treatment was difficult and required administration of multiple antibiotics over a long period. Social contacts were also screened and treated if necessary. Antibiotic resistance was a growing problem with multiple drug-resistant tuberculosis infections.

•••

Everyone at Waverly patients, nurses, doctors and other employees had to say goodbye to everything they knew of the outside world. Once anyone went to Waverly Hills, they became a permanent resident.

Many of the treatments used in attempts to win the battle over tuberculosis were experimental. These experimental treatments were often brutal, causing extreme pain to the patient both during and after the procedure.

Many of those same treatments left the patient with horrific scars and often times, disfigurement. Sadly, many patients undergoing these same treatments did not survive their battle with tuberculosis.

•••

During the early days, in addition the providing care for the inflicted, the facility was also used in hopes of finding a cure for the disease. It was believed that early on that exposure to sunlight and clean air of the countryside, combined with bed rest aided in the fight against the disease. As such, the patients were typically wheeled out in their beds onto the porches or the roof of the facility, where they spent the majority of the day.

The practice continued even when winter would descend upon the facility and the patients would be exposed to the cold winter air and snow. Sunlamps were also employed and sometimes placed at the foot of the bed and blasting the patients with ultraviolet light. In addition, the patients were filled with a diet of fresh meat, fruits, vegetables, and dairy products build up the protein in their system to helped them to stave off the disease.

Surgery also came into play. Balloons were sometimes inserted into the lungs of the patients in an attempt to expand them more. On the other side of the coin, patients' lungs were partly collapsed in a procedure which was called artificial pneumothorax in order to give portions of the lung a chance to heal and close off holes the disease may have caused.

Another surgery removed several ribs and muscles from the patient with hopes that it would give the lungs more chance to expand, because of the complexity and danger of the procedure, this would usually require multiple surgeries and result in as many as seven rib bones was removed. Finally, a lobotomy would be performed as a last ditch effort, which would remove diseased portions of the lung. While there was some success, the last two procedures had a high mortality rate.

●●●

High morale was also a tool the staff of Waverly Hills employed. Patients were given a form of occupational therapy where they were taught how to make baskets, brooms, tablecloths, sheets, and much more. The resulting items would then be sold at the Kentucky State Fair and the money went back into funding the day-to-day routine of the sanatorium.

Patients were also given stations with headphones so that they could listen to the radio of the day and get their minds off their inflection and the sadness around them. A tunnel was constructed at the same time as the main building beginning on the first floor and traveling 500 feet to the bottom of the hill. One side had steps to allow workers to enter and exit the hospital without having to walk a dangerous, steep hill.

The other side had a set of rails and a cart powered by a motorized cable system so that supplies could easily be transported to the top. Air ducts that lead from the roof of the tunnel to above ground level were incorporated every hundred feet to let in light and fresh air.

As antibiotics had not been discovered when Waverly opened, treatment consisted of heat lamps, fresh air, high spirits, and reassurances of an eventual full recovery. Once tuberculosis had its peak, deaths were occurring about one every other day.

The sight of the dead being taken away in view of patients was not good for morale which plummeted, causing them to lose hope or the will to live and become depressed, which only contributed more to the death rate.

With deaths occurring at such a high rate, the tunnel took on another use, and when patients died, the bodies were placed on the cart and lowered to the bottom where a hearse would be waiting to be take them away discreetly, out of patient view, saving morale. The doctors also thought this would combat the disease and keep it from spreading.

● ● ●

Rumors

There was a sad rumor floating around about Mary Hillenburg and Dr. Frank Stewart. It is said that the body of Mary Hillenburg who had hung herself was discovered in room 502. She killed herself because she was pregnant with Dr. Frank Stewart. She was not married, and her body had been in the room for quite a while before it was discovered. Another nurse committed suicide by jumping from the top of the building after working in room 502.

● ● ●

Doctor Larry Williams

With all the horror stories about Waverly, I really didn't care about them. I knew what I was getting into. There were so many rich dying folks here. This was going to be the break I need to get away from this life.

This was going a nice fresh start for me. When, I was a fresh doctor, straight out of college. One of the first hospitals I worked at they handed me the policy of the hospital as soon as my boss turned his back the packet was in the trash. I really didn't want learn the damn requirements. I don't care about any damn policy. I am going to do things the way I want to.

There were patients were just asshole. As they slept, I would go through their things for anything that was worth pawning off or keeping for myself. Those same patients would complain about anything and everything that was bothering them, such as their head was hurting to having sharp pains in their stomach. I would lie to them. I would ignore it hoping it would just go away. While they were in pain, I was in the storage room fucking a patient or nurse.

I wouldn't even report any of the malpractice cases I caused. They helped me cover up my fuck ups such as when I decapitated a baby during birth and covered it up. It wasn't for the sake of the hospital's reputation, I just didn't want my business out there like that. The hospital helped me cover up a lot. Now I was transferred to Waverly. This was going to be a playground for me.

With the way this disease killed people, I was very glad I don't family and friends to keep in touch with. Life should be easy and new start for me. I asked to be sent to Waverly to move up the ladder after all the hard work I put into my last job.

I was moving into Waverly because now I was the new head doctor of this hospital. I was going to have a little fun. I wanted to make myself known and to become a famous doctor that has discovered some new drug at one point, but that was just a dream. This will be the perfect place to do all my experiments.

● ● ●

Three Weeks Later

Soon afterward, Janet the head nurse had come to me. She had found a bottle of succinylcholine, which was a powerful muscle relaxant, which had been reported missing three weeks earlier. I saw that the cap was missing and the rubber top punctured with needle marks, so I dismissed Janet from her employ.

Before anyone else, find out her findings. I waited late into the night while everyone was asleep. I snuck into her room while she slept; I put a pillow over her face until she stopped moving. Once I knew she was dying. I undress her and got rid of her body with the dead patients.

I had to fill the bottle with saline. In other words, I didn't want anyone to know that had been using this dangerous drug. I had forgotten where I left it last. I used it to paralyzed people into a sort of hell on earth.

They would lay inert but aware and unable to get anyone's attention, so I can do whatever wanted to do from cutting them open, raping, and/or put a plastic over their head so I could watched them suffocate. Once I was done with them I would threaten them, about what would happen if they told anyone about what I did.

● ● ●

In the Basement

I loved to go down into the dungeons I had put in which was through the tunnels. I also had torture chambers that had all the fiendish devices, demonically conceived, to inflict suffering on the bodies of my helpless patients. All of the captives here had long chains wrapped around their waists, which prevented them from being able to sit or lie down.

They were slumped in the chains, reeking with their own urine and body wastes. They had been condemned to a slow death, with little water and no food. Some were already dead and the awful smell of death was filled many of the dungeons. I even had secret rooms to hide my fortune and I had any "special" treatment I needed to perform privately.

There was a young girl in here. She was very disturbed and destructive. I kept her naked, chained by a leg to the floor, in a room that was five feet square. I had tried everything, flogging her with a whip and at last tried pulling her, by hanging her by the thumbs. This seemed to keep her in order.

● ● ●

After an examination and advising as to the care and medication, I would instruct that the windows be closed and nailed down, and that cracks and any air holes be plugged shut so that all air be kept out. I further instructed that a heavy blanket be hung over the door so that as little air as possible got into the sickroom when anyone came to care for the sick. Many patients were almost frozen to death in tents and open buildings so they would get plenty of fresh air.

I hated touching and dealing with some of these patients. Many disliked the diagnostic tests they had to go through. There was a man that pissed me off that I took some pleasure in having a steel tube forced down his windpipe, so I could take samples of his lung fluids. It really hurt, but I guess he will learn about his attitude towards me!

● ● ●

Sick and Despair

An eleven-year-old boy who was one of my nurse Clair's son started experiencing chest pains, night sweats, spiking temperatures, loss of appetite and breathlessness. I knew that the tuberculosis were getting worse in this hospital.

He was taken ill with severe coughing and fever and was diagnosed with tuberculosis he was wracked by a cough and fever, coughing up bloody clots. Despite that he wasn't as far along as his mother thought. Being the con artist I was I took advance of his mother, because she was willing to do anything to cure her son's illness. I mean anything!

She'd just lost her husband to cancer, and the thought of going on without him, was killing her. She only had her son now and she would be lost if he died too. There was no other option; she wanted to do anything to see her son well.

● ● ●

At first, I felt wrong for taking advance of Clair but I was horny and she was willing. I wanted to see how far she would go to make sure her son got the best treatment. The first night we had sex it was odd. There was an empty room in the basement where we meet. We started talking as we sat on the bed. She was nervous.

"So what made you come to Waverly?

"It was my wife." I stopped and dropped my head.

"Did you lose your wife?" she said, believing that we had something in common, which we didn't.

"Yes, she died from leukemia, and a bit of me died with her that day," I said, swallowing hard.

"How did you stop yourself, from ending it all?" said Clair, knowing she could sympathize.

I continued to tell her more of my bullshit lies just to get her to calm down. "I had a letter; it was a letter she made me promise not to open, until after her death. She didn't give it to me until two months before she actually died. It simply said, "If you love me, as I know you do, you will carry on, and remember me with all your heart. I love you, and always will."

Clair couldn't stop the flow of tears. She thrilled as she began to talk, "It was the words: I love you that did it. They were the last words my husband had spoken to me before he died in my arms."

I just she felt a need to talk a little while longer. Therefore, I played along and continued to listen to her as if I gave a damn.

"It's hard to let go isn't it?" she said, after catching her breath.

"There isn't a day goes by that I don't think of my wife, but I've always believed I would get to see her again one day."

"I believed that about my husband". Clair said.

"What would you like something to drink?" I said, smiling.

"G&T please," she replied, taking her jacket off and placing it over the chair.

"Sorry I only have whiskey."

"That is okay!"

● ● ●

Finally about 2 AM

She wore a knee length skirt, and a blouse that hugged all the right places. As, I handed her a drink, I told her how foxy she looked, and realized I had made her blush. I caught myself staring at her legs, and a sudden realization dawned on me.

I just leaned forward and kissed her lips gently. Once our lips parted, she was smiling, and kissed me harder, this time with a little more passion. I placed my right hand onto her cheek, and felt her tongue entering my mouth.

In that moment, time seemed to stand still, and nothing else mattered. Clair reached up with one hand, and gently ran it around the back of my neck. I ran my free hand down her shoulder, and felt the sweet shiver of one who hadn't been touched by someone of the opposite sex for some time.

Suddenly, it was like we both wanted to do this for some time, for no sooner did I began to caress her thigh then she ran her hands down my shirt and began to unbutton it. I took my fingers lightly brushing her pussy through her panties. She responded by opening her legs a little more. I took that as a cue, so I commence to slip a finger around the hem of her panties, and gently rubbed her clit.

Clair closed her eyes, and sighed deeply. When, my fingers probed her pussy, she kissed me harder. I then placed one hand onto her left breast, and squeezed it gently. I could feel her nipple hardening in the palm of my hand, as my flesh tightened around it. I entered her pussy, and let out a sigh of built up passion, which culminated with her eyes closing, and her body shuddered with an imminent orgasm.

The last man that had touched her in this way was her husband. She pushed me back, she ran her hand down the front of my pants, and I knew she felt the hardness beneath. She then quickly unzipped them and pulled them down, with one swift movement. At the same time, she bent her legs and knelt on the floor, taking my cock between her lips for the very first time.

● ● ●

I never said anything; I just sat there looking down as Clair's head bobbed back and forth, sending shivers of excitement through my body. The feeling of her tongue sliding along my cock as she kept sucking it in, soon it made me realize if I didn't stop her I was going to explode inside her mouth, and I didn't want that, just yet.

Reaching down, I stopped her, and asked her to lie on the bed. When she did, I then removed what little clothing I still had on, and climbed onto the bed next to her. We kissed as I positioned myself between her legs, and she closed her eyes. I knew by the look on her face that she could feel my hard cock pressing against her delicate skin.

When I started to slide my cock into her throbbing wet pussy, she held her breath, only letting out the air once more as I picked up the pace. I looked down between us just to watch my cock entering her pussy, and then looked into her eyes. She smiled up at me, and then we kissed passionately. We kept fucking for another hour, before finally going our separate ways for the night. This went on for the next few months. I was a fucking God nothing could go wrong. Everything was going as plan for about six months when things started to unravel at the hospital.

● ● ●

Oh Shit

One of my ex-employee who was once employed at the hospital, which was another nurse I was using and fucking. She was probably mad that I took everything she had, and couldn't prove it. She went to the police and stated to them everything I was doing.

She also alleged that I tried to kill her, I didn't but I wish I did now. She made sure she told them about me killing her brother who was a patient with morphine. She neglected to tell them about how she had a hand in her brother's death.

•••

Morphine

In general, the misuse of morphine entailed taking more than prescribed or outside of medical supervision, injecting oral formulations, mixing it with unapproved potentates such as alcohol, cocaine, and the like, and/or defeating the extended-release mechanism by chewing the tablets or turning into a powder for snorting or preparing injectable.

The latter method can be every bit as time-consuming and involved as traditional methods of smoking opium. This and the fact that the liver destroys a large percentage of the drug on the first pass impacts the demand side of the equation for clandestine re-sellers, as many customers are not needle users and may have been disappointed with ingesting the drug orally.

•••

As morphine was generally as hard as or harder to divert than oxycodone in many cases, morphine in any form was uncommon on the street, although ampoules and phials of morphine injection, pure pharmaceutical morphine powder, and soluble multi-purpose tablets are very popular where available.

Morphine was also available in a paste that was used in the production of heroin, which could be smoked by itself or turned to a soluble salt and injected. The same goes for the penultimate products of the Polish Heroin and black tar processes.

Poppy straw as well as opium could yield morphine of purity levels ranging from poppy tea to near-pharmaceutical-grade morphine by itself or with all of the more than 50 other alkaloids. It also was the active narcotic ingredient in opium and all of its forms, derivatives, and analogues as well as forming from the breakdown of heroin and otherwise present in many batches of illicit heroin as the result of incomplete acetylation.

Morphine was an analgesic used to control pain. While pain was subjective, it was often used with kidney stones, etc. Most often, we start with 5 mg of Morphine combined with 4 mg Zofran to prevent nausea associated with morphine use. It's a quick acting opioid.

●●●

My Skill

I had a serial forger and professional serial killer. I fucking loved it. It was a high for me. I can't get enough of it. . I was getting greedy oh well. I needed more money. I loved to poison a betting crony with strychnine. I was able to get the other doctors to confirm the death by accepting my explanations of the natural death of many of the patients who had died this way.

I killed one with aconitine. Another patient was embalmed before the toxicological tests that her father demanded could be done. Oops, the paperwork seemed to disappear.

So many people were all heavily insured. I sexually assaulted and raping my patients and then killed them with sodium pentothal. I murdered five of my other patients with curare after obtaining sexual satisfaction I would watch them die.

I loved the idea of forgering of prescriptions, peoples will a, and then I poisoned many of my patients with a newly introduced morphine.

I had learned a lot with the use of morphine and with a muscle relaxant. The things I could mixed, to get the same result. Clair soon found out that I was killing the patients. She demanded that I should turn myself into the police by the end of the weekday or she would tell the police everything she had learned. I couldn't have her doing so.

●●●

That Monday
Only two months later

I needed to get rid of one of my rich patient. I forger my patient Mr. Smith's last will and testament, leaving me everything. He was rich as hell. Under my direction, Clair injected a lethal dose to him. She didn't know it until I brought it to her attention. Mr. Smith died suddenly of coronary thrombosis to simulate a heat stroke topped up with gelsemine to treat the so-called heat stroke.

After his death, Clair was starting a bunch of shit. She saw me in the hallway and pulled me aside three days after his death.

"What the fuck did you have me do?"

"What are you talking about?"

"Don't act fucking stupid!"

"Clair, get back to work and stop bothering with bullshit."

"Bullshit?"

"Yes, fucking bullshit, remember you are the one who overdosed Mr. Smith."

"You are the one who told me to give it to him!"

"Prove it! Remember your son still needs his treatments. If you say anything about Mr. Smith. Everyone will know about how you suck my cock every night so your son can get the best treatment in the world, that his mother can't fucking afford. Try me...you fucking whore"

"You are such an asshole!"

I just smiled at her and walked away. I couldn't have her opening her mouth about what I was doing. I killed her and her son so it wouldn't get out what I have been doing to save her son and my dirty secrets. It was bad enough that the police knew what they knew.

● ● ●

Time to Disappear

It was too late. I find out that even my partners in the hospital exposed my secrets. I had serial poisoned the three of them with antimony. A cyanide poisoning killed the fourth one. The local police was wondering how the partners died suspiciously. Apparently, one of the partners had left a confession of exonerating.

There were new improvements in the public health, which began significantly reducing the rates of tuberculosis. Now, there was a new arrival of streptomycin and other antibiotics. Although the disease remained a significant threat to public health.

It was only a matter of time before they would come and get me. I would have one last patient to steal from. This new development of the antibiotic streptomycin was going to make things a little bit more effective for treatment and to cure of tuberculosis a reality.

● ● ●

My Last Act

I was going to disappeared and move on with a new life with a new identity. The police were getting closer to finding out about all the other killings, the forgery and everything else I have done. I persuaded one of my last patient that I will ever have. She was a widow of a rich husband who died a few weeks back from the disease.

● ● ●

After days of being by this woman's side I listened to every damn thought she wanted to share. I was able to get her to make me the power of attorney of all of her money and estate.

As soon as the seal was put in the papers, I sold her estate and withdrew all her money from the bank. Once everything was done, I then gave her a bottle of poisoned whisky, which ended up killing her. Before anyone discovered her body, I was long gone.

Sweet Kisses

College Days

𝕴 am so glad that this is my last day living in this hellhole; I have called a home for the last four years. Don't get me wrong I love being in college but I need some space.

As I sat in the middle of my friends at my graduation, I started to doze off, while thinking about how I have to deal with the real world now. I have to find a real job to my likings. Just then, I heard my name being called, "Drusilla De Rais". I jumped up and walked up to the stage. It was time for me to get my diploma. After the ceremony was over, I headed to my room to pack up my belonging.

My girlfriends and I decided to go on a small vacation one last time to France before we all go our separate ways and I thought it would be a chance for me to meet the other side of my family Now, that I am old enough to do what I want. I was going to take this opportunity to get a jump-start on it.

I wanted to be daring and have a one-night stand before it is time for me to go to south to leave near my father. With my luck, I would not even get that far because I am so damn meticulous. On the way to France, all I could think about all the things I wanted to do. I only have a few weeks to enjoy France so I have to do as much as I can.

● ● ●

In France

When I step off the plane, I closed my eyes and took a deep breath. The air was crisp. It was a nice cool summer day. My girlfriends and I headed straight to our hotel. My room was so beautiful with all the fixings. There at my window panel was a crow. It was most beautiful creature I have seen.

● ● ●

Surprise

Later that evening my friends and I had dinner together. They decided to break the news to me that they had entered me into a challenge, which was taking place later that evening in a nearby castle. They tried to explain to how this would be a great experience as I refused to go. I gave in, I'm such a sucker. Great, just what I wanted to do!

●●●

After hours of begging
From the Friends

The challenge was that I had to stay in the chapel at Saint Vincent, the chateau of Tiffauges, where children were killed and sacrificed to the devil. The ruins of what was Gilles de Rais home. It has been said, that the site of his mass murder spree can still be seen in Champtoce-sur-Loire, Anjou.

It is said, that an apparition appears in the ruins. It takes the form of a fiery Gilles de Rais with the flames of hell dancing over his body. When he appears, you can hear the screams and moans of all of his victims echoing through the ruins.

●●●

At the Ruins

After dinner, we all went to the castle. My friends wished me luck and left me there. I got a quick drive by of the rules from the judge and then he left three other people and me there. Thank god, it was a nice night, no rain in the forecast, because there wasn't much of the castle left.

As, I was walking around the ruins, I kept getting chills as if someone was blowing cold air on me. Off in the distance I heard a voice. The voice was getting closer. I stopped to listen to the voice to see where it was coming from. Out of the shadow, a man stepped out.

"Bonsoir Madame"

"Salut. I responded back."

"Parlez-vous francais?"

"Je parle un peu francais!

"Excuse me but my name is, "Michel Barde Bleue and so what is your name?"

"My name is Drusilla De Rais."

"Any relations to Gilles de Rais?"

"Yes, is one of my great grandpas. Apparently, one of my great grandmothers was the daughter of Gilles de Rais. When she little, a servant girl of Gilles had kidnapped Marie. The servant traveled to New Orleans to a plantation until the birth of her very own son. The rest is history. My family never talks about Gilles and why the servant girl kidnapped Marie."

"Is New Orleans in LA?

"No, Louisiana."

"Really!"

"I really don't know much about him. That is another reason why I am here in France. So why are you here?"

"I am your tour guide and to make sure you make it out of the castle safe. To also make sure you guys don't cheat or try to leave and return before the contest ends."

"You don't have to worry about me. Do you know anything about Gilles?"

"Yes"

"Can you tell me a little about Gilles?"

"Sure, where do you want me to start?"

"From the beginning, please if you don't mind."

"No problem at all. You do know that Gilles had a reputation and was convicted as a prolific serial killer."

"Yes but I think it is all bullshit!"

"Honest to god...it's the truth! Let me tell you about him."

"Go ahead I'm all ears."

Gilles was the son of Guy and Marie, born September 4, 1404. He is also known as Giles de Montmorency-Laval. His birth was took place in the "Black Tour" as known as the Castle Champtocé. In 1415, he lost his mother. At the end of that same year, a wild boar killed his father. That made Gilles an orphan.

Gilles was very educated, speaking Latin almost as good as his French. Gilles was always curious to learn. He was passionate about music, but at times, he was always so angry, violent, and wildly arrogant.

He fell under the tutelage of his grandfather, Jean de Craon, who was still upset about the lost of his son Agincourt. Gilles grandfather was old and was totally devoid of scruples.

To complete the portrait of adolescent Gilles, one must point out his well-known aversion to female and his homosexual tendencies. It wasn't well known about the females in Gilles life especially if they didn't have money.

In July 1420, Gilles took part in a victorious campaign against the Penthièvre to free Jean de

Montfort and Duke of Brittany, which fell by treachery in their hands.

Then in 1422, Gilles had married to Catherine of Thouars, 16, which provides Savenay, Pouzauges, Chabanais and Confolens in Charente, but especially the castle-fortress Tiffauges, important political asset between Poitou and Brittany Gilles reside and where most frequently.

Gilles and Catherine welcomed a baby girl in 1949, which they named her Marie after Gilles mother at the Champtoce. No one knows exactly when baby Marie was kidnapped but shortly after Marie was kidnapped, Catherine moved out and disappeared until Gilles hanging.

Around the same time seeking to improving its relationship with the Duke of Brittany, the King of France or rather than with the "Dolphin" Jean de Craon who had charge of negotiating an agreement to be signed in 1425. Jean was rewarded to get a command in the royal army for Gilles de Rais and her grandson. Shortly after, he opened a campaign against the English.

I thought to myself how fascinating it was nice to finally learn about my great grandpa was, but I can't figure out why they never talked about him. I sat back and listen to Michel, while he continued on talking about Gilles.

He surprised everyone with his courage, his endurance, and his poise and sense warrior. He knows the success more often than others do. It is a beautiful warlord, but it is ruthless. At any fault, he understood how punishment was performed by the church. Death would become a new interest for him. He would begin to attend the local executions. He thought the executions was impassive.

I stopped and interrupted him right before he could finish what he about to say, and asked him in a puzzled voice, "Please tell me that there is some kind of excitement in my grandpa's life! It just seems too boring. Is that all? It doesn't sound like much to hide from me."

"Patience... Drusilla!

"Okay." As I tried to stay, awake.

He continued to tell me more about Gilles. That is when he took the taste of blood and death of others. He loved it. He had a little secret. He suffered from a lycanthropic disease.

"What is lycanthropic disease?"

"Lycanthropic disease is where one believes that he or she is an animal or can turn into an animal, is a mental disorder with psychological causes, as contrasted to legendary lycanthropy."

Well anyway, no one really knew about his disease and he kept it that way. He was admired and trusted by his soldiers. Therefore, no one dare to question Gilles about what he was doing. For the next few years Gilles fought aside of Joan of Arc until her timely death in May of 1431 when she was burnt alive at the stake.

He was now 27 years old. Gilles returned home, only to realize how bored he was with his life and how he yearn for some excitement in his life. He annoyed his wife as he prepares for Pouzauages. This is when he began to kill children one by one, from time to time, with refinements unthinkable.

"Are you making this up?"

"No… Just listen!"

I shut my mouth while he continued to tell me more. Now this was getting even more interesting.

● ● ●

After Jean's Death

Now that Jean has just died, leaving Gilles at the head of a colossal fortune. Gilles was becoming more and more reckless with his spending of a carefully amassed fortune. Almost immediately, Gilles starts to make some changes. Gilles gradually withdrew from the military and public life in order to purse his own interests: such the construction of the Chapel of the Holy Innocents. Which I personal think it was a cover-up.

Things are getting worst the killings were happening several times a week, always at night. Gilles would pamper and dress the children in better clothes of his liking. He would eat and drink with the child as if he was their friend. The drinks he gave the children had hippocras, which acted as a stimulant.

Gilles is now torturing, raping and is masturbating over their corpses. Gilles rarely left a child alive for more than one evening's pleasure.

Many times, they were dealt mortal wounds before he would sodomize them. Occasionally, he would perform a sex act with their dead corpse. When the children were dead he would kiss them and those who had the most handsome limbs and heads he would hold them up and admire them.

He would have his people cut open the dead corpse so he could take some pleasure looking at their sexual organs. All victims were killed by decapitation or by cutting of their throats with some kind of sharp object. There were times he would sit on some of his victim's stomach so he could laugh at them while they were dying.

Gilles then had his peoples' abominable conditions secretly put the children's corpses in the surrounding countryside and then the small carcass was burning in the fireplace while he slept.

Gilles was a demented son of a bitch but his faith remains deep and naive. He believes that it's pleasing to God that he kills these children. He believes that by killing a child, that their souls are released to paradise and that they are reborn as angels. He thinks he is doing God a favor.

Gilles's entourage is aware of his actions and provides him with fresh and beautiful healthy boys between the ages of six and eighteen but when there are no boys found to his liking he will settle for a girl from time to time. Hell, he even had the church from the outskirts of the town joined in on the fun.

●●●

The Church and Gilles

The sexual abuse of minors by Archdiocesan clergy and employees was a secret that Gilles loved. Everything Gilles believed about the church was a lie. The abuse and the murders was known, tolerated, and was hidden by High-Church officials, up to and including the Cardinal himself.

One of the priests would come over Gilles's home with a little boy. Gilles's always watched from a distance because he knew once the priest was done, the boy was his. The priest didn't care what happened to the boys.

So as directed the boy would take off his clothes, and was ordered to put his penis in the priest's mouth. Then the priest reversed positions, until he ejaculated on the boy. The priest would tell the boy that God loved him, It was Gilles's turn to do whatever he wanted.

Meanwhile no one has any idea the Gilles is the one responsible for the missing kids. There were so many children killed by Gilles over the next few years.

Gilles was aroused by the idea of killing children; he has somehow brought the devil, the evil infamous Bluebeard and magic into the mix. It was believed that Gilles was involved with a cult that was known for alchemy and demon summoning. That is when things became weirder.

Gilles apparently tried to summoning the demon named Baron in the lower part of his castle at Tiffauges. Barron required offerings of parts of the child Gilles had murdered. Gilles always follow through.

I asked puzzled, "Bluebeard?"

"He was a wife killer."

"How does Bluebeard fit into this story?"

"Let me finish!"

People started to derive a conclusion about Gilles. Now by 1432 Gilles had engaged in series of murders that was in the hundreds. It all came to a stop when Gilles got into a violent dispute with a clergyman, which lead into an ecclesiastical investigation that brought Gilles' crimes to the light.

The locate church was frustrated that it could not charge either the abusers from the outside church in the local church, because the successful cover-up of the abuse. So the local church just went after Gilles. They tried to find all the missing children each place he had lived at. When they went to Machecoul they find forty bodies.

At his trial, the parents of all the missing children and Gilles' own confederates all testified against him. Gilles was charged included murder, sodomy and heresy. He was executed as a witch in Nantes on October 26, 1440. Several of people say till this very day Gilles was innocent, and that he was set up by the Catholic Church or the French state. They believe that it was all about politics. I guess we will never know.

"I can't believe you know so much about him. Thank you that means a lot to me. I always wanted to learn about him, but didn't dare to. I now see why! So, what about you, are you going to tell me what your last name means, it sounds familiar? What is the deal with Bluebeard?"

"I will tell you but don't worry, in time you will find out all you need to know."

● ● ●

Afterwards That Night

Just then, he took me by the hand and led me down a long hallway. The walls of the ruins started to reappear around me. I thought I was losing my damn mind. We stopped at a huge door, he pushes it open. The room was elegant; it was like something I have seen in a movie. There was a canopy bed off in middle of the room.

Michel let go my hand. He walked over to a wooden box and opened the lid of an old phonograph. He then put on some soft music. He walked back over to me and extended his hand to me. I placed my hand into his. We commenced to slow dance. Everything seemed so perfect. I forgot about the contest and why I was here. I could feel his strong arms in my hands. His chest was pressed against mine. I was starting to get hot and bother.

I pulled back away from him. We locked our eyes for a split second and he reached in and started to kiss me. Part of me wanted him to stop but the other part of me yearned for him. Time just seemed to stop for us, just then he stopped and walked me to bed. I sat down on the bed.

I looked up and asked him, "Why did you stop?"

He asked me in sexiest tune I have ever heard, "I will not continue unless you want me to."

I batted my eyes innocently and in a soft voice I said, "No don't stop!"

He continues to kiss me, he slowly moves behind me and continue to kiss the back of my neck. He pulled back my head, holding it into his hand. Something came over me. A warm sensual came over me until like any other I have never felt before. I closed my eyes and let him have complete control of me.

● ● ●

The Confession

For just a second he stopped and whisper in my ear that he was Gilles and Bluebeard in one. I was in shock. Out of nowhere, I felt a sharp pinch on the side of my neck. Blood poured out of the neck, while Michel sucked at it. There wasn't anything I could do. I felt myself slipping away.

●●●

While Passed Out

Flashes of Gilles's, Bluebeard's, and Michel's life ran though my head like a movie. It all made sense now, they were all the same person, who never really died. Michel was a vampire who traveling through history leaving his mark on the world. Michel has lived in different forms.

●●●

Two Nights Later

When, I came though I find myself in a crypt lying on a stone table in a white gown. Seating right there next to the window was Michel. He was staring at the moon, which was shining through.

Michel turned to me and said, "Welcome home my Queen!"

I try to jump off the table. I was so weak that I fell right into his arms. "What did you do to me?"

As he held me in his arms he replied, "The contest was a set up to bring you back to me. You will live here with me and you will be my wife."

Just then, he bit into his wrist. I watched as the blood flow out of his wrist. He brought his wrist up to my mouth. I hesitated for a second. I can't resist I was so hungry. With each drop, I could feel my body fill with life.

● ● ●

Nowadays

The life I once live has become a distant memory. Now, I walk the earth yearning for blood with my master lurking near. I feel his presence and see what he sees when we are not together. I do not know if I approve of it.

This is the life I was destiny to live. Among the living, while feasting off their blood. I had a deep love, devotion to the God I did not really know personally, and I yearned to give my life to him completely. I see what the church has done to my family and I really can't be a part of the church anymore.

My heart was bursting with idealistic devotion and love toward the false goals I had been taught would please and honor God in my life. I was now learning how strong and tenacious the old soul ties to a demonic religious system could be. As for my thoughts about God...we will just leave it at that.

Guilty Pleasure

In New York City

How can I live without sex in my life? Sex in the morning, in the evening and sex at night every minute of the day sex......sex......sex. Sex was so great and bad at the same time. I would have sex today, tomorrow, and every day when I am in sorrow. I loved to have sex on the bed, unfamiliar places, at work, and on the floor. I would have it every day; I craved it like a drug.

●●●

Nowadays

I graduated Harvard, and then went to Law School. I ended up making the Law Review. I got a great job on a partnership track at a top firm in New York. All my dreams were coming true.

I was now a beautiful sexy and smart woman, a 29-year-old executive in a law firm I presently was working at. I stood five feet seven inches, weighed 115 pounds, and had long black hair that fell down over my shoulders and gorgeous brown eyes.

I had sprouted a fantastic perfectly perky set of breasts at the end of middle school. They were perfect grapefruit-sized beauties that stood out from my chest with the arrogance of youth. They were capped with the kind of large brown nipples that a person usually only saw in girlie magazines. My slender waist flared out into rounded hips, and from there on down I had nothing but long, perfect milk chocolate legs. I kept myself fit until this very day.

• • •

Back in the day

When, I little I heard about *Playboy* being the thing it was porn to my parents, but the thoughts about masturbation were very much in vogue.

Hearing about porn growing up made me a very curious little girl. It made my escalating porn addiction seem normal to me for years. I can't imagine the long-term effects on society brewing in the generations behind me. My introduction into sex was from hardcore porn, even by today's standards were discarded in a common restroom in a medical complex.

● ● ●

Turning of Events

I was there with my mother to a doctor's appointment. While I was sitting in the waiting room, I find a *Playboy* magazine that was hidden behind a coat rack. I took the magazine and began to read it. I was amazed by what I was saw that I took half dozen glossy pages torn from a magazine. I folded them putt them in my pocket. I putt the magazine back as soon as I heard my mother's voice.

● ● ●

Later that night, by the dim nightlight in my room, I masturbated for the first time to the torn pages I had. I was hooked. I have been masturbating since I was 16. There was an old-fashioned claw tub in my parent's house. It was based on the original cast iron tubs, which were made by the millions between 1890 and 1940.

It was a vintage roll rim tub. I would sit up under the faucet in my bathtub and let the water hit my pussy. There were times I tried to avoid from masturbating when I was in the tub. As soon as the water began to run down my body. Well my hands started wonder as if they had a mind of their own. My parents thought that I just loved taking long baths. They didn't worry about me being in the bathroom for so long.

My mind was a tangle of dark thoughts, unholy fantasies and images that I had never thought of in my 16 years, but overall, overwhelmingly, the desire to cum. The frequency varied, I had to masturbate about seven times in a day. I used masturbate to run from the things that made me sad at times. I used to get a temporary high after I would masturbate. I find it easier to sleep at night especially if I masturbate before going to bed.

There were times I would wake from a deep erotic dream, in which my naked nubile body was stretched out into an X and being fondled by anonymous men, and in which I was having orgasm after orgasm. Then I would realized I was alone, in own bed, and that my pussy was wet with excitement.

●●●

My First Time
November 1983

I lost my virginity to the thirty-one year-old pastor's son from the church my family and I went to when I was 15. After about six months of having sex with the pastor's son, I realized that boys my age were so pathetic that they had probably even would pay me for sex or anything in that natural. I started having sex with guys all over the place, all the time.

To tell you the truth, most of them didn't know what they were doing, and some of them lasted for about 10 seconds before they cum in their pants especially if I just touch their cocks on the outside of their pants or took off my clothes. There were a few I was able to have sex. When I did, I loved the feeling of their cocks ramming away inside of me. I would cum like crazy, and it was a great way for me to make some money. If my father found out what I was doing, he would have killed me.

I would charge the guys $25 for a blowjob and $100 for a fuck. I now had more than $2,000 saved up so far. I just wished I had thought of it sooner. Fucking was about the greatest thing in the world. For me to be paid for it was even better! After a while of being paid to have sex and other things, were getting old, but in time I will find a job close to my likings. I am going to keep what I earned tucked safe away.

When I could not have sex, I would feel like curling up and crying. I craved for it every waking moment. I fantasized about it. I dreamed up scenarios where I was enjoying mind-blowing sex. In fact, one of my biggest fears was that I would die without knowing what lung shattering, explosive sex was like. I was obsessed with finding it. The sexual urges were becoming quite strong at times, particularly at night. I would take a shower, listened to music or do something to divert my attention for sex or masturbating.

●●●

Playboy Bunny Job
April 24, 1984

I wanted to be able to put myself though college. I had two more years before I was going to be in college. I apply for a job to become a playboy bunny. I was always my dream to be a bunny. I was able to get an audition at the local Playboy Club. The club's atmosphere was of a private men's club with jazz music playing and top notch entertainers. It was a glamorous club in New York.

After the audition, they made me seat in a room with other girls who were done their audition, just to find out who was going to be a bunny. I was nervously chewing my fingernails while waited. Only hours after the audition I find out, I was hired. I had a lot to live up to since the first African woman was hired back in 1965. I wanted to be the best bunny I could be.

● ● ●

Before I could start working at the club, I had to get a pelvic exam despite that I was only going to be a waitress. It was must in order to report to work. If I didn't I wasn't allow to work and my gynecological health had to come back clean. Despite how sexual active I was, I secretly went to the family doctor to make sure I had my birth control up to date and I was clean from any STDs. I didn't tell a soul were I worked at.

Once I was cleared to work, I received my costume. The costume wasn't that bad but it hurt to in for a long time. My costume/uniform was of an ultra-right rayon satin corset, satin bunny ears, cuffs, collars with a bow tie and a pair of black inch heels, sheer support black stockings, plus a bunny tail. I had a nametag on a satin rosette, which was pinned over the right hipbone. My name was Bunny Chastity.

Before each shift, they inspected all of us to make sure that we were the perfect bunny. I learned to deal with standing for hours in my heels. They hurt like hell.

I had to watch my weight which was up and down but I never let them find out how much I gained because I knew they would make stay home for a week just to lose my weight. So I kept my weight under 112 pounds. I had to be well groomed at all times with freshly painted fingernails. I had to always keep my hair styled in a Bunny Mother-approved way. I was never allowed to change my hair color and style.

I learned about the Playboy Empire and the rules. The club and Bunny Mother were strict and I learned quickly not to get on their bad side. Bunny Mother taught me on how to walk and serve food and drinks, including the famous Bunny Dip, Bunny Stance, and the Bunny Perch. I learned the many kinds of alcohol and the difference between each. I had to join the union, which was a good thing to have down the road if we bunnies got into trouble.

The men were dogs at times, playing on my tail for fun or hitting on me. We were forbidden from sleeping with any of the customers, but of course, I broke the rule from time to time. I did accept the flattery and favors that was bestowed onto me by any of mine high-end customers. This was where I master the act of flirting. Before I knew, it had received plenty of gifts. I was able to earn just as much as the girls who were working here before me. I had a colorful adventurous life and I was learning how to control my never-ending desire to masturbate or to have sex with a stranger. I was able to keep this job until I went to college.

• • •

Sometime in 1986

I finally went to an adult bookstore. I brought a few things especially some Ben-Wa ball. As soon as, I got home I ran to my bedroom and locked the door. Despite I was home alone it would be hours before anyone would return. I didn't want to take the chance. I reached into the bag that was on the floor and pulled out a small box. They were two small metal objects slightly smaller than Ping-Pong balls.

They were hollow metal balls, which was partially filled with mercury. It was known that women use them to masturbate with. They would fit snugly up inside a woman's pussy so when she walked, they would shift the center of gravity repeatedly, stimulating the inside of her pussy. The result was a spectacular orgasm for women.

I pulled off my jeans and panties. I began to push one of the Ben-Wa balls into my swollen sopping wet pussy, and then I put the other one right after the other one. They were cold, but strangely, I didn't mind it. I was horny and wanted to cum so badly. The doorbell rang...oh shit! I jumped up and put my clothes back on. I shuddered at the thought of these awful foreign objects inside me.

●●●

As I walked downstairs to answer the door, I could feel the slick balls slipped and tumbled inside me. As a huge wave came over me, I stopped halfway down the stairs because the Ben-Wa balls were moving in a more stimulating way, I thought I was about to cum. I gathered myself and answered the door; it was Malik the Jehovah witness. Just great! Just what I needed right now! I couldn't tell him to leave, because he was a friend of the family.

I in visited him and offered him a drink. All the while, the Ben-Wa balls stuffed up inside me rolled and rolled, a constant reminder of my horniness. Although the Ben-Wa balls were stationary, my pussy was suddenly leaking a trickle of juice down my thigh.

My clit was throbbing, and I thought about reaching down with my hand, pulling my panties aside and masturbating while he sat there and witness this but I forced myself to be focused. I wiped my thighs, went back into the living room, sat down, and listened to what he had to say. Only a few minutes went by I couldn't take it anymore.

I stopped Malik in the middle of his lecture about the ending of world. I sat back on the couch. I pulled off my jeans revealing my dripping pussy. He just sat there drooling while he looked at my sweet pussy. I ordered him to put his fingers up to the opening of my young pussy. I had him hold his hand out.

I pushed the Ben-Wa balls out. He was so excited and drooling from his lips. He was very obedient as I pushed them out, the two metal balls pooped out into his hands. They were wet with my pussy juice. They left my pussy wide open. I took the balls and put them in his mouth.

He licked them cleaned. Then I pushed his face into my pussy. He pulled my pussy lips wide with both hands. My little clit popped out from under its hood, looking like a small, moist pearl, glistening with desire. "Yum yum yum," murmured Malik.

He licked his thumb, and then pressed it down, gently but firmly, on my hot, throbbing clit, and began to massage it in a circle. It felt soooooo good. He kept massaging my clit, which was getting bigger and bigger, redder and redder. It was as if the tiny organ had a mind of its own and was straining upward for release at his hand.

He roughly gripped my clit and shook it from side to side, like a dog playing with an old sneaker, and went rigid with an overwhelming orgasm. I was going to cum so hard, as Malik's thumb was moving faster and faster. I made him stop and lick my pussy clean. I came all over his face, and then I made him leave with his dick in his hand before my parents returned home in the next ten minutes. This was my favorite little secret, along with so many others.

● ● ●

At Harvard University
In 1987

During college on a "good" day, I could hook up with three or four different people, but never at the same time. Group sex was never was my thing, so it was always one-on-one.

Afterwards I would still have to go online to watch porn to get another one off. I could meet up with some of my clients at a hotel. It was mostly in a hotel a since the guys were usually married, from the burbs, or in some sort of relationship.

• • •

My First Girl on Girl Experience
April 1989

By my junior year in college, there was a girl, who just kept hanging around me when I wasn't out fucking. I met Sophia in one of my law classes. She was a nice girl but something about her was weird. Her hair was shorter, a slightly lighter auburn streaked with stunning gold highlights. She always wore a loose cotton blouse, khaki Capris, and sandals that showed off her tiny, pink-painted toes.

One day she was having problems with one of upcoming test and wanted to know if she could stop by and get some tips. I agree for her to come over a Thursday since I lived alone and off-campus.

• • •

When that Thursday night came around, she was my house for hours. It was three in the morning. I told her she could sleep over and instead of driving out so late. I gave her the spare room and took a shower. When I got out of the shower, she was sitting on my bed.

"What's wrong?"

"Nothing."

"Okay then good night."

"I really wanted to thank you for your help."

"Okay you are welcome."

"No, I don't think you understand I REALLY want to thank you for your help." She then grabbed me by the hand and pushed me down onto the bed. I really didn't know what she was up to and what to do. So, I just went along with it.

She began to kiss me. I closed my eyes and went with it. I was enjoying a woman's touch. This was so different from being with a man. Her touch was so soft and gentle. I jumped up and closed the curtains as I secretly hit a button on the wall. It was a hidden camera. Which I had molded inside a book that was on my bookshelves. I wanted to record everything.

I sat back down on the bed. She slowly took off my robe as I was pulling off her clothes. We stood there, staring at each other, both of us frozen in place. Finally, I managed to draw a breath of air and my lips parted in a smile. The expression that flashed across her face seemed to be a look of joy and wonder and fear all at once, and then suddenly she threw herself into my arms, hugging me close.

Her body was warm and soft against mine as I held her, and I knew that the pounding of my heart had to be obvious. My eyes drifted to her lips, full and tempting. The tip of her tongue slipped out to moisten them. The thrill of what was happening had started a low thrum of electricity running through my body. Every nerve in my body was alive!

She dropped her hand and turned back forward, and I continued my work, rubbing my thumbs up the back of her neck, her soft moan sending my heart skittering out of control. "That feels so good," she murmured, and I suddenly became aware of certain dampness between my thighs.

My hands traveled lower down her back, and I was rewarded with another sigh of bliss. I slowly eased each button undone on her blouse. The edges of my arm brushed against the already hard tips of her nipples as I moved down, sending goose bumps skittering across my arms. It was almost too much for me, this slow agony of anticipation. I fought down the impulse to simply rip the buttons off and take her in a wild heat.

Her skin felt beautiful, warm and inviting, and I let my hands play further downward, caressing every inch. I realized her breathing was already heavy and I had no doubt her heart was pounding with anticipation and excitement, and probably an air bit of nervousness, too.

I reached for her, drowning in the feel of her breasts pressed against mine. I leaned backward, pulling her on top of me, my hands exploring lower. I cupped the roundness of her bottom, spreading my legs and pulling her hips tight against my body. My own hips thrust against her, once, twice. Through the haze of passion and need, I remembered that this was my first time with a woman, and I forced myself to slow down.

Sliding down slightly, my lips found the softness of her breasts. I traced light kisses over the heat of her skin, my tongue dancing toward the sensitive tips. I thought she was going to explode when I finally took one hard nipple in my mouth, sucking and nipping, as I had wanted to for so long. Her scent and taste went straight to my head like a fine wine, and I was instantly drunk with her.

My hands splayed across the smoothness of her stomach, stroking and tantalizing as my lips kissed every inch of her luscious breasts. Her hands clenched the back of my head, winding through my hair, holding me tight. My fingers found the front of her pants, and I quickly unclasped them, sliding the zipper down. I pulled away, and she immediately lifted her hips and helped me slide them down.

Black lace panties that matched her sexy bra were the only thing left clinging to her body, but as enticing as they were, I tugged them off, too. I settled myself between her spread legs, and my lips traced her collarbone in teasing little circles before moving further down, my body rubbing tortuously between her legs. Her hips arched forward, pressing against me, and my lips dipped lower to kiss the softness of her belly.

She whimpered as I rested there, my fingers finding the softness of her inner thigh, stroking and caressing in rhythm with my kisses. My lips moved further down, and her hands found the back of my head again, any hesitation or inhibition completely gone. Her hands urged me lower, and I slid my body off of hers, my hands spreading her to my view. She was so wet, the evidence of her desire coating the damp, curling tendrils. The scent of her flooded through me, and suddenly nothing existed in the world except for the two of us.

My mouth claimed her, and she cried out as my tongue found the sensitive bundle of nerves. Her clit was hard and swollen, ready for me, as I sucked and stroked, my tongue dancing a slow line of fire across the sensitive flesh. I slid my hand up between her thighs, sliding two fingers, then a third, into her, relishing the feel of the rippled flesh inside as my tongue drove her higher and higher.

My mouth and my fingers stroked a dancing rhythm, fingers curling and tongue swirling, and I knew she was lost in utter delirium. Her hips bucked against me. She threw back her head and fists tightly clenching the sheets. In a flash, she was screaming, her wordless sounds of passion bringing a fresh rush of desire to my body. Repeatedly she thrust, her wetness soaking my hand, screams ripped from her throat. Then she shuddered, muscles clenching my fingers still inside of her, and finally lay still.

I pulled away, my own body throbbing with desire. She laid there, a fine sheen covering her body, her breath still ragged and the pulse pounding in her throat. I slammed my eyes shut, clenching my teeth furiously, trying to drag my raging hormones back under control. I didn't want to push her, to take her farther than she was ready to go.

She reached up with one hand and began to play with my nipples. The sensation of having my nipples stimulated added to the delicious incredible oral reaming of my asshole, and I felt myself getting closer and closer to orgasm I felt her hand pushing against my rectum, pushing in slowly, gently, and eased her fingers up into my ass.

It was so tight, hot, and moist. She pulled out slowly, and then pushed in again. As she stroked, my ass relaxed and opened up even more, very soon he had a slow but steady rhythm going, in and out, in and out, pumping her fingers up inside me.

She pushed forward, inch by inch, letting her finger luxuriate in the feeling of my rectum. Finally, she was all the way in to the knuckle. I screamed with pleasure. My hips bucked up and down wildly, my entire body tensed and went rigid, the muscles in my rectum clamped down ferociously on A's fingers.

She kneeled on the so that one knee was on either side of my head, as she faced my feet. Her ass hovered above my face, and slowly she started to lower it. She wanted to feel my tongue up her ass. She lowered her well-fit frame so that her soft smoothed ass hovered just an inch above my mouth.

I stuck out my tongue as she lowered her buttocks the last inch and settled her own ass crack right onto my mouth. I moved my tongue a little bit. "Oh, yeah, Princess, that's right, use that tongue. Lick that ass," ordered Sophia. I complied, licked back and forth along Sophia's ass crack.

I gave her the sweetest rim job she had ever had in her life. She bent slightly at the waist so that she could rub her hand on her clit, which was swollen with blood and oozing with cum.

I moaned into her asshole and continued to work my tongue. It was all so nasty, so humiliating, and yet so wonderful. My whole body was on fire.

● ● ●

"God, I need you to touch me." Raw need clutched at me, and I tugged her hand down, wanting, begging for release. I placed her hand between my legs. Her fingers found my clit, and instinct took her over. She stroked me, the tips of her fingers sliding down into my wetness and back up, rubbing just the right place to drive me over the edge.

It took only seconds and then I was coming, grabbing a pillow to muffle the too loud screams that would have been heard all the way to the neighborhood. My body convulsed against her, the waves completely overcoming me as I simply let go and fell crashing over the edge. The explosion was blinding, a free fall of fire and pleasure rippling through my entire body.

My hips ground into her hand, my back arched into her, my hands clenched tightly into fists. It seemed forever before the waves passed, slowly ebbing away and leaving me wordlessly. Sophia rolled to my side, nestling her naked body against mine. It was several minutes before; I could get my breath and control the ripples that still sped, every few seconds, through my body. Once I cummed, I stopped to gather my thoughts.

● ● ●

She climbed down off the bed. I ordered to lean over the desk. I got up from the bed. I walked over my briefcase and pulled out some handcuffs, then stripped her down to the desk with her ass up.

"What are you doing?"

"I am going to finish playing with your ass."

"Please don't. I still in pain from the last time you fucked my ass! Rimming my ass was good enough for me"

"Don't worry I will be gentle. Just breathe and relax. Do I have to remind you about what our deal is? Do you remember what it was?"

"Yes"

"Do you like the cock up your ass?"

"Yes or I should send you home naked?"

"No, I am sorry I will do anything you want me to do."

I pulled the strap on out of my briefcase and put it on. I walked behind her, added a few drops of lubrication and started to slowly fuck her ass. Then I pulled it out and stopped.

She then lifted her head. "Don't stop!" she moaned. "Please don't stop! Make me cum! Fuck my ass! Please fuck me, fuck me, fuck me, fuck me, don't stop!" After that night, we never spoke of it ever again. We finished out school and went our separate ways.

●●●

New Life in 1997

Now working in a law firm I could have any man I wanted to and fuck him. When I was at work if I was horny and I couldn't get away, then I would lock myself in the private ladies' room, watching a porn on my phone. Something about the fear of being caught really turned me on.

There were times my boss Mr. Moretti; the senior partner in the firm would have me host one of his retreats. My boss was a middle-aged man, about my father's age. He had a sexy voice, and kind eyes. He was good-looking, and he smelled nice.

●●●

Flashback

He was sponsoring a small retreat one weekend with some powerful lawyers at other firms, but I was not to tell anyone at the firm, because it might be construed as favoritism. He tried to take advance of me but I had the last laugh. I slept with my boss at that retreat. That was when he made me full partner in the firm, and in return, I never told a soul what we did.

That weekend was fun and I had it all on tape. I would not show anyone the tape that I had of us. I wished you could have seen him when I told him that I had everything on tape. I thought his eyes were going to pop out of his head. It was a risk I knew it. He could have had me arrested, but I gambled that most women would not do even when they faced with the opportunity. Mr. Moretti took the low road, the testosterone highway just to save his ass.

Not only did he pay me nicely for the tape, but also I signed a contract, that if I ever needed legal representation, he would provide it pro bono and do whatever he can to make me a partner, with the best high-end clients.

●●●

At work

During office, some of the office meetings I find myself squirming in my seat. I would slide my ass forward and back, forward and back, rubbing against the wood. As I rubbed my butt against the seat, I would cross and uncross my legs.

I would swing my right leg over my left, crossing them in mid-thigh, and squeezed the muscles in my legs. I had a terrible itching in my sweet pussy, the itch that spread deep up into her asshole. I was afraid that if I wriggled too much more, my boss would say something in front of everyone.

● ● ●

At times when I wore a pencil skirt, it would climb up my thighs, before I knew it, my skirt would ride up high enough to expose my white panties in front of my boss. Mr. Moretti was droning on about the different clients in front of the other workers. I was too pre-occupied with the uncomfortable feeling in my pussy and ass to notice how often Moretti was looking my way.

He didn't stop talking, but he would keep his eye me. It gave me a feeling of power, and even, sometimes, made my pussy a little juicy, just thinking about how many horny all the guys were looking at me.

● ● ●

I was biting my lip, and rubbing my ass against the chair for all it was worth today. I was super horny because my period was coming. I wished that I stayed home.

"Miss Lloyd is there something wrong?" asked Mr. Moretti, interrupting his lecture. He stared at me. The entire room stared as well.

"No sir, I'm OK," I squeaked out.

"Then why are you squirming so much in your seat and making noise?" asked Moretti. His eyes glittered with a touch of evil; his cock was beginning to get an idea what was wrong with me. It stirred in his slacks.

"I'm sorry. I'll be alright."

"See me before you go home today." He went back to lecturing us about the new clients. I really wanted to take my panties off and shove his face into my throbbing pussy. After work, I had to meet up with Mr. Moretti after the meeting in his office. I knew exactly what was going to happen.

●●●

Later that day

Mr. Moretti shut the door behind me and started to a necking session. "What do you have to say for yourself, Chastity?" he asked. His dark eyes burrowed directly into mine. I didn't answer him.

I was too horny to care, and I knew what I was going to do to this man in just a few minutes. I squatted down, unzipping his fly, and pulling his cock out with my tender fingers. He sprang to life, hard as a steel bar.

I leaned forward and placed my lips around the head of Moretti's cock. I reached a hand into his open fly and began to fondle his balls. I pulled my mouth off the engorged cock, then stuck my tongue out and swirled it over and over the head, Moretti moaned.

I opened my lips wide, and ran my mouth all the way down onto his cock as far as I could manage. His kinky pubic hairs tickled my nose. I pulled back, and then started bobbing my head up and down, faster and faster.

My hand seemed to be on automatic pilot, rolling his testicles around in his scrotum. I could feel them start to inch upward and his scrotum tightened as his orgasm approached. "Oh yes, ohhhhh yes," he moaned.

My pussy spasmed slightly, I was so damned turned on I reached down with my free hand without even thinking, pulled aside my panties and started rubbing her exposed pink clit with two fingers.

Suddenly, Moretti's cock exploded into my mouth, pulsing out wave after wave of hot man's semen. I started swallowing dutifully. I kept working my clit, faster and faster, approaching my own climax. He stopped me from finishing him and myself off.

●●●

My pussy felt warm and opened. He lifted my ass up off the desk and somehow quickly pulled off my skirt and panties together. He had poured honey all over my pussy and ass, parted the tender labia with his rough fingers and dribbled the honey deep into my pussy, then parted my ass the same way and applied honey there.

My body had taken over, and I was inching closer and closer to an orgasm. I moaned, thrust my tender breasts out, and humped my pussy frantically against Moretti's fingers.

"Oh yes! Oh yes!" I cried out. I teetered on the verge of a powerful orgasm. My nipples seemed to be more sensitive. I could feel them pushing against the inside of my bra. When the air hit my nipples, they instantly sprang to life and became erect, jutting out like little erasers. God, they felt so good and tingly.

"Oh God, yesssss," I moaned. He licked my asshole with his tongue. The anus was as full of nerve endings as the vagina, and properly stimulated it's one of the most intense erogenous zones on the body plus saliva makes a wonderful lubricant, as I relax, so I can soon be able to take in something a little harder than a tongue.

He was able to push his tongue further and further up inside my warm, moist rectum. "Rim me out with your tongue". I screamed. The farther he put his tongue up my ass, the bigger the orgasm got. Well, fair's fair. I was getting a hot tongue stuffed up my ass, and now it's time to reciprocate.

●●●

I felt the desk shift and Moretti, was now naked. He turned me around and laid me on the desk. Just for a moment, he stepped back with his erect cock in his hand and smiling as stared at my wet pussy. It felt wonderful when he plunged his firmly erect cock into me. He thrust his cock deep inside me harder and faster as I moaned, "Fuck me harder." It felt very good when he came inside me, very good that I came too.

●●●

Before I met my Fiancé

Nowadays, when I didn't connect with anyone I would be on my computer searching for porn for hours. I would tell myself that I'm just going to log on for a minute, but once I was on, I couldn't stop. Some days I wouldn't leave the house I would work from home.

It got to the point where I would have to force myself to turn off the computer at night so I could get some sleep. I would negotiate with myself almost every night about the amount of time I would spend on the computer. 15 more minutes and I'm done, but once those 15 minutes passed, then I would say just another 30 minutes and so on.

● ● ●

Chastity and Jack

My addiction was creating problems between my fiancé Jack and me. Jack was a traveling sales manager. He was 30 years old. When I first started going out with Jack, he was thrilled that I wanted sex all the time. I met Jack just before my 29th birthday. We just clicked.

We had a strong sexual attention that I couldn't get from anyone else. Every moment we spent together was exhilarating and fun. Sex with him was like a fire to where I could never put out the flame. We would have sex until we came or until it hurt.

During sex, when he started to grip on my ass, I knew he was ready. He was fulfilling my every desire and my favorite word was now his name. I loved it when he brings pain into sex, I am exposed. I was very flexible so it was always fun to be in different position.

When I asked him to go deeper and put it all the way in, he did it without a single pause. I liked have crazy sexy sex and maybe a little wild limitation but it doesn't faze me because the rules are not our style. Jack loves to be in control in bed. Like any other normal guy. He had his fantasies too we love to act out.

From the beginning, he was very turned on when I was the aggressive one. He got a big ego boost when I wanted him so desperately, but as the months passed, he went from loving and attentive to not even wanting to touch or see me, because my addiction was getting the best of me.

I was so sad and wanted to have sex so badly, that there was a time when I put my arms around Jack's legs and begged him to have sex with me. He would actually walk to the door, dragging me along the floor with him. He left me there, crying. I'd never felt so pathetic in my life. We would have fierce fights over my addiction. We use to do all kinds of wild and kinky things but it wasn't enough after a three months. I wanted more.

● ● ●

New Fetish

I started looking into a new field of sex it was BDSM. BDSM was a type of role-play and lifestyle between two or more people, who use their knowledge of pain and pleasure to create a sexual atmosphere. The BD stands for Bondage and Discipline, the DS was for Dominance and Submission, and finally the S&M was Sadism and Masochism. The people involved in BDSM make sure that others know it's not a form of abuse and that it's an understanding between two people.

A submissive was someone who completely gives into his or her partner, and follows his or her every command. The dominant was the person in charge and was the one who gives the orders of what was going to happen. BDSM goes beyond only chains and whips. It's also deeper than just sex. In this culture, sex was pure vanilla, people who enjoy giving pain are typically called sadists which was me, but the person who enjoyed receiving pain was the masochist also known as my slave.

It's easy to perceive BDSM as self-destruction. The physical behaviors may be further subdivided into the following categories: bondage, physical discipline, intense stimulation, sensory deprivation, and body alteration. These categories are not meant to be mutually exclusive.

Bondage or restraint ranges from being held down or tied in such a manner that the person could escape if he or she tried, to behaviors, which involved elaborates restraints that leaves a person completely immobilized. This category also included the partial immobilization with handcuffs, leashes, constricting clothes such as corsets etc. This was something I was willing to give a try. I would have to go shopping.

Physical discipline ranges from slapping to whipping to caning. These behaviors could be of low intensity such that no marks are left, of moderate intensity such that only a redness that would disappear in a few hours or days was left, or of high intensity so that extensive bruising, welts, or other lesions are left for several days or even weeks.

Often, the recipient of these blows has not recognized what level of tissue damage has been inflicted nor does the intensity of the pain experienced necessarily relate to the tissue damage inflicted. Power that was erotic to them and the pain was just a method of achieving this power exchange.

Intense stimulation activities include scratching, biting, the use of ice on skin, hot wax on the skin, etc. These are activities that produce strong sensations with little or no tissue damage. The range of these behaviors usually involves duration or manner. Scratching someone's back a few times could be quite pleasing, but scratching someone's back for an hour could be quite painful.

Also included in this category was any behaviors or devices that increase sensation. For example, a spanking on wet skin was more intense than on dry skin. The dropping hot wax from several feet above someone was a very different sensation from dropping it from a few inches above him or her.

Sensory deprivation could also heighten sensations as well as intensify feelings of vulnerability. For example, a blindfold deprives the wearer of knowing when or where the next blow was to be struck. Not being braced for the blow may increase the sensations as well as focusing the recipient on the sensation without any other distractions. Other examples of sensory deprivation devices included hoods, earplugs, gags, etc.

Body alteration activities involved tattooing, piercing, branding, burns, etc. While many of these activities are meant to be permanent, they often are not. These behaviors may be seen as proof of S/M commitment, beautifying, or as sensory enhancements. The psychological pain was induced by feelings of humiliation, degradation, uncertainty, apprehension, powerlessness, anxiety, and fear.

● ● ●

Weeks Later After Learning About BDSM

I went shopping for some new clothes and shoes. As soon as I got home, I put on the new clothes and shoes. I pulled the skirt on and found out it was made out of Spandex, and stretched to fit. I tugged it over my thighs, up to my waist. Jeez, this sucker was tight, but finally it was in place. The black Spandex skirt was a micro-mini.

When, I looked in the dressing room mirror, I couldn't believe my eyes. It clung to me like a large black rubber band. That's practically what it was, anyway. It came down just two inches below my crotch, and the bottom moons of the cheeks of my ass were half an inch away from being plainly visible. My long bare legs were magnificent and the high heels made my walk with a hooker's strut, rolling my hips and pelvis. I looked like I was auditioning for a Penthouse video.

● ● ●

That Evening
After Jack Came Home

I headed to Jack's office in my new outfit. Jack stared me up and down. I could see he was getting a hard one just looking at me. "Hey, honey, are you up for some role-playing," I smiled diabolically at him.

"Oh hells yeah, give me a minute. Go back to the bedroom I will be up in a few."

Heading back upstairs and got the bedroom ready for excitement. The walls in this house are so thick they're virtually soundproof, so if Jack screamed no one would hear him. Jack walked into the bedroom as I lay across the bed, so what was my role, tonight?

"You are going to be a slave." He didn't disagree. I forced him to concentrate on our position and his body. I gave him a feeling of helplessness and remind him what his status was, he showed that he was submissive and devoted to me. I had easy access to his body, so I could do whatever I wanted to do to him.

● ● ●

I examined his body as if I have never seen it before. I ordered him to strip, and I gagged him with my own panties, so his screams are muffled. I attached alligator clips to his nipples. Then I lay him face down on the wooden chest, and strapped his wrists and ankles to the legs, immobilizing him. I put him in a position where he couldn't fight lose.

I grabbed a couple of pillows from the bed and pushed them under his tummy, raising his ass up, presenting it as a target. I reached into my briefcase and pull out a thin, supple switch, and proceed to just beat the bejeesus out of his ass and the back of his thighs for a good half hour.

I found that whipping his ass until it bled got me good and wet. He was covered with raw, bleeding welts.

"Please?" he asked plaintively.

"Please what, baby?" asked me, as I was teasing him.

"Please don't stop what you were doing," he said softly.

If his hands hadn't been cuffed, he would have finished himself off right there in front of me. I knew everything had felt so good to him. My heart was pounding, I was shaking and sweaty, I wanted to cum so damn bad. I just wanted to give him everything I could dish out to him!

"I don't think so," I ordered.

"Pleeeeeeese," he begged.

"Let's hear what you want," I said briskly.

"I want to, you know," he said. He wanted to cum.

"I want to have an orgasm," he begged.

"Maybe later," I said coldly.

You ready to cum?" I whispered. "You ready?"

"Yes! Yes! Please!" he begged. "Yes, mistress, I want to cum."

I sat back on the bed and smiled at him. I was debating the idea if I should finish him off or put on a show. What should I do?

Giana's Bayou

In New Orleans

The first time we meet, it was in May of 1998, I was eighteen years old and he was thirty-five. His name was Edgar. I met Edgar at a place we both worked at when I was sixteen. He was a relaxed young man. He stood about 6'0". He had jet-black hair, and hazel blue eyes.

He was the sort of guy that everyone adored, well spoken, well mannered, incredibly handsome, and sexually magnetic. As soon as I looked into his eyes, I felt an instant attraction. Physically he was everything I wanted in a guy and we got along so well.

He was mysterious, extremely funny and entertaining with a mischievous smile. He had money, it was never a problem for him do what he wanted when he wanted. His family fortune was in the billions. So of course, that was a plus for him. He enjoyed golfing and gardening on the weekends. He preferred classical music, and reading the newspaper every morning.

●●●

Giana Jennings

I was a quiet girl who usually kept to myself unless I was upset. I was very cautious of giving my heart to a guy. I was about 5'3", black hair and brown eyes. At the time, I rented a chair in a salon doing hair as a licensed cosmetologist in New Orleans, Louisiana where I had moved in with my boyfriend and his parents. I also would work my salon schedule and appointments around certain weeks when I was able to do some modeling at conventions that frequently came to our town.

It was good money. I enjoyed doing it. I didn't really like to call it modeling because it wasn't as glamorous as print work and runway, but I had fun doing it anyway. I modeled clothes, shoes, accessories, electronics, computer programs, just whatever came to town. I never took jobs out of town because I didn't have enough money to travel.

●●●

My So-called Family

My family was poor as hell let me correct that. My family did have money until my father stop working as much. My mother became a fucking alcoholic. My brother and I were abused as a child.

We were lucky after my father's death that he had a nice 401k and some bonds tied up for my brother and me. It would be nice to be able to live comfortable without having to worry about money. Edgar and I were both in relationships at the time when we met, but we both remember having a sense of attraction to each other.

●●●

Over the Years

We exchanged numbers to keep in touch. I never thought it would go anywhere because of what was going on between us. Then it was nonstop visiting and ridiculously long and frequent phone calls which we really got to know each other. We became the best of friends, and fell in love.

Edgar had just been saved and he was serious about wanting a woman that would help with his dreams. However, the person he was, I did not share the same goals and dreams. As for me, I was involved in my first serious relationship but it wasn't a good one. I really had other plans that would kill Edgar. After all the shit I experienced with my father, the things I was doing for the sake mine own interest.

My boyfriend and I fought all the time and eventually he cheated on me and we then broke up. In 2001 after my boyfriend and I called it quits, I moved out on my own. Edgar and I started dating Edgar made me laugh; we both enjoyed many of the same interests. We had the same family values, and wanted similar things for our future. I felt safe with him.

●●●

Fat Wednesday

As the years passed, Edgar and I would see each other at the Mardi Gras events in town once a year. We began to realize that there was a connection. Our failed attempts to get each other out of our minds and attempts of being with other people, we both realized we were just meant to be together and it wasn't worth fighting it anymore.

We had missed being in each other's lives so much. We knew we loved each other but I just didn't know where he would fit in and where it could go.

●●●

We decided to give it a try. When we first dated, Edgar knew that I was the one for him, but since I had been hurt in my last relationship, I wasn't sure what I wanted. It was love at first sight. He was very romantic. He'd bring me flowers. He wrote me poetry and love letters all the time.

We could not stand being away from each other. We loved driving in the country and going to shows together. He brought me out of my shell sexually. He always took me out for fancy meals and bought me stuff.

He regaled me with stories of this huge fortune he had amassed in his days as an aviation engineer guru, and amazing stories of his travels to exotic countries around the world.

●●●

As Time Passed

We then dated for nine months. I was young and about to leave home. I had planned to live with my brother until he asked me to move in with him. His behavior had become obsessive and controlling. It didn't helped that he was stressed out all the time. I just overlooked it because he had so much to do out of Africa for work. I ended up quitting my job and became a stay at home wife.

We've moved four times, and though he was successful in his profession, many sacrifices were made in order to secure his position. He had bought some diamond mines. I was happy to hear that because now we would be richer and the fortune was growing even more than I had ever could asked for.

● ● ●

Dream Come True

We finally got a twenty room brick home that was completed with a picket fence and automatic sprinklers. The house was along the bayou in Louisiana. The bayou curved like a crescent around the point of land on where the house stood. Between the stream and the house laid in a big abandoned field, where cattle were pastured when the bayou supplied them with water enough.

Through the woods that spread, back into unknown regions I had drawn an imaginary line, and past this line, I never stopped running along.

This was the form of my only mania. We own two cars. We were members of both the Rotary Club and the Chamber of Commerce. He introduced me to the high-class scene. He bought me presents, took me to the theatre and generally made me feel special.

I had all the nicest clothes in my closet, which was brimming with the season's must-haves. He let me pick the biggest room in the house to become my own closet. Everything was looking great for us! I decided to pretend to be a princess. I finally felt like I was becoming an adult.

●●●

He even gave me my own unlimited Visa credit card. I never owned one in my whole life. The day he gave the credit card, I ran out to a nearby mall to go shopping. I walked into the first store closest to the entrance of the parking lot. My eyes sweep the room. I could see rows of shirts, neatly folded.

Oh my god, there was a lovely printed velvet, beaded silk, embroidered cashmere, all with the distinctive signature of many famous fashion designers. They're everywhere. I don't know where to start. I thought I was going to have a panic attack. This was a girl's favorite dream come true. My adrenaline sweeping through me, as I hopped from one store to the next. I got so much that it all barely fit into the car.

When the first bill came in a month later, I panic. The bill was nine hundred and forty-nine dollars, sixty-three cents. In clear black and white I can't believe I spent that much. I thought Edgar was going to be pissed. As soon as he came home, I waited until he went into his office. I knocked on the door, I sat down near his desk I really didn't want him to see the Visa bill.

"Something wrong?" inquires Edgar.

"No," I mutter but I can't bring myself to smile. I told him about the bill but he just kept telling me; it was only a *VISA* bill. It's just a piece of paper; a few numbers and he wanted the best for me. He kissed me on the forehead and threw the bill on his desk. Wow, I thought…it felt great to be with someone who had some money.

● ● ●

On Cool Evening

Everything felt like a fairy tale. One evening he took me to see a new movie at the theaters a remake of "*Les Miserable*" I was so excited because it was my favorite Broadway musical. He rented out the whole movie theater out for us. It was so amazing! At the end of the credits flashed on the screen "WOULD YOU MARRY ME, MISS GIANA JENNINGS".

I jumped up and down, as he dropped to one knee with the most beautiful diamond ring I have ever seen. I had to make a decision now.

I said, "YES!" I decided to go for it. I knew if I didn't that I might regret it the rest of my life. I knew that I loved Edgar but at the same time, all I could see was green. I had a hidden agenda, so I was surprise when he popped the question.

●●●

Short but Sweet

Our engagement only lasted four months and then we were married on June 13, 2005. However, after six months together I knew something wasn't right. Our marriage was wonderful at first. Edgar was if different people, one who was violent, and then one who was fun. I noticed that Edgar's behavior tended to swing back and forth between controlling and loving.

●●●

What the Hell

He started to change for worse, after he found out that his dad was dying from colon and lung cancer, it was too much for Edgar to deal with. Edgar was the only child and was the next one in line to take over the family business.

He was afraid that the company was losing business especially knowing that just started to bounce back from 9/11. Now with being hit with the Hurricane Katina that swept through our town in New Orleans. Edgar wasn't sure how everything was going to work out.

Edgar put me on an allowance and limited the bank account so I was only allowed to take out so much a week. Even though I had a few hidden accounts that Edgar didn't know about. He regularly visited his friends down the pub to forget about his woes, leaving me in the house.

It was then that I found a huge collection of bottles of vodka, gin, and whiskey, hidden in a storage area in his office. All the times he'd locked himself in his office, he was drinking.

It would be honest to say that I haven't wondered what would have happened I had married someone else, but in all the years we spent together, I never once regretted the fact that I had chosen him and that he had chosen me as well. I thought our relationship was settled, but in the end, I realized that I was wrong. I was hoping that I wouldn't do the same things to him as I have done to others.

●●●

Of course, all marriages go through ups and downs, and I believe this was the natural consequence of couples that choose to stay together over the long haul. I found out his true age was 40. He explained that he lied because he feared losing me.

I forgave him, believing we could overcome our obstacles. Over the next couple of years, I progressively lost my independence, and my self-esteem. A cycle had started as emotional abuse. Over time, it got worse and worse. I was hoping I would never be physically abused.

I felt I had got myself into something that perhaps wasn't very good for me but I wasn't going to let my friends and family know I had made a mistake. Edgar was really threatened by my friends and my social life.

He hated that other guys would look at me, Tiny things that had not even occurred to me as being possibly offensive would cause enormous rage.

• • •

The Pain

My fear escalated when the physical violence began. He put his hands on me for the first time. He punched me dead in my stomach. I never felt so much pain in my life. I wanted to go to the hospital I didn't have the balls to tell the doctor why I was there.

When I was about to say something to the nurse, she was paged and had to leave the room. Edgar threatened me to not to say a word about what happened. He hissed and cursed under his breath, just then he lunged for me and struck me viciously with his fist. Just to make sure I didn't talk. He had knocked lose my front teeth. I got a black eye.

Then he threw me on the floor and kicked me in the stomach. I received a huge knot on my head when he knocked me down. We left the hospital before the doctor and the nurse returned to my room.

• • •

He was jealous of everyone and started treating me like his possession. Raw terror and cruel punishment bring absolute and unquestioning obedience in the convent to every rule and order, no matter how unreasonable or trivial it was.

• • •

This was a new low for me. He performed one of his favorite torments on me at least once a month. It was always when I was washing clothes. He would catch me in the laundry room, which was in the basement of the house. He would ordered me to prostrate myself on the cold, wet, soapy, floor.

This was done, with a cruel sneer he would then ordered me to would lick his cum off the rough cement floor with my tongue, after I would sit at his feet like a dog as he masturbated. He watched intently to see if there was the slightest flicker of anger, distaste or hesitation on my face as I cleaned the floor.

If he did, he would whip me until I would start to cry. Believe me, my tongue was always raw and bleeding before he was satisfied that I cleaned all his cum off the floor. I was unable to eat or drink for a day or two because of my mangled tongue. He would especially do this after an abused moment or he was drunk.

●●●

Another favored punishment was to crawl up and down through the house all day, upright on my knees. After I made it through the house at least five or six times, my knees were killing me. When I was drain of strength, I could not continue and ended up collapsing in a fainted. Edgar would shook me roughly, pulled me back on my knees and commanded me to resume crawling. I desperately tried to finish my daily house routine.

He'd screamed and yelled at me about everything that made him mad, and called me an idiot. Edgar was shoving me, spitting at me, lifting me up and shaking me. I was very intimidated by him.

From that time on, even though the physical violence was occasional, the fear of it happening pervaded my life. He would threaten me with it often. At other times his anger became such a white-hot rage that the veins on his forehead and neck would pulsate and he'd be unable to talk.

There were some nights that he would force himself on to me. Eventually after being raped so many times, I became pregnant, only to lose it a few months later.

●●●

This relationship was going to work I keep telling myself. In many ways, I thought I brought this upon myself. He felt he had to have control everything, and so I did. He used to hit, punch, and slap me. At times, he would tell me that I was no good, but on good days, he would apologize and make me feel better about the things that were happening as if it was a dream.

The few sweet words he said were always as an apology for shouting at me, locking me out of the bedroom or for throwing his dinner across the room. I was living on the memory of the good times we'd had and hoping that he would change and things would go back to the way we were when we first met.

●●●

Three Months Later

He had done his worse. Deep into the night, we begin to argue. This argument turned into a fight. I did not want anything to happen. He punched me in my stomach. He grabs me by the throat.

His fingers tighten around my throat. As I was fighting for my life, I can feel the air slowly slipping away. He then let go. As soon as I was free from him, I started pushing him back away from me. I began to punch him back. He turned and punched me in my stomach again. Soon after that he pulled my hair, I had no choice but to pull his hair back.

He released his hands from my hair and went back to choking me. His hands were tighter around my neck than before. I could see the darkness in his eyes. It was a darker than any other darkness unlike any other I've seen before in his eyes. Just when I thought he wasn't going to let me go, he dropped me from his death grip. No more, I threw in the towel. I stopped trying to fight him. I must have thought I could knock him out. I was wrong.

● ● ●

Only a month later we were at it again. This time he struck me in my face. I can hear the crackling in my jaw and the taste of blood emerged across my lips. Of course, my dumbass tried to fight back. He didn't do anything else that night.

● ● ●

The more I was attacked, the more I became withdrew. I kept feeling perpetually blamed, inadequate and not doing enough to keep the relationship together. I isolated myself from my friends, my family and from everything that I used to enjoy doing.

●●●

Questioning Myself

Why did he hurt me? When he promised to love me! What did I do to deserve the pain he has given me? He promised to honor and cherish me! Every punch, kick was like a stone shattering glass, chips of my love for him was falling away with every strike! Why didn't we have a normal relationship? I gave him my all, my everything. In return, he would slap, punch, kick, rape, and threaten to kill me!

●●●

On a Quiet September Evening

One day I decided to confront him about the abuse. "Why?" I asked him

He was drunk I should have known better to talk to him when he was like this. He laughed in my face and said," Because I can! It was all your fault why I do the things I do to you. You annoyed and piss me off. Therefore, you should take the consequences. You are a worthless piece of shit."

He blamed me for everything that went wrong in his life. He went on to tell me, he wished he'd never met me and wished I was dead. I sat there, feeling the weight of his words like stones around my neck dragging me deeper into a deep dark hole. I hated him. I hated everything he put me through and I hated myself for letting him.

Almost everything I did, made him angry and there were rarely a day when he didn't yell at me. I became more and more isolated, more dependent on Edgar, and more afraid of Edgar's temper if I didn't do what he wanted. He would call me a whore, bitch, liar and fat. This isn't love! Why did I stay so long? I should had killed himself earlier but I stuck on cloud nine.

●●●

Only two months after the last fight, we broke out into another argument. We were on our way back from Pennsylvania after visiting some business friends. He was driving along I95 in the pitch-dark night. He was complaining about his friends and how I wasn't talking, how I was making him look like a fool.

His words poured into me like venom I clenched my fist, screamed "I hate you" and punched him across the face causing the car to swerve off the road. As soon as the car stopped, I jumped out of the car and began running.

He chased me down and threw me against the road, smashing my head repeatedly on the gravel only stopping to punch me in the chest. Eventually we stopped. He finally let me up. I wiped the blood from my head and we got back in the car. We continue on the way home in silent.

At the house, we both got out of the car. Edgar began to speed race to the door. Once he reached the front door, he turned and pushed me onto the ground. He ran for the door and he was planning to lock me out but I got up just in time before he could. We started fighting again. This time he didn't fight back. He just stood there as I kicked him and yelled "Fight me, you miserable coward. It's not much fun now that I'm fighting back, is it?"

We ended up back in the house where he threw me on the bed and pounded my chest with his fist. He then started strangling me. His face was contorted and I could read his lips saying, "I am going to fucking kill you!" then everything went black. When I came to, he was beside me and had put a wet towel on my forehead. He looked at me and said, "Now look what you made me do you little piece of shit."

● ● ●

Turn of Events

That was the last straw. In my head, I decided there and then that the relationship was over but I needed to think things through before I did. It got to the point that if I wasn't home on time or gone for more than an hour, I was interrogated repeatedly about where I was, whom I talked to, even what I wore. If I spent too much money, talked on the phone for too long, or argued with his point of view.

I knew I wanted to get out so I could get what I really wanted from him, which was his money, but I just didn't know how to end it. I was scared of what he'd do if I divorced him. He would make sure I didn't get any of the money. All I had was five cigarettes and the clothes on my back. I was scared of him and didn't know what to do.

A better life, a life without fear or intimidation, no more walking on egg shells or awaiting the next beating or rape. He left me with emotional scars and physical. I now am going to be complete control of my life. I was broke, depressed and suicidal. Other times I felt homicidal.

He had promised me all kinds of things including riches and wealth. He had guaranteed it would be one sweet ride. I wonder what I could do to show my appreciation to him. I gave him my heart in return all I have is fear to show. I feared that he would file for divorce and lock me out of his family fortune.

•••

A New Dawn

Away from our abusive fights, I was able to build my self-reliance in small ways. I learned to have fun without Edgar, to make decisions and to be okay without seeing him every day. I slowly built my self-confidence back up just so I could get back to my original plan. I defend myself on my own terms, rather than seeing myself as Edgar's trophy wife.

•••

Two Months Later
One Evening

He arrived home at his regular hour. I pleasantly surprised him by preparing his favorite meal. We ate dinner together. A bottle of wine stood on the table between us, I reached over and poured me another glass better the bastard finished it.

The wheels were rolling in my head of what I need to get his money and to get rid of him. Our meal nearly finished when I got up and started cleaning the kitchen. Afterward, I began collecting all the dishes from the table, and when he was finally done eating. My plans to end this were drawing near.

"Are you ready for tomorrow?" he asked me.

"Yes"

"Good, I don't want to be late, so I am going to go to take a shower and head to bed."

"Ok, I will be up soon." I said with a mischievous grin on my face.

Little did he know I didn't book our trip to Hawaii, I booked a one way to Hell just for him. He headed upstairs. I just stood there for a minute as I watched him walk up the stairs. As I turned back into the kitchen, I heard the faucet running. I grabbed the carving knife and headed upstairs. I turned the radio up loud enough so no one could hear what was about to happen next.

While, he was in the shower I brutally put an end to this so-call promising life. I had stabbed him 27 times, shot in the face, and I slit his throat from ear to ear.

● ● ●

Here I am, stumbling up and down my backyard. The rain was pouring down. I stared at my foot that is when I noticed that the splashing on my feet was my own tears and not the rain. They are salty and bloodstained from my agonizing pain. Nobody could be madder at me than I could. Why was I so stupid? I was so stupid I lost track of what the plan was and instead I fell in love. I pushed this one too far. Never again will I trust anyone. I went back inside.

● ● ●

The Cover-up

I called my brother Damien, to help me get rid of the body. Thank god for him, he was truly a saint. Damien owned a funeral home in New York. I gave Damien everything he needed so he could cover my tracks. We didn't want anyone to find out it was me who killed Edgar. I made sure I cleaned up the house with perfection. I file a missing person report with the police but a few days after the event.

● ● ●

Moving On

Only a few weeks later, they find his body and his car in a back alley in a prostitute and drug infested area. He was believed that he was killed and robbed. The police asked to come down to the city morgue to identify Edgar's body. I could barely identify his decomposed body. I put on a show. I acted as if I was going lost because he was gone. They had no evidence. There was no one to fight for Edgar's case. It was easy case that was closed just as quickly as they find his body.

Two days after the release his body to me, I put together a wonderful funeral. I put his body to rest. The lawyers didn't worst any time after the funeral. They had a meeting with me. Apparently, I was the only one listed in the will, which I already knew. I inherited everything; I tied up most the money, for my baby brother. I sold the family business and mines while I started to move on with my life.

I got what I really wanted in the end...his fortune. I went through hell to get it but I think I did look him at one point as the love of my life. I think I am going to take a trip to New York. It was time to change my name again. I must disappear and start a new life, maybe I will find another sucker I can swindle more money from.

Blood and Honor

Somewhere in New York

It was always a dream to become a police officer. I was one of five siblings born to Robyn and Wyatt Demarcus. They were in search of a better life and settled in Manhattan. My parents divorced, my mother remarried, and the family moved to the South Bronx. There was where I received my primary and secondary education. I decided that I would enlist in the Navy after I graduated from Theodore Roosevelt High School.

•••

Once in the Navy

I was deployed near the village in Afghanistan. On that day, my unit was engaged in a firefight with Afghanistan military soldiers. The shrapnel of an enemy grenade seriously wounded three of my comrades during that firefight. I was awarded the Navy Commendation and Purple Heart Medals.

●●●

After I recovered from my wounds, I was discharged from the Navy and I returned to New York. There I met a young girl by the name of Angel Sherwood whom I married. I worked in various jobs among them as a factory worker and ambulance driver. On various occasions, I would apply to become a police officer in the New York Police Department. I was not accepted. It took a few years before I applied again. I was finally accepted as a police candidate in the NYPD.

●●●

New York Police Department

I graduated from the New York Police Academy after six months of training and was assigned to the 13th Precinct in Brooklyn. The 13th Precinct was located in northern Brooklyn in the Williamsburg section of Brooklyn.

It was primarily a residential and commercial area consisting of factories, warehouses, one and two family private homes as well as numerous apartment buildings. The five primary commercial strips are Graham Avenue, Grand Street, Lee Avenue, Havemeyer Street and Broadway.

My identity as a police officer was not so much a unifying force as a tool that allowed effective functioning in spite of differences. When I put on my uniform, I am not white or black. I am blue. We are one big happy family. We were a bunch of dysfunctional motherfuckers.

As a police officer was taking his oath of office, he was making a sworn statement to act ethically and judge fairly while performing his duties. We are supposed to lead by example.

Police officers must be held to a higher standard of moral and ethical values than was expected of the average person. Police officers needed the trust and respect of the public to perform their duties and responsibilities effectively.

This trust does not come without the officer knowing and understanding his sworn oath and code of ethics. All police officers throughout this country must take a sworn oath before they are authorized to perform the duties of a law enforcement officer.

• • •

Police Culture

My life as in the police culture was actually less mysterious and exotic than outsiders believe. There wasn't a secret handshake. We are social isolation comes not from corruption or brutality but from the grind of daily shift work combined with doses of unfiltered and politically incorrect reality.

Many of the potentially good police are turned off by a shamefully low starting salary not even enough to wipe my ass with. We must learn to stand at attention, salute, and skills of problem-solving, independent thinking, quick action, and the ability to articulate everything.

There are some tricks of this trade which involved of knowing which corners to cut and why, what form to fill out and how, and when to modulate your radio voice so backup started to head in your direction before trouble starts.

Fresh out of the police academy I was placed in high- crime districts because these areas are the least desirable to work in. I learned faster in the hood. I learned about the importunate demands of the dispatcher, the futility of rapid response, and the persistence and harms of the drug trade.

●●●

It's unfortunate that the ghetto becomes a real-life training arena. I made mistakes. High-crime areas are where the best and most experienced patrol officers are needed. The enthusiasm of the young was no substitute for the wisdom of the old.

The academy doesn't really teach much, it's the job that educates police officers was really productive. Criminals and the community don't want to work with the police any more than police want to coddle criminals. Young police learned that the job has more to do with public control than with public service.

●●●

After Years on the Force

One night my partner Damien and I were driving to a police call when we saw a person running a red light. We rolled up behind the car and ran the license plate. The call we got was to check the car because he was a drug dealer.

We decided to stop the car. As, I was approaching the driver's side of the vehicle, the driver gets out, and started to walk backwards as he's looking at me. I tell him to put his hands on the car and he says "Can't do it man." He then takes off on foot. I give chase. This traffic stop turns into a foot chase with a gun.

While doing so, I'm running with my gun out as I can see he's holding his right front pants pocket, which led me to believe he had a gun. I could see that there was definitely something bulky in his pocket that resembled a gun, and wasn't taking any chances. While running right behind him, I've got my gun in my right hand and my radio in my left, telling dispatch 242, foot-chase, Broad, Northbound through the yards, black male, red shirt, black pants, about 6' 0", possibly got a gun, he's holding his waistband.

● ● ●

This was done in 4 seconds. After about two blocks, I lost him through the yards of trees and brushes but I believed that he was hiding out nearby. We set up a perimeter. My partner spotted him a few minutes later. We started chasing him through the back of people's yards and over their fences.

Damien grabbed the fence with his hands, using his momentum and flew over the fence. Then the guy we were running after jumped over the fences without his hands, like a professional runner, damn he was good.

When we finally apprehended him, whatever was in his pocket was now gone. We tried to trace back his steps we recovered nothing. We arrested him and brought to the station where we learned that he's already been arrested three times for carrying a gun, dumb ass! You would have thought he would have learned his lesson the first time.

●●●

A Few Months Later

I was given to a police officer trainee at 17:00 hours. Damien had the day off. While training the new officer, I was approached by a woman who was screaming and crying hysterically that her baby wasn't breathing. I advised our dispatch and entered her home.

We found the 7-week old infant; he was lying on his back and looked like he was sleeping. He instantly reminded me of my little girl who was about the same age at the time. I did everything I was taught how to do CPR and didn't stop CPR until the ambulance arrived. He was transported to the hospital where doctors made several attempts to revive him, but no luck. He had passed.

After he was pronounced legally dead, I had to stay in the same room with him for about an hour until the detective arrived. The father of the baby came in the hospital; he looked at the baby and just lost it. My trainee tried to calm him down as I went to the vending machine to get him a cup of coffee to calm down.

He grabbed my trainee's gun and started to shoot up the hospital. He manager to kill four nurses and a doctor by the time I came around the corner. Without even thinking, I empty my gun into the father.

● ● ●

Time for a Change

It was the first time I ever cried on the job. After that, things just got worst for me. I didn't make enough money to keep my house. I was losing everything. At least I still had my wife and daughter. Even my partner quit after the death of his sister. I moved to Philadelphia. My mom helped me get back on my feet. I was hired at 69th District Precinct in Kensington.

●●●

In Pennsylvania

Kensington was a neighborhood in between the Lower Northeast section of Philadelphia and North Philadelphia sub-neighborhoods than a clearly defined area. The Kensington area of the city roughly coincided with the former Kensington District, Richmond District, Aramingo Borough and Northern Liberties Township.

The area was just a couple of miles northeast of Center City and just to the West of the Port Richmond neighborhood. Kensington was home to a large population of Irish Americans, Hispanic Americans, mainly Puerto Ricans and Dominicans, African Americans, Italian Americans, and Polish Americans.

Deindustrialization eventually took its hold on the neighborhood in the 1950s, leading to a significant population loss, high unemployment, economic decline, and the abandoning of homes in the neighborhood. While most of the large manufacturers have left, the area had many small shops and large renovated factories and warehouses for newer artisans to set up shop.

● ● ●

What the Hell

The way I looked at things was very different now. I don't who I was becoming. I wasn't really myself anymore. Here was where I learned that there were good police officers and as well as corrupt ones. The majority of the police officers who served our cities, towns and counties are good law-abiding men and women whom we could look up to as heroes.

Many of these officers are seldom charged for their crimes and often the only punishment that those who are accused receive was a minor and limited suspension from their jobs.

I am sure that you as I, have asked yourself, why was it that some of the officers who are so cruel could get away with the things that they did. Well, they did get away with it. However, that was not the worst of it, the most amazing thing of all it was that there are many corrupt officers within the police forces that it wasn't funny.

Which are associated with the worst criminal elements known to society and the fact that they are officers of the law made them worse than your common street criminal. In many cases, other fellow officers knew the corruption and criminal acts committed by other officers. They would rather keep quiet and look the other way instead of doing something about it.

●●●

Corruption

For the first time I noticed the illegal acts committed by some of my fellow officers were often ignored and seldom reported by others, including some of my superiors who believed in a code of silence known amongst them as the "Blue Wall of Silence" in which reporting another officer's error, misconduct, or crimes were regarded as a betrayal.

Those who had engaged in what they regarded as less serious misconduct for example, operating an off-duty security business; accepting free gifts, meals, and discounts; or having a minor accident while driving under the influence of alcohol.

At the same time, most police officers indicated that they would report a colleague who stole from a found wallet or a burglary scene, accepted a bribe or kickback, or used excessive force on a car thief after a foot pursuit, especially if they didn't get a cut or was a snitch. A police officer, who reported the criminal acts of another officer, was considered a traitor by his fellow officers and often has to go through hell because of his honest acts.

If the colleague were an asshole, the corrupt officer would find a way for the traitor to be fired or killed in the line of duty. I was warned to pick my friends wisely. Forget what you learned at the police academy. My new partner keeps telling me every day that he would show me what police work was really all about.

●●●

A Change

Well I finally got to find out what my partner meant. My partner Christop discovered a burglary of a jewelry shop. The display cases were smashed, and it was obvious that many items had been taken. While searching the shop, he took a watch, worth about 2 days' pay for that officer. We reported that the watch had been stolen during the burglary. I kept my mouth shut. I didn't want to make any waves.

When we returned to the precinct, Christop handed an unmarked envelope with $300 in it to Captain Bobby McKinley. Captain Bobby McKinley who was connected to the Department's Chief Inspector in the Investigating Unit of the same police department I worked in. He would make cases disappear.

• • •

The next ride with Christop we unlawfully stopped and searched a vehicle because we believed it contained drugs or guns. We falsely claimed in police reports and under oath that the car ran a red light, which was a traffic violation. We then claimed that we saw contraband in the car, which was in plain view.

• • •

To conceal an unlawful search of individuals who we believed that one guy was carrying drugs or a gun, we would falsely assert that we saw a bulge in the person's pocket or saw drugs and money changing hands. We would get him to start paying us a percent of his drug sales. If he fell to do so, we planted some kind of contraband. This started to become natural to me.

• • •

There was a regular pattern of trading collars. The purpose of this practice was to accumulate overtime pay for the officers involved. In this scheme, the police officer who actually arrested the defendant would pass off the arrest to a colleague who was not involved or even present at the time of the arrest.

Trading collars were done to maximize the overtime pay because the regular day off, of the officer taking the arrest coincided with the likeliest date for a required court appearance. The officer who took the arrest would get all the details from the actual arresting officer just to fill out the arrest papers.

● ● ●

My Life and Angel

After six years of marriage, my wife Angel finally was pregnant. I knew I couldn't stop what I was doing. In April she gave birth to a baby girl, we named her Adela. My wife only knew a little bit about how I would get money under the table. She seemed fine with it.

It was great being married and I loved my little girl. My world just seemed to make sense. I didn't dare to tell my wife about the things I was doing. She had a big fucking mouth and that was all I needed, was for people to find out how I got my money.

●●●

Dirty Secrets

That following summertime I was assigned to work the street on my motorcycle. For the first time as a motorcycle cop, I pulled over some guy on the 11th street, because he has exceeded the speed limit of 110 in a 25-school zone.

He was some 50-year guy for Levittown. I informed the guy that he was facing a fine of $5,000 and that his violation would not be registered if he pays me $500. Without a single blink in his eye, he gave me the money. This was easy cash. This was an everyday route.

●●●

The Ultimate Dream
A Wet Dream Come True

Wow, I would never forget one motorist. A young teenager driving a 1972 Dodge Charger that was rebuilt from the inside out it was a beauty. I pulled him over around midnight one night. He was driving very reckless. There in the back seat was his girlfriend. He didn't want to lose his beautiful car to a DUI violation.

He offered his girlfriend as payment but he wanted to join in fucking her. I agreed. Since I was married to Angel, I never had such an experience of having a threesome. I had to give up a risqué life, which was the price I had to pay for being married. I made them give me their keys and cell phone. I put them in the back of my car.

While driving down we scanned the almost dark road, searching for a place to do business at that they had promised. I looked in the rear window she was smiling wryly. Finally, a few scattered buildings came into view. I pulled into the empty parking lot and grabbed a blanket out my trunk. We walked into the building and placed the blanket on the floor.

She grinned and said, "I always wanted to fuck a cop."

"Well this is your lucky day!"

● ● ●

I looked her up and down her threadbare tank top hugged her body too tightly, outlining every curve of her full breasts, and at this point, she didn't even care that the thin cloth was nearly transparent. The heat poured through my veins as she started to undress, my heart fluttered. Her boyfriend sat there and watched he kept rubbing his cock through his pants.

My hands went to the back of her neck and began to rub gently. I rubbed harder, my hands finding the curves of her breasts as I began to kiss the back of her neck. I came back around her to see her breast. I teased her sensitive nipples and squeezed them gently.

I started sucking on her nipple deep and hard, with my tongue flicking and swirling, you can tell it was driving her wild. She grasped my head, pulling me tighter against her as I switched to the other breast.

She leaned back against her boyfriend, letting him support her. My hands traveled lower, reaching her thighs, then the sides of her hot pussy. I spread her lips, one hand on each side, as her boyfriend reached down, too, sliding his fingers between mine, right to the slick wetness of her center.

Fuck yeah, I thought. She was soaked and dripping wet. I think this bitch must want some black cock. Her boyfriend looked back over her shoulder at me while smiling in amusement. Apparently, part of him really like what was going on. He was already rock hard. He backed away from her as I stepped behind her.

I thrust once more against the small of her back. Then my hands urged her forward, bending her over at the waist. She instinctively spreads her legs, knowing I was about to take her, and the reality of that impending moment made her whimper with anticipation.

I was going to fuck her, right here and now, with her boyfriend watching every thrust and grind. She looked up to meet her boyfriend's eyes, finding them glazed with his own arousal, his cock hard and thick as his hand stroked.

In a flash, I was with her, my big, black cock impaling her completely, and she screamed in pleasure as I took her. I began to pump hard, slamming against her ass, burying myself to the hilt in her soaking wet pussy and then sliding out slowly, only to pound forward furiously and do it all over again.

● ● ●

Her boyfriend stepped in front of her, and from her bent over position, he pulled his cock out, and she gasped at the sight. She reached out a hand, sliding one finger along his white rippled skin. She wrapped her hand around the shaft. She slowly slid her tongue from the base to the cleft, as she had her finger moments before.

She flicked the velvet underside of the head with the tip of her tongue, and smiled as she was rewarded with an involuntary twitch, followed by a low moan from above.

Then she took him inside the warm, wetness of her mouth, wrapping her fist around the base, because she had no hope of being able to deep-throat a cock. He began to pump in and out of her mouth, copying my rhythm that I was still doing from behind her. She was caught in a whirlwind of pleasure.

When I reached underneath her to find her swollen clit, she bucked back against me, knowing I was about to make her cum. Her body began to tremble. She screamed out as she came. Only the strength of me holding her hips tight to me as I thrust kept her knees from completely buckling as pleasure flooded her entire body.

I was pounding harder and faster, my cock swelled as I came deep inside her, spurting and filling her as her pussy clenched me tighter, milking me of every hot drop. Her boyfriend cum in her mouth, we all got dressed. I took them back to their car and let them go. I loved this new power.

● ● ●

Sex and Money

I was coercing sexual favors from prostitutes so in return for not arresting them. One night I was getting a blowjob from a nearby prostitute, when one of my colleagues had called me on my cell, helping him cover up a shooting, this was becoming bullshit cleanup for this guy.

Did what I needed to do to get any money coming my way. I would get money and sex out dumb ass girls. People were trying to stay out of trouble. Then there were those who didn't want to go back to jail.

• • •

Just Some Shooting

I helped cover up three unjustified shootings in 2007. The first was a shooting early May 6 in which a few of my colleagues fired at several unsuspecting gang members that were a little rally up. They were firing their guns into the air about midnight.

I helped collect the officers' expended shell casings so there was no evidence of the shooting, but had to put them back when officers discovered that they had wounded two of the three men. The incident was covered up. We all reported that the men were pointing their weapons at police when, which wasn't true.

●●●

In the second alleged cover-up, I witnessed a few officers place a gun next to a 21-year-old man whom they shot. As Jacob Clifford bled to death, we intentionally delayed summoning an ambulance as we huddled with a supervisor to concoct a scenario that justified the shooting.

●●●

Towing

The towing company frequently was affiliated with a repair shop, and thus loomed the possibility that the repair shop would be contracted to repair the accident vehicle. To gain an advantage, some towing companies enlisted the services of Philadelphia Police Officers.

For the right price, an officer might look the other way, as a tow truck driver sped to an accident scene. For a slight gratuity, an officer might intercede on behalf of a tower by convincing a driver that the tower, in question, was worthy of repairing the driver has damaged vehicle.

Some officers openly recommended the services of one tower over another. There were officers who would notify their favorite tower via pay phone, upon arriving at an accident scene. Soon I was getting a payment of 20 percent of the repair bill from the shop owner.

●●●

Helping Officer in Need

At 02:00 AM on Monday May 10, I was on duty, driving my patrol car on a deserted road. I saw a vehicle that has been driven off the road and was stuck in a ditch. I approached the vehicle and observed that the driver was not hurt but it was obvious intoxicated. I also found that the driver was a police officer. Instead of reporting this accident and offense, I transported the officer to his home.

●●●

Drugs

When it came to a drug bust, I would keep money and/or narcotics confiscated at the time of an arrest or raid. I was selling narcotics to addicted informants in exchanged for stolen goods. I would pass confiscated narcotics to police informants for sale to addicts.

I even planted narcotics on an arrested person in order to have a law violation. I accepted money or narcotics from suspected narcotics law violators for the disclosure of official information financing heroin transaction.

• • •

I would lay, hid evidence, distorted facts, engaged in cover-ups, paid for perjury and set up innocent people in a relentless effort to win indictments, guilty pleas and convictions. All the money, sex and cover up were spinning out of control, but at the same time, I was a God!

I participated in a drug bust, which ended my career as a police officer. In October of 1999, some members of the police force that was involved in the same drug bust as I had framed me. I found out that the officers were pissed because I was pulling more money than they were. Oh well, fuck them they should have done a better in getting what they wanted.

• • •

Oh, Shit...

Now I was scared of my life. They wanted to indict me by a Special and Extraordinary Grand Jury in Philadelphia for one count of Burglary in the First Degree; one count of Grand Larceny in the First Degree; one count of Grand Larceny in the second Degree; six counts of Grand larceny in the Third Degree; and, one count of assault in the Third Degree. The witnesses against me were drug dealers involved in the drug bust who were promised to have their indictments dropped if they agreed to testify against me.

●●●

I was worried about everything I had done since I moved in Pennsylvania. I was even worried about my family. I got into an intense argument with my wife about if I was found guilty. I try telling my wife what she should do.

She was not trying to hear it, but in the middle of the argument, she made it clear that HER daughter wasn't going to visit me in prison. That was weird, especially knowing that she was very protective about me going to any school and doctor meeting with her.

•••

I was starting to have doubts about my daughter's paternity. I took my daughter out of elementary school and swabbed her cheek at a nearby fast food parking lot. Two weeks went by, that was when I found out that someone else fathered the 6-year-old girl.

I called Damien my old partner because I knew he still had a connection to the police department. I sent a swabbed of my daughter to him. I asked him to run it though the database to find out who was the father. Within days, Damien broke the news to me. It was one of the officers I worked closely by. It was Jason Hamilton. He had helped me in the drug bust that, I was now on trial for.

•••

Breaking Point
January, 2000

I planned a romantic night with Angel. I had sex this lying cheating whore for the last time. I handcuffed Angel's naked body to the floor. She thought we were going to do something freaky and went along with it. I covered her eyes and gaged balled her. I slipped my cock back into her pussy she just started to climax. Before she could fully cum, I began to strangle her with a computer cord.

I killed my wife, Angel of thirteen years of marriage, and my so-called daughter Adela. I went into Adela's room as she slept. I stared down at the Adela. My heart was boiling all this time I was living a lie. The man I once thought of as a friend was the father of my child.

Once I was done, I looked at her bloodied and mangled body. Her skull was crushed by the repeated slams against her bed frame. I packed up a few of my things since I was still fired up, decided I was going to take of care Jason before I skipped town. I threw my suitcase into the back seat of the car. I went over Jason's house.

● ● ●

I drove up to his house. I knocked on his door. As soon as he opened the door, I opened fired. I empty my gun into his chest. There he lay on the floor dead. Oh…shit what have I done. I needed to escape. I skipped out of town. The hunt for me was on. At night all, I could think about was how my life was going so good and quickly turned to shit.

● ● ●

Aftermath

Tightness in my chest I can't breathe. The only time I could escape was when I fall asleep. It's a constant worry another would strike. I worry about everything that has happened in my life all the time; it makes me lose my appetite. My sight darkens my life flashes. My worries control my thoughts. You have no idea what it's like to live one day in my shoes.

Maybe if you did you wouldn't judge me as you do. Their face was always on my mind. A smile I have seen a million times, two eyes that would light up the sky at night. One last battle I could not fight. The day was long, and then night then morning, I knew that soon I would be gone. Soon I would be out of time.

A million pieces went my heart, now a photo I look at to see my once loved family's smile, what have I done. I had no choice, but the great memories I would always keep with me. Their love was in my heart for eternity. I never got to say goodbye but I didn't have the strength to say goodbye either.

I had to wake up and face the truth every day. Angel was nothing but a menace to society. She was a fake bitch and a pitiful excuse for anyone to call a wife. She was not even worth having the title of being called a woman. All the misery all the pain all the tears and agony she has dished out. I don't want to this shit to come to haunt me and bring me down anymore. I have nothing to live for.

I was stuck in a place of pain, torment and no end. There was no way out, only a black hole without an end. When was it my time to end, that's all I could think about why was it me in this awful place, ruby red slippers I wish to be in reach. I was harmed in a way I can never forget; fearing every day was the only thing in my way.

My mind, my dignity was completely distracted by someone who I once trusted and by the things, they have done. My words have no meaning in anyone's eyes; all I ever did was made her cry. My child was not mine and now had to suffer the same fault as her lying cheating mother.

No more walking on eggshells, sitting on the edge of my seat trying to please everyone. I don't have to huddle in the corner apprehensively or sobbing my heart out to anyone. I am so sick of putting on a brave face for those who see me on the street. I will stay in hiding until my death.

Cruel
Punishment

In 1954 in South Carolina

I was born in a little town called Demark in South Carolina. My name is Damien Grissom. I was born into a medium class family. My parent's Bill and Eve Grissom were well known in the community. I was the couple's second child. My mother was the beauty queen back in the day until she married her high school sweetheart the school's all-star quarterback.

Everyone loved them; they were the town's favorite duo. They were so happy together until my mother became pregnant. They had a daughter together; she was fifteen years old when I was born. They named her Evelyn, after my mother. My father was forced to have a quick wedding so no one would know that they were going to have a baby out of wedlock.

We dress just like everyone in town. We went to church every Sunday with a smile on our face and the Bible in our hand. We wasn't your usual family despite how well known my family was. We still had our secrets. My family kept things to themselves but when they were home, things just did not seem normal. It was completely different world when the doors were closed. We kept to ourselves and never had company.

● ● ●

I hated my father. He was a no good for nothing bastard. I remember how he uses to beat my mother to death. Every night she would tuck me into bed, as my father would stand in the doorway, with a bottle in his hand. He wanted to make sure my mother wasn't telling me any secrets.

Then within minutes you can hear them fighting, I just covered my eyes and fall asleep. Many of the fights were wild. I could never figure out why she dealt with it. Then again, she wasn't wrapped to tight herself. She always seemed to be drugged up. If he was not getting his way, he let it be, know.

• • •

As my sister got older the less, I saw her around dad only but she was barely home. She would walk around the house with her head down. When she talked to me, she won't even look me in the eyes. I would go in her room and watch TV with her until dad would call for her. She would disappear for hours but when she returned, she had tears in her eyes and even blood running down her legs.

• • •

I would soon find out that my dad was having sex with my sister until she was too old for him. There was a time when she was coming out of the bathroom after her shower. My father would make her drop her towel and he always wanted "a hug."

If she were ever in the bathtub, he would always come in and wanted to wash her. This also frequently occurred when she was in the laundry room as well.

• • •

The abuse he uses to do to my sister was now happening to me. When I did something he didn't approve of, he would pull me to him and pulled down my pants and underwear then would bend me over his knee and spanked me.

My father started to beat me then it grew into other things. My dad loved to slap me around and treat me badly. He always needed to drink alcohol, day to day.

All the hurt and pain he was a flicking on my sister and I. I remember the nights when he was half-insane I never wanted to be home.

● ● ●

When I was in middle school, he used to come into my room late at night. He would wake me up and make my sister and I follow him to the basement. The look on his face as if he was enjoying in flicking pain on me. I got my father so mad that he placed a hot metal pipe on my back, leaving a scar that I was ashamed to show to anyone or putting me in an Iron Maiden for hours

He enjoyed taking my sister to his office, which was in the basement. No one was allowed to go down there not unless he was with you. There was no way out of his basement. It was cold and damp in his "office". There were locks on both sides of the door which lead down into the office. In his office was a bed. The sheets were dirty and stain with blood. On each side of bed, chains with handcuffs were connected to the bedposts.

● ● ●

Fucking Insane

He would molest me and do sexual things to me. He would make me kneel on rice, as I had to give him oral sex. As the years passed his huge collection of pictures of my sister and I grew on his office wall. Now, he was forcing my sister to have sex with me as he took pictures of us. Sometimes he would masturbate while he watched. He would tell us how to perform all different types of acts on each other.

My mother knew what was going on but turned a blinded eye to it. She would never interfere with my father. I hated this horrible life I lived in. Each day was filled with different conflicts. The quarrels and strife that always ended the same. I was being raised in prison. When was I ever going to see any sun through this darkness? Love was what I craved the most, but this was how he showed his love. My bedroom was my jail cell.

●●●

One summer day in 1966

At the age of twelve, I could not take it anymore. I was sitting in the kitchen when he yelled at me to follow him down to his office. I screamed at the top of my lungs "NO".

Saying no to him was never an option. He stopped dead in his tracks. He stopped walking towards the basement door.

He turned around. He gave me the nastiest ass look I ever seen. He ran down into the basement. I really did not why he ran down into the basement, nor did I care. I got up from the table and commenced to go to my room. My father bolted up the stairs to the basement. He had in his hand some rope and some weird metal thing. I had no idea what he was doing.

He grabbed me by the arm then twisted my arm to make such I didn't break free and dragged me to the table that was in the foyer. His face was so red I wished I was dead. I was kicking and screaming. I tried my hardest to break free, it was impossible. He had a death gripped on my arm. He tied me down to the table.

•••

My hands were tied down to each of table legs. I was crying and yelling at my dad to stop. He pushed a piece cloth in my mouth. I was terrified. I really didn't know what he was going to do to me. I didn't see his belt or anything else he liked to beat me with. I had no idea what he was planning to do to me.

"Well, who do you think you are, talking back to me? You are nothing but a spoil little brat. Your mother and sister are nothing but whores. You will learn to respect me. You are your mother's seed. You deserve whatever I give you. You tell anyone what happen I will kill your mother! God told me to punish you for all the bad things you do."

Just then, he disappeared behind me. Just then, I felt him pulling on my pants. I started to kick back at him.

"Oh, you want to kick back." he growled back at me.

I pushed the cloth out of my mouth. "Mom, help me! Please mom help! Evelyn. Help me! Please do something! I cried but no one came to my rescue.

He shoved the fabric back into my mouth. He then stopped and looked at me. He walked over to the foyer closet and pulled out more rope out. He tied down my legs even more. He ripped off my pants. I was crying harder than I have ever in my entire life. He walked back in front of me; he then bent down in front of me and smiled. Now, I was shaking. He stood up then back up and pulled the cloth out of my mouth. I begin to scream for my mother and sister once more.

"Scream all you want, your mother isn't going to hear you. She is in a coma as usual."

He pulled out special clamps that I have only seen in the dentist. He put the clamps in my mouth to keep it open. As he stood in front of me, he said," See you like to talk back. I am going to fill your mouth and you will learn the meaning to swallow"

Just then, he pulled back his bathrobe and revealed his penis. He walked up to my face and pushed his penis into my mouth. For the next few minutes, the room was quiet. His penis started to get harder and harder. He pulled it halfway out and pushed it back in until he was fully hard. Then he pushed his penis further into my mouth. He pushed into the back of my throat. It hurt so badly that I could taste the blood in the back of my throat.

With each stroke, he pushed harder and faster. I could feel his scrotum tighten and his balls prepare to release a massive load into my mouth. He groaned loudly as he did. I could feel a rush of liquid spilled in the back of my throat.

"You're not my son; you are just another whore like your mother and sister. Today you are my little bitch ass...son! You want to act like a bitch well I am going to treat you like the bitch you are. Now, swallow bitch," he yelled some more, "Swallow you fucking cunt all of it and better not drop any."

I cannot believe what he was doing; this was not my father anymore. This man was a monster. He took the clamps out of my mouth. The clamps were covered in blood and white fluid." Stick out your tongue." he ordered me.

With tears in my eyes and blood in my throat, I did as he commanded me to do. He watched me lick the clasps as I swallowed every drop at the same time as he stroked up and down on his penis. Once he was hard again, he walked behind me and raped me. A few minutes went by when he finally stopped I wish I were dead.

● ● ●

He walked back around to me. He looked me in the face and said, "I do not think you understand me. I want you to get it through your head. By the end of the day, you will thank me for what I have done to you. You WILL respect and obey me. This will help you to be a better man."

He closed back his robe. He walked to a nearby closet and pulled out a baseball bat. I jumped as he slammed the bat in his hand repeatedly as he walked towards me.

He disappeared behind me again. This time he rammed the baseball bat into my backside. I could feel my insides being ripped apart. A minute too late, I saw a light come on upstairs; it was the light in my parent's bedroom.

I yelled," Help."

My father was mad. He kept doing what he was doing. My mother came running down the stairs. She stopped in front of me and started crying. She kept saying, "Oh my god, if you have to hurt someone. Hurt me!" She ran over to my father and tried to pull my father off me.

He then said to me, "You see those purple bruises on her arm, she does that to herself when you're not around. Let's leave her alone to moan and groan and pray. She rather prays to her stupid God than help you. Hey, that deserves another beating, wouldn't you say?" Just then he punched her in the head sending her to the floor she was unconscious.

• • •

My sister was watching from the top of the stairs. She was talking on the phone. She was asking them to hurry up. My father saw her on the phone and stop what he was doing and began to run up the stairs after her. Before he reached the top stairs the front door flew open, it was the police. I was fully exposed to them. My father kept running the police ran after him.

Some of the cops untied me. I was so weak that one of the police officers wrapped a blanket around and carried to the ambulance that was waiting outside. I had blood all over me. Just then, I heard gun shots go off. About ten minutes later my mother and sister came running out of the house crying. They both ran to me.

The paramedics went in with a white cloth and a stretcher. A few minutes went by before they came out with my father covered with the white cloth. As they walked down the stairs from the house, they lost control of the stretcher and dropped the stretcher. Down the stairs my father's limp body fell. He was dead.

Blood was coming out of his head and chest. When he landed on the ground, his eyes were still open. They were still looking up at me. My mother tried her hardest to turn my head away, but I pushed her hand away. I ran over to my father and spat in his face. My sister ran over but was pulled back as the paramedics picked my father off the ground and laid him back onto the stretcher.

●●●

Moving On

After this event, we moved out of the state. My mother was ashamed to be seen in town, especially after everything that has happened. Things were never the same between the three of us. My mother and sister tried to put everything behind. They acted as if things were perfect.

You can say my sister and I were sick fucks but after all the years of abuse. We became "REAL" close. My sister and I were still having sex. When no one was around us or especially when our mother was in her drug-induced coma. My sister moved out a year before I did. She got married to a millionaire, she wasn't happy. She even changed her named to Giana.

●●●

In the meantime, my mother acted like a saint when she was away from the house, but once the doors are close, she was a demon. She now drank so much whiskey from day in and day out. My mother forced me to hold my open hand over a flame, beating me if I cried and tried to talk to her about what had happened with dad.

•••

The Nightmare Continues

She burned her cigarettes on me when I didn't listen to her. My mother and I fought constantly. My mother was now the abusive parent and the sexual abuser one; it's almost as if she picked up from where my father left off at. She forced me to perform oral sex on her.

There were times she made me fingered me until she was completely aroused. She kissed me and I thought that would be as far as it would go. She then would undress me and started feeling my whole body. She pulled off my pants and immediately she gave me a hand job, when I was hard she forced me to lie on the bed and suck on me.

•••

My mother was so lazy to get a job, but the new sick obsession she created to do. She brought home strange man, to have sex with, but there were times she would allow them to come into my room, to force different sex acts to me. When, they left she would force me into a bathtub filled with extremely hot water to wash off the stench of the man and my sins away so she says.

I begged to Christ to rid me of my demons, so I could be a good Christian boy, but counting my sins didn't seem to help me. I asked God to forgive me, for the thoughts that were in my head and for the things, I was doing.

● ● ●

In 1972-1986

When I was old, enough I moved the hell out. I left my mother in that rundown apartment in Camden, New Jersey. I put everything behind me, hoping that I do better with my life. I now live in New York City as a part-time pathology assistant in a local funeral home in the morning and at night a police officer. I had one more year left of school before I can become a full time forensic pathologist, but for now, this would work for now; it was a job and a fresh start.

I had to do 4 years of undergraduate training, 4 years of medical school, 4 years residency in anatomic and clinical pathology and 1 year of forensic pathology fellowship. It was well of overdue for me to get a bigger paycheck. I am the first one to make this far in any career.

●●●

I could see my first real morgue, today instead being a class setting. As the pathology explained the reasons why people ended in the morgue and why they are there. The first was an unexpected death. The second was a doctor has not seen them in three months three died from accident or injury. The fourth died in a violent or unnatural way.

Others died as a result of an anesthetic or within 24 hours of an anesthetic 6 was unidentified and last seven died while in state care in a prison / mental institution / or while in child protection I really didn't realize all the reasons why people came here, but also thought everyone had to get an autopsy. The class was kicking my butt today. I need a break.

●●●

September 1995

It was time for me to get dinner, it sucked I had to get drive thru dinner. I had to work the bet. I was going to meet up with a few of my friends while I was out. I wanted to meet up with my sister but unfortunately, I had to work tonight.

She was up here to get her life straight, especially after her husband left her. It didn't helped that my sister and I were so close that we had to be careful when she would come into town. She even changed her name so people wouldn't find out the truth about her past.

I guess the good thing was that she met a person that she was seeing for the last few weeks, so I don't feel too bad not seeing her today. I just parked my car at a nearby fast food place; I received a call, which came over the radio.

●●●

It was Officer Shirley asking, "If there was anyone near Hell's Kitchen. I need an officer at 34th Street at the New Yorker Hotel. There has been a shooting at one of the suites." 10-68 she repeated over the dispatch.

I took the call and headed to the hotel. I keep praying that it was not my sister's room. My nightmare was true; it was my sister's suite. I tried to keep it together as I approached the door. I pushed opened the door. There was broken furniture everywhere. Apparently, there was a struggle.

There was her estranged boyfriend sitting on the couch with a gun in his hand. I pulled out my pistol and slowly walked towards him while repeating, "You have the right to remain silent. Anything you say can and will be used against you in a court of law. You have the right to have an attorney present during questioning. If you cannot afford an attorney, one will be appointed for you."

He put the pistol to his head and said, "I loved her and I am sorry."

Before I could stop him, he pulled the trigger. There before me I watched as his brain matter spread a crossed the wall. With a single gunshot, just like that he was dead. There across the bed, laid my sister faced down in a pool of blood.

I ran over to her and started to shake her, she was not responding. I tried to wake her as I began to weep, but all my pleas she could not hear me. Oh, if I could have only kept her near or even stopped by to visit her before my shift maybe I could have stopped her from being shot.

● ● ●

The paramedics rushed and started to work on her. She was barely breathing. They took her downstairs and put her in the ambulance while they still tried to get her to respond. I rode behind the ambulance. I was in shock. I couldn't believe it was my sister. I kept repeating to myself that she was going to be okay. I didn't flinch as I parked the car behind the ambulance.

The driver jumped out of the ambulance and slowly walked over to me. He held me back. I knew exactly what happened, she was gone. "I am sorry, Damien, she is gone."

I dropped to my knees as they pulled out her lifeless body. I clasped her cold hand in mine. We wheeled her down to the morgue, which was in the basement of the hospital. My teacher was working tonight. I asked if I could do her autopsy despite how much I knew I was not allowed to do it. He agreed. I didn't even bother calling or even telling my mother.

● ● ●

My Lost

After this, my life was never the same. My sister's face was always on my mind. A smile I have seen a million times. Her two eyes that would light up the sky at night were no more. One last battle I was hoping that she would pull through but this was one fight she could not fight. The days were long, then night then morn. A million pieces went my heart. Now a photo I look at to see her smile. I kept her number on my speed dial.

A video I watch to just to hear her voice. This I do... I have no choice, but the great memories I will always keep with me. My sister's love will always be in my heart for eternity. I could never say goodbye the way I wanted to. I am always hoping that we would have grown together just a little bit longer. She will be waiting in heaven from this moment on, until god asks her to bring me home. I am finding it very hard to believe that you have gone and I must grieve.

I tried to call out her name in the middle of the night but she does not answer. Where are the soft brown eyes of affection, the laughter and talk of childhood reflection, the loving care when I was sick or sad, the generous soul for which I was glad, the forgiving and understanding heart, and where are the bonds that were there from the start?

I missed all the little ways she showed me that she cared. Since there were so many good moments, we shared. Looking back on my life's assorted scenes, I realized she taught me what love truly meant. She was my trusted confidante and best friend. On whose loving support I could always depend on.

I looked at her smiling face in all my photos.

Memories flood my mind as I touch the mementos. From happier times, she and I have had, but now these memories bring tears and make me sad. For the time together went by in a wink. Life was not as long as we'd like to think.

Sometimes memories bring comfort and make me smile, but there are times when grief takes over for a while. Friends offered gentle words and prayers to console, and tell me what has happened to her loving soul. Could it be true what they say of time healing grief? Was it enough when they say death has given me relief?

Could we believe what others say about a better place? Where our beloved ones rest in God's warm embrace? I should be happy she was free of pain and sorrow, and rejoice that she will always have tomorrow. How could I then be so heartbroken and selfishly crying? Return to me from that peaceful place where she lies!"

● ● ●

Now I look down at her name on a cold hard stone. That says little of the loving light she has sown. It tells nothing of the wonderful person she was, and only serves to remind me of the painful loss I endure, but I knew her kind soul wanted no tears or pain. Instead, she wanted warm memories and love to remain here with me.

Although, I cry and stand grief-stricken by her grave, I promised not to forget the loving memories she gave me, but still I miss her so very much. Her caring words I once again learn to hear. My heart's only solace was one day I will see her as before. Beckoning me to come join her on that white distant shore.

● ● ●

December 1995

I was able to quit working as a police officer. I kept in touch with my partner Dante, but I can't do this anymore. I started my own funeral home. I brought the house right next door of the funeral so I didn't have to go too far to work. Something about death was taking a hold of me. I welcomed death. I needed to do something to get my mind straight. Therefore, I went out to a bar almost every night.

● ● ●

January 1996
One Late Night

As sat there drinking my problems away, off in the distance a woman was staring at me. I tried to look away but I could not. Before I knew it, she was standing next to me. We started talking; she asked to go back to my place. I was so wasted but we did.

By the time, I closed the door to my house she was all over me. Guess what I needed, some good night sex. I pulled her shirt over her head and started sucking her nipples, wow, I was so excited but images of my father started to play in my head. I tried to shake them out. I reached down and put my hand up her skirt to tickle her pussy but instead I find a penis. I jumped back.

"What is wrong? She asked surprised.

"You know damn well what!

"What…you do not like it?

"Get the fuck out of my house!"

"Oh, come on! It will be our little secret. Are you afraid? You do me and I do you."

All I could do was think about what my father did to me. I could feel my blood starting to boil. I screamed even louder, "Get the fuck out my house, you fucking freak!"

"Who the fuck, are you calling a freak?"

"This is my last time I am warning you, GET OUT!"

She stood up and started to hit me. She was screaming at me. I was not even listening anymore to what she had to say. All I could hear and see was my father. He must pay for what he did.

I snapped I reached under my couch and grabbed the hammer. I stuck her in the head and she fall to the floor. I hit her repeatedly until she stopped moving. What have I done? Lying in front of me, her body battered and bruised. Pieces of hair were ripped out and on the hammer. The hammer stained with crimson.

I sat back down on the couch and stared at her lifeless body. Her blood was all over me. There was blood splattered on the walls and ceiling. My clothes are bloodstained, ripped, tattered and torn. I need to change out of them but I am so tired.

I loved the way the blood looked in the moonlight. It almost appeared black. The blood poured out onto the floor. I watched as the blood trickle down my arm. Blood was dripping from my fingers. Blood slipping through my fingers and felt so warm.

•••

Next Day
At 6 AM

I went to my funeral home and grabbed a body bag. I put her cold body in the bag. I picked her body up; carried her to the funeral home through the back door of my house. I put her on the table and left her there. Then I went back home to clean up the mess, but instead I fell asleep on my couch.

•••

About noon, I finally got up and cleaned up the blood. There was dried up blood on my white hands. It gave it a nice rosy color. Thoughts and images of killing the girl, made me thirsty for more. The rush was so thrilling. Once I was done cleaning any evidence of her, I commenced to go take a shower.

As the water ran down my back, all I could do was think about what I have done. I never knew what it was like to kill someone. I felt so confused about being right and wrong, but it felt good to do what I did. I was yearning for the desire and pain to do it again. I was so enthusiastic, that I started to get an erection. I could not help it.

Looking at my erection and the blood on my hand was so electrifying that I just let myself go. I began to stroke my penis as the images became more and more clear in my head, before I knew it I cum in the shower. This was unlike any other feeling I was ever having in my life.

● ● ●

My New World

I finally made myself over to the funeral house two days later, there was a stench coming from the home. I needed to take care of her body before anyone noticed it. I had a funeral to plan for a customer so I knew exactly what to do with her body.

For the first time I saw my first decomposed body only two days later. The stench was intoxicating but it did not bother me. All I could was to think, about what I learned in school about a body after death. When a body died, it does so slowly.

● ● ●

The Human Body

A shot through the heart immediately stopped blood flow, and the brain ceases to function a few minutes later. The cells of muscle, skin, and bone live with dying only when metabolic waste products build up, sometimes days later.

Upon death, the body temperature begins to drop at about 2.5 degrees F an hour. The muscles relax, and the skin sags into new shapes. The blood settles in body parts closest to the ground, turning the top grayish white and darkening the underside, except where pressed to the ground. The resulting liver-colored stain, livor mortis, was most pronounced about 10 hours after death.

Within 6 hours, rigor mortis sets in. The eyelids stiffen then the neck and jaw, and finally the remaining muscles. The reason, still poorly understood, was probably a combination of chemical shifts and protein coagulation. After roughly a day, the muscles slowly relax again in the same sequence that they stiffened.

Meanwhile, the bacteria have begun to eat through the gut. The first sign was usually a greenish patch marbling blood vessels on the lower right belly. The putrefaction spreads across the stomach, down the thighs, over the chest.

The skin changes to olive to eggplant to black. The bacteria produce gas that bulges the eyes, protrudes the tongue, and pushes bloodstained fluid from orifices. That's why coffins were constructed with lids that can burp. I was able to get rid of her body when I buried my customer's love one.

● ● ●

Sex and Death

My sex life wasn't what you would call normal. I picked up girls who had the weirdest fantasy. I was having sex with some girls who wanted to have my way with them while I was holding my pistol in their mouth. Then I would tell them the truth that I was going to kill them.

They wanted to run after a little bit of them fighting to get away. I would kill them. When it was time, I had to dispose of the body. There were times I used an acid bath. I then took the remains and packed away inside coffins. Killing became something of a habit. It was an adrenaline rush.

After, I decapitated some of them. I placed their heads on my fireplace mantle and used it as a dartboard. It was very entraining. I took my time and made practice runs throwing darts at them. Once, I was done playing with my victims. I got rid of them and their heads.

● ● ●

October 2001

I had no perfectionist of what my victims would be. On one occasion, I kept a 23-year-old man for two months in my basement but only after, I remodeled my basement in a soundproof sex dungeon. I even build a secret chute that dropped into the basement of the funeral, so I could get rid of his body when I was done with him.

• • •

I tortured him daily with electric shocks, anal penetration and other abuse. When I sexual abuse him, I would put my hands around his neck and started to strangle him, to the point he couldn't breathe. I would put a gag ball in his mouth so he couldn't scream too much.

The whole time he was screaming but nothing could come aloud enough for anyone to hear. After, I repeated rape him with objects. He had developed a rectal rupture and was bleeding profusely. I treated him with animal antibiotics and injected bleach into his eyes. I didn't intentionally murder him. The young man died because of the countless injuries inflicted.

• • •

March 2002

This one girl was 18 years old when I met her at the stripper club. She would come over and hang over my house, but she was very disrespectful. She would always find a way to make up for her rudeness. One day I was having a bad day and she was pissing me off.

She was just being a bitch so I thought maybe; we should have sex just to relax and get my mind off the bullshit. She answered her cell phone while we were having sex, this sent me into a fury so blinding that I strangled her.

●●●

May 2003

There was a cute red hair 29-year-old girl. We meet at a local pub. We chatted briefly then went back to my place to have sex. After receiving a slight rebuff from the fucking bitch, okay I had to done something to this whore; I left my bedroom to make some coffee.

When I returned, I brought two knives in addition to the coffee; she didn't notice me placing the knives on the nightstand. Soon after we began having sex again, I just stabbed the bitch repeatedly. She lay there naked; rape her until her vagina turned into blood. I continued to have sex with her lifeless body until I cummed. After I cum, I pushed the bitch off my bed and went to sleep like a baby.

●●●

August 2004

I meet a man who was hitchhiking along I-95 South. He claimed to be heading to an old friend up state. He wanted to stop by a bar before I dropped him off. We had to be in there for hours before I realize how late it was getting. Out of nowhere, he started to brag about a killing he had done but someone else was doing his time. He then tells me how he hated being married.

He tried to make it a happy home but his love to have sex with men was getting in the way. He loved his life outside the house, but it was hell living in a lie. The last straw was when his wife had told him she was three months pregnant.

The two already had two young daughters, Olivia, 9 and Stacy 5. He and his wife got into agreement one day that was when he beat his wife to death with the butt of a .357 Magnum and then he shot the two girls. Olivia was shoot in the face and Stacy in the back as she tried to run away.

His story sickened me. I allowed the man to stay at my place for the night because it was too late to drive. He agreed to stay especially knowing that he had to tell his friend he was coming to town tomorrow.

● ● ●

I gave him the bed in the basement and I went to bed, as a whisper in my ear to go kill him. I couldn't take it. I fix him a drink that was laced with some strychnine. A sure way to make sure he didn't fight with me. I put on my bathrobe, then I head down to the basement, there he was laying there.

"Wow, I love your basement!"

"Thank you!"

"I thought you were never coming down to see me!"

"What do you mean?"

"Oh come on man, we are both adults."

"I fixed us a drink."

● ● ●

He then got up from the bed and took the glass out of my hand. He started to kiss me. It felt weird to feel his whiskers against my face. He then took off my robe. He then dropped down to his knees and commenced to suck on my cock.

The scary thing was I actually like it. He slammed his head into my pelvis. He sucked until hot cum rushed out of me and into his mouth and asked if I'd rather have sex with him. I didn't say anything.

He quickly got undressed. He jumped on the bed and got in doggy position. He looked over his shoulder and asked me to fuck his ass. "Have you ever done it with a man? He asked

I said, 'No way, what do you think I am?" I never had sex with a man before but now I was curious. "Give me a min I need to get something." I said to him.

"Make it quick I am starting to get sleepy."

I slipped over to the corner of the room. I put on some gloves and a condom.

"Why do you have gloves on?"

"It is better to handle my cock, once I put lube on it."

"Oh…okay!"

I pulled him closer to the edge of the bed, closer to the nightstand. I slide my hard cock into his ass. He moaned out harder.

• • •

As I pushed harder and faster into asshole, I reached into the nightstand and grabbed my Taser X26. I fired barbed electrodes at him; they landed in the back of his head. A shot released two probes. The back of head started to smoke. All voluntary control over his muscles was gone and he was helpless. I could feel all the electrical bolts flowing through his body.

It was so stimulating, I kept sending electrify shots though his body, as I fucked him until I cum. A regression to infancy was erotic stuff. There he lay with cum coming out of his ass and his back of his head was smoking. Perfect, the bastard wouldn't be missed.

• • •

July 2005

My eyes are so tired. I can't sleep at night anymore. My mother and father haunted my dreams. I wake up hearing yelling, was it me or the other person in me? I always wonder who it was then I realized it was I. I thought I was dreaming and I would wake up feeling scared. The feelings were real and I realized I was in my bed depending on the dream.

I wonder if anyone heard me screaming and shouting. I am helpless and afraid just a lonely man. When I turn out the light, they are like faded dreams. Alone in my room it was a dark black, but my nightmares come back. They won't leave me alone. I need someone to free me from my deep hurt pain of all the regret that makes me insane.

Many nights I drowned myself in tears, because of what was causing my family so much pain over the years. My mother lived off in her own little world at times. My sister and I would have been better without her and our father in the picture. Old memories old actions, old regrets, all to seem to never go away. They seem to return repeatedly.

● ● ●

September 2005

Weeks have passed I started to get a nagging feeling to talk to my mother. A week later, I went to visit my mother. My mother was now suffering from dementia. She still lived in her apartment I left her. There were good days when I visited her, and she called me by my name. She's grateful for the company, and thankful that I came. Most of the time it's difficult, to see my mother that way, all I could do was love her now but it was so hard, because of the memories of the pass.

She was trapped inside the prison walls that used to be in her mind. The woman that she used to be has long been left behind. There are times she's quite alert her memory's still intact. She sits in the darkness as her memories serve as her only company.

Then there are days when she disappears and I knew it was not an act. No longer able to care for herself, I couldn't leave her alone for too long. Her safety had to be assured, so I was going to place her into a home but I really don't give two shits about her to put that much money out.

●●●

I was able to convince her to come to my house for a month. She agreed. Only three days after she got there I was ready to kill her. Memories flashed through my head of the hell she allowed to happen and the hell she put my sister and me through.

● ● ●

Asked my mother to go with me to have a midnight picnic, and relax in nature on the outskirts of town. Today was a good day; she seemed to be like her old self.

● ● ●

I knew a nice place that police don't go in but it was known for people having midnight picnics and bonfires. She loved the idea. When we got to the wooded area, I helped get my mother out of the car.

My mother and I made our way to a closed off area. I rolled out the blanket. We sat down and started to talk, before I knew it my mother started to yell at me. I forgot that I was a 33 year-old man and returned into that 16-year-old boy, I was so afraid of her.

She had a devilish grin on her face. Damien, do you remember who the boss is? You don't speak to me in that tune! Now I must punish you. You know what to do."

● ● ●

I slide over to her; I ran my hand over her large saggy breasts through the flimsy bra. She whimpered as I squeezed one, then the other soft one. I felt nervous as my hand moving along her smooth flat stomach, then between her legs, moving back and forth. I felt her pussy twitching; sucking inward as her my palm rubbed the growing wetness through her panties.

I made the decision to kill her. I couldn't do this anymore. I stopped what I was doing and ran to the car to get a few things. When I came back, she was pissed off.

"Why the fuck did you stop for, you fucking piece of shit! You are a worthless of flesh! I wish I never gave birth to you and fucking sister! You both ruin my life!"

My blood was steaming. Now I knew what I need to do to get rid of her." Mom, I have a surprise for you."

"What is it? I hope you are going to finish taking of me like a good little boy."

"Well mom, I have this toy just for you."

"What is it?"

"I find this 12 inch long dildo just for you."

"Hell, what are you waiting for? Give me the surprise."

"I have to get you warmed back up."

"Ok" she said as she lay back on the ground.

I began to plunge my fingers in and out of my mother's pussy. My finger thrust into her, the wetter she became. I then slid in the dildo. I rammed the 12-inch cock into her really hard as I did so I pushed a little button on the handle. When I did so, it released Tetrodotoxin into her pussy. Once the poison was in her, I pulled the dildo out.

●●●

Tetrodotoxin

Tetrodotoxin was one of the most powerful neurotoxins found anywhere in the world. When put to use by the puffer fish. The substance was employed to keep predators away while it was alive, and apparently, to extract revenge upon humans who dine at the fugue sushi table following its demise.

In its fugue sushi state, the blowfish can have enough of the neurotoxin left in its little filleted body to kill more than thirty full-sized people, even me.

●●●

I watched as she went motionless. She had this shock look on her face. I took a water bottle out of the picnic basket and washed my hands off. I put on some latex gloves. I leaned over her and told her how she was a horrible mother, I explained to her what was going on and what was about to happen to her.

●●●

Now seeing the fear in her eyes was a turn on. Before I started on my plans, I gave her the news that her daughter was died. Tears rolled out of her eyes as she just laid there.

I inserted the dildo back in her one last time, this time I twisted the handle. Little razors popped out. I fucked my mother with the razor sharp dildo. Chucks of her pussy oozed out, as I did so I looked into her eyes, despite that she was my mother I wanted her dead.

I then slit her throat just enough for the blood to slowly drain out of her. She was barely alive when I poured gasoline over her, and set her body on fire. A piece of me that was part of my mother was gone. Once the fire was out, I took her remains;

what was left of her remains and dropped them into a nearby lake.

• • •

My life was now filled with an endless chain of horrifying sexual abuse, torture, and mayhem. What was my motive? I lay in my bed alone at night and wonder why I'm here at times. I have become the perfect "Jekyll and Hyde" of my time. These two people lived in one body. There was always a struggle in my head. This would be my only friend, the voices in my head. I tried to be careful so others wouldn't find out my secrets.

A perfectionist I have become. I believed that some people simply give birth to monsters. The sadistic bastard I have become. An eye for an eye I have always believed. What kind of monster I have allowed myself to become?

• • •

In the light of the day, I lead a normal life, but when it becomes night, I become someone else. I have killed an immense unbelievable sum. At times, I have no memory of the people I killed.

Some memories of what I have done remain in some kind of haze. There were times that I remember their bodies and who they are where as others I can't remember them for shit. From what I knew I have a sadistic taste for blood. I disposed the bodies in coffins with other people's love that are being laid to rest.

Occasionally I have flashes of my family ran though my head. I remembered the last thing I said to each of my family members. My eyes closed. I was holding onto my memories with hatred in my head. The pain I carried secure behind my eyes hoping no one else could see my pain. I could never let out the pain. The misery I headed to hell with my dignity and pride.

That person I was was gone. I am no longer human. I am a monster with many faces. I can't deceive the darkness that lives within me anymore...I must let it. I'm losing control of myself. There was no way back into normal society. I have crossed the line. My place is in hell. Hell has been booked and paid for by the blood of your victims.

Some people look at me as a hero from when I was a police officer. I just took it one day at a time, while being patience and enjoying my time. The people I used to work for, the one's I worked with me now, have no idea what I am doing, and the person I have become.

Alone in my head, I felt so low, nor will I understand. No one could know. I was trained in anatomy so my murders were very precise. I congratulated myself on my precise work. I must be careful and not be dumb enough to be caught. I will never keep a few souvenirs as a reminder of what I have done.

I will only keep memories of my work. With pride and no remorse, I wanted to continue to torture, raped, and killed my victims. After it was all completed, I had a morbid sense of pride. In my sick mind I am having fun as I watched my victims take their last breath but I am always going to be haunted by the pain my family and what it has done to me.

●●●

Fuck This Shit
My Birthday
June 6, 2006

Therefore, I sit here at this desk writing my final goodbye; only after killing and destroying anything, that was causing me so much pain.

For Suicide Note:

Dear whom this may concern,

Most people kill themselves because of a mental condition. Well this was true in my case. The condition, which I suffer from, roots all the way back to my childhood. Everything I love was taken from me. The child I once knew was gone. I am not like every one of you "sane" people. You are more fucked than you think if you think you are sane.

I am not normal in the sense that I am not like every other one of the brain –a dead zombie. I can observe and learn from life but over time, it has taken the best of me. I can make my own decisions and follow through on them. I can't fucking take it anymore.

Since everyone in my life was a fucking retarded drone who revels in his or her ignorance and unintelligence, I must put an end to my misery. I truly wish I could have the same conversations day in and day out about sports, politics, and really don't give two fucks about the damn weather.

Of course, you will see this note and say Damien was crazy. You can carry on my legacy and talk about how pathetic my life was. Go ahead call me every name in the book, everyone else does. Then, return to your happiness of everyday mindless monotony.

My only wish was that the bullet I put into my head doesn't even kill me but only leaves me fucking brain dead. For if ignorance is bliss, is truly happy, then living a life without a brain stem in a coma, devoid of any cognitive ability must surely be utopia.

Leave my fucking machine plugged! If I die there was no need to do an autopsy, this was definitely a suicide. I have enclosed with this note all my journals from my childhood and up until now.

Yours truly,

Damien Grissom

•••

Once I was done with the letter. I took a shower and put on my favorite tee shirt and jeans. I laid back into my bed. I stopped and reflected on the good times in my life. There wasn't much to remember. I put my .38 calibur to my temple. I could feel the cold steel. It brought peace to me, a warmth of happiest swept over my body. I closed my eyes and pulled the trigger.

Bommmmmmmb!!!!!

Revenge is Sweet

Jackson Tennessee, 2006

As I drive into work, I can't help but to think about my boyfriend of three years. Andre had to live with his aunt and uncle when he was nine because his father died of a massive heart attack while coming home from work. Then, only three months later, he woke up to find his mother lying at the bottom of the stairs. She had fallen and died of head trauma. Suddenly Andre and his brother had no parents.

Andre was desperate to ease the pain of his profound loss. He turned to drugs and alcohol to numb the pain and to make him to forget everything that was going on in his world. He began smoking cigarettes at the age of 13, and then using pot.

When that wasn't strong enough anymore, he find others ways to his buzz on. He began drinking heavily, and he hid it well. Soon he needed to smoke and drink before school just so he could look normal. Andre's friends saw what he was doing to him and asked him to stop, but he wasn't ready.

●●●

He began using heroin and sleeping pills. The heroin was to numb the emotional pain and to get high with. The sleeping pills was use to put him to sleep after staying up for days from his pill popping. His grades were dropping dramatically.

He had always been a straight-A student and athlete. He always studies hard. "You will find a high-paying job with great benefits", his parents used to say to him and his brother, but they were nowhere to be around to encourage him to do better in school and stop doing drugs The heroin made him violent and suicidal.

At the age of 17, he carved the words "Love and Hate" into his arm. As soon as his aunt and uncle find out what he had did. They sent him to a psych ward. No one could understand why he did this. He never told anyone why he did it.

Eventually he stopped going to school. From then on out, he was in and out of psych wards.

There was no point in going to school. He thought he was immune to everything and nothing bad was going to happen to him.

His addiction led into some trouble, which resulted in him going to Hardeman County Correctional Center for a few years. He had only one friend who was his cellmate Adolf Crawford who was later transferred to Alcatraz Island.

Andre was in Hardeman for his meth lab. In Jackson, Tennessee, it was notorious for meth problems; many illegal methamphetamines were being produced in large quantities. Motorcycle clubs then dominated the manufacturing of crank or speed, jealously guarding their cooking methods but recipes began appearing on the Internet, many formulas calling for anhydrous ammonia, a common corn fertilizer.

● ● ●

New Hobby

That was how Andre found out how to build his lab. It was built from such innocuous materials kitchen matches, cold pills, tubing, and brake fluid and requiring no more space than an ordinary kitchen or motel room. Of course, Andre had the perfect apartment and location for his lab.

That's why Andre was in county for the meth lab in his apartment, making and selling illegal drugs. He started to teach a network of friends and few high school students who were trying to make some quick cash to "cook" speed and sell the drugs. The local teenagers began to drop out of school. Many of the teenagers in the community were now making, selling or abused the drug themselves. Things were getting out of hand.

His mini industry had grown ultra-violent. Andre started to use his own product. The community group had alerted citizens to lookout for things that they should be aware of such as the acrid smell of a lab in operation, discarded sacks of batteries and light bulbs. They supposed to report when they saw a wonder drug addict walking the streets.

Even if they noticed, a person who was suddenly showing signs of losing weight and was paranoia. The residents took notice and the tips began to roll into the police department.

The police finally had an enough evidence to go after Andre. When the police kicked down Andre's door, Andre started a fire. He ended up burning down his apartment to destroy a lot of evidence of any drugs and anything that helped him to make the drugs.

One of the friends shot a deputy sheriff. Another one had allegedly murdered and decapitated an errant one of the drug runner before the police opened fire on him. When the meth lab's toxic chemicals exploded, it had killed a few firefighters that were trying to put out the fire. Andre was looking at some serious time but he only got half of the time he was supposed to serve because the case wasn't handled properly.

● ● ●

At 36 years old, Andre was tired, broken and headed for prison again. It was just another series of drug charges, which would lead him back to jail. It was a revolving door of incarceration. His drug use seemed to be only thing that keep Andre away from the world he was running from. Andre had been to rehabs before. That didn't work. Andre lied to the Probation Officer about where he intended to live when they released him from jail.

The truth was he was homeless and had nowhere to go. Just before his arrest around the Easter holiday. He was living in elevators and on rooftops and eating out of dumpsters. He was forced to go to a drug court program instead of going back to jail.

It was really a rigid program. The program involved a fixed schedule of appointments with therapists, probation officers, and social service workers, set number of 12-step meetings each week, and regular court appearances, as well as frequent random urine tests. He was doing great. He was clean and had a job.

●●●

He had a catheter in his heart and had osteomyelitis from shooting drugs. He also had a bone infection in his ulna and metal rods sticking out of his arm. He was a hot mess. This was when I met Andre. We were both at the hospital one day. That same family doctor was seeing us both. That was when he told me his story. He was cute and we kept running into each other a lot. We finally decided to go out on a few dates.

●●●

Two years later

He moved into my house. We were expecting our first child in January. We named him Clint; soon after Clint was born, I got pregnant with Gavin who was born in October the following year. We didn't waste anything and had a third child, which we named him, Quinn. I had him in August. Everything seemed to be great. We were both working and he was clean for two years.

● ● ●

Trouble in Paradise

By time, Andre lost his job things were looking up for us. Andre was going to go back to school. At first, his boss thought it was funny. His brother laughed at him too about losing his job, but I had hope for him, and that was all he needed to get back on his game, at least that was what I thought.

Six months went by and Andre still didn't have job nor was he in school. It was fine to do nothing at all. Bullshit! It's fine to recline on the flat of one's spine, with never a thought in one's head.

I wish I could sit around the house doing nothing. It must be fucking nice for him while I did everything. I tried even asking him to help me around the house and with boys but all he wanted to do was sit around the fucking house feeling sorry for himself. This was really driving me insane!

Then there were times he would sleep the entire day away like the single fucking hermit he had become. Hell…on our anniversary he saw a flower delivery truck parked outside and stole flowers from the truck.

He stopped looking for a job. I would come home he was always spaced out. Quinn would be still in the same diaper I put him in before I went to work. I had to ask my sisters to come over and help me.

With him just lying in our bed or couch he won't help us through these hard times and stormy weather. It was time that he stop talking and do what he was going to do because just dreaming about what he wanted to do, wasn't pulling us through the problems we were having now. If only money grew on trees, things would be so much easier.

It wasn't as if his drug problems were getting any better. The fucking bastard was shooting heroin like it was candy. He acted as if had nothing to lose. I put up with everything because when he isn't using he was a great friend and father. When he was using, I get to hear all the sorry ass stories why he can't work or how "the man" was holding him back, which I knew he was full of shit.

● ● ●

Stealing from me

One night I was going through my bills. I happened to check my bank balance on-line and discovered that $500 was missing. That was a lot of money to me; I was working two crummy jobs and trying to save up. Therefore, I tried talking to him, I was crying and stuff, he was so sympathetic, and worried, and all the things a good boyfriend should do.

●●●

The next morning I called the bank with my terrible news. They kindly did an investigation for me, and subsequently sent me a letter with all the exact times and dates that my debit card had been used to steal my money. Well, I checked and compared, and yes, they were all the times when I was at work, and the location was right by our house.

So of course, he denied it when I confronted him. Then came clean the next day, about EVERYTHING all the massive, weird, huge lies he had been telling me about everything in his life, that was when I find out that he was using again and how bad his drug addict was getting!

Turned out he memorized my PIN from the supermarket or something he wasn't sure. Then he took my card from my wallet, stole the money, and replaced the card when he was done with it. He told me he was getting high while I was at work. He begged for my forgiveness and that he was sorry. I felt so bad for him that I didn't have the heart to kick him out. He promised to stop using and seek help. He never did.

●●●

Growing some balls

At first, he was only using heroin on the weekends, but after a while, I had to use it all the time. At first, it was one bag a day, then two, and then it was four, then it was 14, and by the time, he finally was arrested. His probation officer had stopped by unannounced to do a check-up to see if Andre was clean. Yes, his urine was hot.

As soon as, he was back home he was up to 20 bags or more a day if he could afford it. Affording it became the hardest part but he always found a way to get his fix.

He was stealing property and selling it. Money was another big problem. Successive rent periods came where he would spend all my money on gambling and alcohol within 48 hours of receiving it, leaving me to pay all the rent with any other money I had hidden and then provide food for the family for a fortnight. This was becoming impossible and it meant instant poverty. He found his lost love which was the needle & spoon.

The needle & spoon came into our life and changed everything. I watch him one day, pulled out a Ziploc bag of pot and several rolled joints, and scattered them on the table. He also laid down a mirror with several lines of cocaine laid out. He actually started to get high in front of me. This was making me sick. I took my boys and went over my sister's for a few nights on many occasions.

●●●

K2 and Friends

One evening after sleeping over my sister's, I returned with the boys, only to find him out in the garage, smoking K2 with friends. Apparently, some of his old friends from high school had returned into town for a class reunion, they find out where Andre lived and wanted to catch up on old times.

They stopped by and told Andre about a legal substance called K2 it was like smoking marijuana. It could be easily purchased in stores and a few of the guys had purchased some that weekend at a local corner store. K2 was very dangerous.

Many people have gone into comas after smoking K2. Of course, Andre was all about trying everything new in the drug world. He had been smoking marijuana regularly for some time now so was curious about K2. I was piss! I kicked all his friends out that night. We ran into the living to continue to argue about what was going on. Andre and I started to get into a big argument.

"What the fuck are you thinking?"

"What the fuck do you care? You always at work…anyway!"

"You are fucking piece of shit anymore. All you do was sit on your fucking black ass, eating everything in sight. You don't even help me around the house. Do you even recall the final time you invest time with the boys and me? You can't even get a fucking job. You are lazy piece of shit! You are fucking useless!"

"Fuck you, bitch!"

"No fuck you! You are always in my face popping lies after lies. You are such as fake ass nigger. You treat me so coldly like nothing but your personal slave and banker. All you know do is, how do some fucking do drugs, between selling and shooting I don't know which one is worst. My mother was right about you! You are a fucking nigger!"

"Fuck you and fucking mother! I got your fucking nigger." Just then, he punched me in my jaw. I dropped to the floor. I looked up at him as he walked away and sat down on the couch. I picked myself off the floor and didn't dare to say anything else to him. I stayed in my room for the rest of the night.

It worries me deeply. He was now smoking, large doses of K2 that it was creating an increase in the risk of suicide. It was causing terrible anxiety, difficulty thinking, and depression for him. For a while, there I got him to decrease how much he was doing.

●●●

There may be hope

Andre even started to look for a job. I think he was only doing this because he knew his probation officer was coming around soon. It seemed like nobody was hiring. Every place he went to turned him down. Many companies claimed that they were trying to save money, by downsizing.

The damn bills were piling up every day. He claimed he was doing application after application when I wasn't able to take him to do so, which I knew he was full of shit. The only thing he cared about was his drugs and probation officer.

I was so sick of everything and the way things were going. He was even offered a minimum wage job, he turned it down as if he was too good to work his way up the chain just to get where he needed to go. Driving him around to get to these job interviews were killing me because the gas prices just keep getting higher.

He bragged about having big dreams but no job to follow his dreams. There are people who started with nothing and now look at them. He was just full of fucking excuses. I have to get things together for my boys. I can't wait for him. I don't want to follow him around like a puppy hoping and wishing for him to change. He has to want to get a job.

●●●

At one point before things hit the fan and went to hell. Andre and Clint were the always so close until Andre lost his job and started back into drugs. It was to the point when Clint wanted to spend time with his father, Andre would push him away like a fucking dog. Despite how young Clint was, he would continue to try to get his father to play with him or spend time with him. Andre was so worried about himself and his drugs that he didn't care about anyone else.

●●●

I can't remember the last time we had sex. He was spending so much time on the computer looking at porn. Despite how many times I tried to have sex with him.

There was a time when I tried to do something nice for him. I put together a special evening and cleaned up nicely. I cooked his favorite dish. Afterwards I put the sexiest piece of lingerie on. It was a red short baby doll dress with lace on it. The edges of the dress had a split that ran up my left leg. I put on some black garter belts and a pair of sheer pantyhose.

I did my hair. He told me to leave him the fuck alone. This lazy drug addicted asshole, it was more important to watch his fucking porn and beat his fucking meat. I tried to brush it off as if it was my fault. Things were getting so bad with the drugs and the porn.

●●●

One Evening

A few months later, I try to repeat the romantic evening of looking nice and doing something different. I endeavored to give myself to him but this time he was so strung up that all he wanted to do was get high and read his porn. The day before, he threw the porn magazines out and he promised he would try to spend more time with the kids and me.

That night, as I tried to throw myself at him, he ran outside before it started to rain and went through the garbage to get the magazines out of the trash. I even followed him outside half naked to get his attention but he was too high to even notice me. After that night, I basically gave up trying to empress him while at the same time he found time for his fucking porn and damn drugs.

• • •

Clint

The death of my older son changed my thoughts about Andre. I really didn't like Andre watching the boys anymore. Andre was always dipping in and out; he was always so fucking high. The last time I saw my son Clint alive was before I went to work one day. It was a weird day and I had a bad feeling not to go into work. I tried to work but after being there for only three hours I received a phone call to come home now.

Once I arrived, I find Clint in the pool facing down. He was dead. The coroner ruled as an accidently death, despite that he had a deep cut up near his heart. Gavin was in his playing in the room while Andre claims that Clint was at his friends playing, but he was so fucking high to remember anything.

●●●

Two Years Later

Tonight everyone was at my house. I had my both of my sisters and their daughters and sons over to do school work and makeovers for the prom. They were staying over late because I was work so late. I was hoping Andre wouldn't show his ass. Usually he was good when my family was over.

The neighbor wanted to come over to pick up daughter but since it was almost 2 am. Thank god, she had called to have Holli to come home in the morning instead so that was perfect. Despite that, my house was too small to have all these people over but oh well.

Just like any other day, Andre was high and out of his mind with the heart of evil and darkness in his eyes. He saw his niece lying on the air mattresses. He wanted to be a jackass so as she lay asleep he let out air. He started to do different kinds of things to piss everyone off.

He was drunk and fueled by eight balls. We left him on the couch falling asleep. We all called it a night and went to sleep. It was six o'clock in the morning when all of nowhere I could hear Andre screaming.

He started to go on a rampage. He was screaming and throwing shit around the house. He was running from room to room looking for some to scream at. Just then, my baby sister was coming out of the bathroom when he had punched her in the upper part of her chest; she passed out from the pain.

My youngest niece hid in a crawl space in the closet. As my older sister ran to get to the phone, as I could hear my baby's son was screaming for his mother to wake up who was lying on the bedroom floor.

Andre came into the bedroom where I was laying. Andre jumped onto the bed. He put the knife up to my throat. He ordered me to get out of the bed. As Andre rolled off the bed with the knife up to my throat, we walked into Gavin's room. Gavin was crawled up in a ball.

Andre could barely stand up straight he was so in toxicity. I climb onto the bed to get my son and escape but I knew wasn't going to work. Andre grabbed Gavin. Quinn was at his great grandmom's house sleepover. All of a sudden, there was a knock at the front door. Thank God I thought.

Andre dragged the knife across Garvin's back. Andre wasn't paying any attention when Gavin started to whisper, "Mommy, I remember that sound." I looked him puzzled. I tried to figure out why he would know that sound from.

He continued to whisper to me that he heard it when my brother was murdered. My heart sunk in my chest, it was clear to me who had murdered my son. Something snapped in Gavin but I didn't have time to figure it out.

Andre dragged Gavin into the bathroom and told me to get rid of the visitor. It was my best friend's husband Cyrus to drop off money for my birthday party. I opened the door. I acted as if my hands were busy and wet from washing dishes. I had him come into the house. I told him to put it into an envelope that he could find in my desk; thank god, my desk was by the door. He put it in an envelope.

Just then he noticed that there was blood on the walls and asked if everything was ok. I then pushed Cyrus out the door and whispered to him to call the police Cyrus shook his head ok. Then I slammed the door in his face. Now it was a race to stay alive before the cops would be here. I just needed to but some time until they do.

Once everything was cleared, Andre came out and dragged me into the bathroom. As soon as the bathroom door opened Gavin ran, pass Andre. Gavin ran into the kitchen to get the sharpest knife he could find. Andre tried to run after Gavin but he ran out of breath. With no shirt on, Gavin climbed up the walls of the house and ended up on the bathroom ceiling. I really didn't know what Gavin was up to but I was terrified for him

● ● ●

There was a look in Gavin's eyes unlike I have ever seen before. Andre tried to jump up and cut Gavin but he was too far for Andre to get him. Andre was so mad at Gavin that I could see the veins popping out in his head. Andre stopped and turned around to walk out the bathroom. Just then, Gavin dropped down to the floor.

That was when the both of them began into a knife fight. Right in the middle of the fight Andre stopped. Andre dropped the knife when Gavin had the tip of knife in the Andre's nose. Gavin slowly knifed one of the nostrils in half. On tip of knife, there was a big snot bubble and skin was hanging off. Andre just stood there screaming with his nose in his hand.

Just then, Gavin pushed the knife into Andre's eye socket. With just enough force, Gavin pushed the knife straight though Andre's skull just before Andre fell to the ground. I grabbed Gavin and ran out the door as the police was pulling up to the house.

● ● ●

The Nightmare was over

I moved to New York with Gavin and Quinn. We got help and moved on with our lives. We tried to keep what happen between us. At last, we were stronger and better family without Andre in our lives. The boys were doing so much happier.

A few years after Andre's death I met a wonderful man. It was everything I could have dreamed of. Only after six months, we got married. Then I gave birth to a baby girl that following May. We named her Chastity.

Cold Vengeances

In Croydon Pennsylvania in 1994

I'm counting down the days, until the bitch gets exactly what she deserves. Her days are number, I would have my revenge, and this woman would die. I would see to that! As I make my way to school each day only to see the girls who break my soul. I wish I could tell the bullies in my school to fuck off. I could pretend it does not happen. I couldn't be a tattle teller, or tell a teacher, must less fight back, letting her know it hurt me.

High school was a battleground, where rumors fly all around. The rumors sometimes never stop. They fill your head right to the top; no two rumors are the same. These girls think that this was just a game but they don't think about the people who are getting hurt when rumors are spread. These rumors could make them wish that they were dead. There was no way of hiding from the secrets and rumors that hurt me the most.

••••

Truman High School
September 1994

For my final two years of high school, I was in an Opportunity Class. This meant that I was academically selected. It was here when things just got worse for me. I don't remember ever doing anything to upset her, but I believed it might have been because I was smarter than she was. This class happened to be for the brighter students that go into selective schools and classes. Unlike this girl was in this class then she went from being the top of the school to average and struggle to deal with it.

Furthermore, my class was composite and only had eight senior students, four girls and four boys. This also limited my ability to meet peers and make new friends, leading to a social isolation that left me vulnerable to bullying. The people that I called my friends they were like monsters.

••••

I have been a victim of bullying for at least seven years. Over the years, I watched her grow into a bigger bitch than anyone I have ever seen. Most of the students at my high school had grown up together, being at the same school since preschool. I believed that entering the last year in school, where friendship groups had already solidly formed, was one of the contributing factors to my bullying. I felt so lonely, I stopped and I wondered what I have done to deserve this.

Her and my so-called friends were now ignoring me. I never expected that my friends would become my bullies. Sometimes one of them would nag the shit out of me by saying they weren't using me properly like a punching bag.

My health, my physical abilities after the injuries, brain-numbing pain, what I looked like particularly my face and my damaged eye reminded me daily of my ordeal. I had to cover up the bruises, scars and hurt too. I wished I could have hit them back, but I was too scared they could have made another attack. It seemed impossible but still I tried playing her and the others off.

I even tried to be nicer to her and the others but all it did was bring tears to my eyes, but then I realized I couldn't change a person by myself. She and the others have to try to change themselves. She was now laughing and teasing, as she called me names every day.

I had to hear things like "You're freak!" whenever she got a chance to make me feel like shit. Even the other kids started to call me weird and fat. There times when a kid would threw something at the back of my head while yelling, "You are fucking freak!"

As, I walked down these scary halls of this wretched school as they would say, "You're ugly and fat, and that's all you'll ever be, I ask myself, do they know what trouble they are causing me.

She laughed with glee when she sees that her words hurt people. Her harsh words would fly through the air, right into my head. Her evil and nasty words were cutting into my heart and soul! They always say that sticks and stones may break my bones, but words will never hurt me but they do.

● ● ●

I'm sick of all her little games. Who was she to pick me apart, throw things at me? I'm not a board for her darts. Just because I'm tiny and fat in her eyes, she needs to quit hitting me. It's not fair, she stands up there on the corner at every hallway I turn to, giving me looks and hitting my books to the floor. I have to put up with her pain and bullshit every day until I graduated.

Always someone makes me cry. I have gained so much pain and hurt inside as days go by. I wondered if the big solution to all my problems was a fire, gun, or even a knife to end my suffering. I wanted to get a knife and carve away the pain. Wouldn't this be easier if I was dead?

Even if I had cried aloud, I still wouldn't have been found. She pushed me away, like a freshman leaving home for college. With her secrets to spread around school and her suspicious looks on her face, she was always staring at me as her and the other kids spoke softly to one another as I walked by. Her eyes are like knives that cut right through my heart. Her cruel gestures that come from her body, they even affect me directly. They strike me and break me down!

She judged with every action I do, as if I am a follower. Am I a real person, who doesn't matter? Do I really matter? In my family's perspective, I do but in my friend's perspective, no. My feelings towards her and "the friends" has drifted further away from being real.

I have no friends because she has done such a good job turning them against me. I have been feeling alone in the dark. It seems to all be too much to handle. The bullies are strong and hurtful in every way, but I would get through this because I am strong. I kept telling myself things will get easier.

●●●

Flashback
At Kasdeya's house

When Kasdeya announced her sleepover to the whole school and I knew all the "IT", girls were going to be invited. This was just before I knew was a bully. She and the so-called friends invited me over Kasdeya's house for Slumber party. I can't wait to attend. There was going to be laughter all through the late night, food tucked into bathrobes, dares and truths about boys, private jokes to reference the following Monday.

●●●

I arrived there with my sleeping bad and enough junk food to feed an army, there was only Kasdeya and three other girls. Many of the other girls couldn't make it. Which I thought was weird because Kasdeya's slumber parties were the most exciting event that happened every year.

The other girls asked me to sit in a circle with them. They whispered and laughed under their breath. Kasdeya seats down behind me. While she was braiding my hair, she asked me whom I liked. I am afraid to answer her because there were a few guys that I knew she liked or dated. I just sat there blushing. Nothing sounded better than sitting with my knees tucked to my chin.

After only being there for only an hour minutes, no one else showed up. I started to get a bad feeling in my stomach. Before I could sneak off to the bathroom so I could called my mother to come and get me, the girls ripped my clothes off and pushed me outside in the front yard. It was cold and raining outside. I ran back to the door, hoping that one saw me naked.

"Please let me in, stop laughing. Don't laugh at me crying. Give me back my clothes. Please don't make me stand here in the cold rain. Please." Why me? Somebody help!" I yelled.

They stood there at the window, laughing at me. One of the girls was taking pictures until Kasdeya's big brother Mason came home. Mason slammed his brakes as soon as he seen me in at the front door naked.

●●●

My Knight

Mason jumped out of his car and began to yell at his sister. Kasdeya just stood at the window laughing. Mason ran into my arms and threw his coat over my arms. I wanted to run home but he insisted on taking me home. He was the nicest person I have ever met. After everything that happened at his house, I now had a huge crush on him. I wanted to write him a note, but don't know what to say.

I wondered how he would act if I approached him in such a way. I tried my best not to stare or stutter when he passed me in school. I am afraid that if I talked to him. I admired everything about him, from his eyes to his smile. I guess that I'll sit back and just wait for the right moment to say something to him.

His light tan skin, his luscious lips, and oh my god his muscle-filled arms was to die for. If he were magic, I'd buy a locket and make him my lucky charm. I guess that this was silly because it's just a crush. Now every time I see him, my body turned to mush.

I couldn't believe I'm acting this way. Oh well, too bad, I just don't care. I can't help the way feel. Why do I feel this way I stutter, and don't know what to say. What makes him so special?

I've studied his face and his eyes that sparkle. The way he looks at me makes me weak maybe I've fallen in too deep.

What if he didn't feel the same way? What if I'm only dreaming? What if I'm only imagining these things? Why do I feel this way? I wish I had the answers. I wish you could fix it. I wonder if he felt it too.

● ● ●

On June 13, 1998

We all graduated and moved on with our lives. I moved to Mount Holly, New Jersey for a little bit. I didn't return to Croydon until 20 years after trying to get myself together.

I live in a life of isolation and desolation as I have become bullied and pushed around; I wasn't even able to make a sound to stand up for myself in school. I know the day will come and I will be free to embrace the person that I am. I hope that I can look back as scream at the top of my lungs to say to tell those bullies, how they fucked up my life. All my depression leaks into my head as flashbacks of my bullies teasing me haunt me every time I close my eyes.

● ● ●

As Time Past

Over the years, I finally came to a decision to get plastic surgery. I hope to erase some of mine, pass and the scars of my bullies. A bit off here, some more up there. What nature gave me isn't fair! I wanted to feel. I wanted to be a more self-confident version of me.

● ● ●

Lipo-suck my tummy, please I begged my doctor, to make me thinner surgically. I had the doctor take a bit from around my knees. He was able to enhance my breasts to improve my chest to make me feel and look my best. He enlarged my breast size up to cup size D. It was a sexier, bustier version of me.

My nose was crooked. My face has sagged. My eyes were surrounded by great big bags. I couldn't stop now. My face now looked like my sixteen self. It was a brighter, tighter version of me. With age, came wrinkles, and crinkles I hated. I really don't want to look old. Now I got some Botox injections that would fill a smoother, expressionless version.

I'm hairy in places I don't want to be, and waxing was getting me down. It was too painful.

Therefore, I had most of my hair removed with lasers. I was less furry, more womanly.

My lips were too small, so they were enlarged. It was simple, accessible. I wanted to be sexy like actress Jolie just a little more pumped up. My lips were more kissable.

I got my teeth to be whiter and straighter. I couldn't leave my smile down to fate. Fixing them with veneers and whitening should hold the key. My looks are important. It was vital to stay, looking my best in every way. I was still me inside, but what people couldn't see was the pain I still hide inside. The cosmetic surgery version of me was nothing like the girl I was in high school.

●●●

**At Superfresh on
Route 413 in Bristol**

One day, while I was scanning items in a supermarket aisle -near my 38th birthday I felt eyes upon me. I commenced to move my head back and forth while pretending to check out items. I was hoping that my peripheral vision would catch a glimpse of the gawker. Just then, I noticed a man had stopped a few feet away, just staring at me.

It was early afternoon on a weekday, a time where most stores are quiet, so it was just the two of us in the checkout lane. There was no doubt his eyes were fixed on me. I felt my cheeks getting very hot as I became self-conscious of his blatant gazing. I really owe it to my bullies to look the best I can.

I wanted to move out of that lane but I wanted to move out with poise, slowly, calmly, without showing any signs that he had in fact intimidated me. I had no idea what had possessed him to stop and stare. Was he some guy who routinely tried to meet women in a supermarket?

Was he a creepy character that I should be concerned about? Would he follow me around the store? Into the parking lot? I didn't know. What I did know is that he was making me nervous. Still, I wasn't going to grant him the satisfaction of watching me flee in fear. I decided to stop to see what he wanted.

I'd turn around and looked at him straight in the eyes as I walked right past him. I turned to look at him as I moved past him with my shopping cart. I found myself face to face with one of the handsomest faces I'd ever seen.

My heart skipped a beat or two. My eyes got big and round as my legs turned to jelly. I could hardly breathe, move, or take my eyes off him. Now I was staring. That's when he said my name.

"Is your name Maribeth...Maribeth Stone is that you?" "Excuse me," as he touched me on the shoulder.

Huh? He knows me...what the fuck. This gorgeous hunk of a man knows me? How? From where? How could I not know him? Who could possibly forget someone who looks like *this*?

"Do I know you?" I asked.

"Yes" He smiled. Moreover, the universe shook. I swear there was a halo around his head. The more I listened to his voice I could tell you it was from a long, long time ago. Holy Shit! It was Mason my bully's brother. Wow, he looked sexy as hell better than high school. I couldn't believe my eyes.

● ● ●

My Knight has returned

Oh, how blessed these days must have been. As he told me was new in his life. I had to remember to pick up my jaw that had nearly dropped to the floor back in place. This dazzling, tall, Italian stud, eye-catcher was the same all American football player that I had spent many days playing with as a child before his sister became my bully. Who saved me from my bully, was once again standing before me, and talking to me.

Reduced to the awkwardness of an adolescent, I nonetheless tried to retain my composure and make casual and coherent conversation. It took tremendous effort to stay focused.

As he spoke, telling me a little bit about himself and his news, my mind wandered off and I could barely make out what he was saying. I was too preoccupied, wondering if I looked okay, chastising myself for not having taken more time to fix my hair or polish my make-up or dress nicer before I left the house.

What was I thinking coming here without making more of an effort on my appearance? A girl should be prepared at all times. You'll never know whom you'll bump into at the supermarket, right? I was even filled with anxiety when I couldn't remember whether I had any pimples on my face or if I had recently plucked my eyebrows or shaved my legs or put on deodorant.

● ● ●

Well, it turned out he was still single and lived close to my town in New Jersey. OH MY GOD! Then he asked about my situation by using three words that had never sounded so obscene in my life: "Are you married?"

"No, why you asked?"

"I would love to take you out and catch up."

I wanted to run through the store screaming. I was so excited. We set a date for him to pick me up this coming Friday.

● ● ●

Friday was here before I knew it. I put on a nice burgundy velvet dress. It had been just tight enough for him to see all my curves. Believe me after the work I had done on my body, I was not a shame to show them off.

● ● ●

That Friday

He was picking me up in 1998 Ford Mustang GT. I was in heaven. I loved mustangs. He took me to a nearby Italian restaurant. We talked so much about anything and everything. We were having so much fun that we forgotten what time it was. We went back to his place and watched a few movies.

He put his arm around me. I wanted more but I didn't want to feel like a whore. It was two in the morning, when he finally took me back home. When he arrived at my house, he turned off the car. We made plans to see each other in a few more days. I looked away for a hot minute just when I turned back my head to look at him. He planted a kiss on my lips. It felt sweet. I could barely sleep that night. In three days, I was going over his house to hang out. He lived out in

● ● ●

Three Days Later
On that summer day in
Cherry Hill NJ

After a day of working, he picked me up again at my house and took me back to his house. He wanted to take a shower. I sat on the couch watching TV waiting for him to get out of the shower.

Once he got out of the shower. He got dressed and sat on the couch next to me. He started to show me old pictures of him. He smelled so fresh. I wanted to fuck the hell out of him, but I behaved. As we watched a movie, Mason was talking about how commercials cut into a juicy kissing scene. At first, I didn't catch the comment, but before I knew it, he was reaching in for a kiss.

I reached in for a kiss, and then he pulled away. Oh my god, no he didn't, I thought. I pulled him back in for a real kiss. Before I knew it, we were making out. He pulled off my dress revealing my lace panties and matching bra. I pulled off his shirt to see his muscular chest. Boy was he sexy as hell!

● ● ●

Before I knew it, I was on the edge of the couch and he was seating between my thighs with his face deep in between them. My pussy lips were swollen and the pink amidst my brown pubic hair.

His eyes grew big just from the sight of my pussy lips. He put the tip of his tongue at the top of my luscious slit. Then the eating began in earnest. I was trembling as he worked his tongue on my clit with each lick I climaxed, and I finally forced my head back against the couch as I cum.

Once he was done, I lifted my head and dropped to my knees, and pushed Mason back onto the couch. I slipped his cock into my mouth. I sucked hard, enjoying the heat of his cock against my tongue. Mason slipped his cock out of his my mouth, then he rammed it back into my mouth but this time he pushed it all the way down my throat.

• • •

Mason started fucking my mouth. He pounded his cock into my mouth hard and fast, banging the base of it at my lips. His balls were beating on my chin. The round head of his cock plunged into the back of my throat. He moaned out my name. Just hearing my name and his moaning made me even more wet. I was enjoying the hell out of his cock.

• • •

He stopped himself before cumming. He got up from the couch. He laid me down on the couch and jumped on top of me. He sled his hard cock into my tight wet pussy. Once pushed his cock deep into my pussy, he stopped for a moment to feel my pussy wrapped around his cock. Then he rammed his cock harder into my tight pussy. He grunted ramming powerfully into my pussy, his balls beating at my swinging ass cheeks.

• • •

"Fuck me…fuck me…fuck me!" I moaned. I couldn't believe what I was saying. I have never said these things before. My body was being swung back and forth by the powerful thrusts by Mason and his amazing cock. I was urging him to fuck me faster and harder. Mason plunged deeper and deeper into my birth canal until the very tip of his penis penetrated my cervix opening. His entire dome shaped cock head entered.

Mason could not hold off any longer. I was yelling, and screaming that as I came repeatedly. My throbbing pussy was bathing his penis with my creamy cum juices. The scalding his way, my pussy was squeezing his cock. His balls grower tight at the base of the cock, this made him pump his cum juice into my dripping wet pussy in a huge quantity. Before we could lay back and enjoy ourselves, there was a knock at the door.

●●●

Who the hell, could this be at this time of night? It was his roommate Chris. I couldn't straighten my legs must less get up, so I grabbed the couch pillows and covered myself, while Mason put back on his pants. Mason opened the door to let Chris. You would have thought his roommate got the hint when he seen our clothes all over the floor.

No, what does he do, he sits on the couch that was next to us and started to talk to us. An hour went by when he finally went to bed. I was so cold. All I could do was get dressed as we just laughed it off. Mason drove me home. We couldn't stop smiling. Well the rest was history.

●●●

May 3, 2010

The crush I had on him, started up again. The feelings I had for him was blossoming into something I had only dreamed about. Only four months into dating, we secretly were hitched and didn't tell anyone.

●●●

After being married for a few years, we were having our first son together. After the baby was born, Mason finally took me to his old house where his sister still lived in Croydon. Kasdeya didn't realize who I was. Mason and I didn't dare to tell her.

●●●

The New Kasdeya

Kasdeya was fat and disgusting. Her once long beautiful jet-black hair was now dirty looking. She was now a blonde-haired person. She had really let herself go. I was surprise that she was even dating. I wonder how she caught him.

Kasdeya probably knocked him out and drugged his ass. She introduced me to her boyfriend. Only to realized that he was secretly cheated on her. I knew this because he was fucking two of my friends. He was degusted about Kasdeya's personality.

Kasdeya was worst now than she was in school. Kasdeya was a straight fat nasty lazy ass cunt. He tried to leave her several times but stayed because something happened at the house to make him stay with her.

Deep down inside me I hide a secret about how I really felt about Mason's sister. I continued to have a happy life with him, but deep down I wanted to tell him the truth about the things his sister did to me, but the time will come.

• • •

Only years later

I watched as she torn down her family. Kasdeya treated her brothers like shit. She called people niggers but yet she was the biggest nigger I'll ever see in my life. Kasdeya took advance of the people around her. She never gives back anything in return.

Most of all Kasdeya treated her own nephews as if they weren't even good enough to be a part of her family. She had the nerve to talk about people like dogs. I don't think she has looked in mirror lately Kasdeya wasn't a pretty sight. She had let herself go in embarrassing way. Kasdeya was not the woman she thought she was.

They said beauty was in the eyes of the beholder while Lucifer has her number. Bitch it's almost time to give her what she deserves. A change was coming and she was going to hers eventually. The next time Kasdeya pushed me too far like she use to do when we were in school, she would see me standing over her with a smile on my face.

Every time I saw the fat bitch all I could think to myself was "Bitch you think I'm bitter I'm beyond being bitter." I hated how Kasdeya treated her own nephews and me. I even hated every time I would log into my Facebook account, I would see her profile picture made me sick to my stomach. I put up a picture with my head tilted to the side with a smile on my face. To be honest I was laughing at her expense and she didn't even know it.

● ● ●

No more drama

No more being afraid to speak up. No more being afraid to walk. No more crying in my world which was now filled with love respect and most of all empowerment for me. I just knew that I could never forgive her for what she has put me through.

Now I stood tall as a proud human being and shared my purpose in life to everyone I knew because I matter and the power was mine to keep, she wasn't going to take that away from me. I felt angry and still had a desire to seek revenge on her.

Life has treated me badly. I just wished that I could have had a normal life and being free. Not all those memories will ever fade away. I felt my anger growing stronger with each passing day I saw her.

My anger was driven mad if frustration. If I don't act soon I will never forget her. It was a cruel world and wicked things happen she deserved to die. Kasdeya has to pay the price for my suffering.

● ● ●

It was time

On a weekday evening while Kasdeya and her boyfriend were watching the late comedy show on television, laughing and smiling when others were dining out romantically.

When the extended show at the cinema was almost ending Kasdeya and her boyfriend was going to call it a night. While at my house, my husband had helped our son prepare for the next day's mathematics test.

My family had already had their evening prayers. My loving husband had kissed me a goodnight kiss. He took his sleeping pills and we both went to bed.

As he slept, I rose from the bed and got dressed then headed over to the bitch's house. Most of the lights in the houses in the neighborhood were switched off with only amber streetlights shining. While most of the people in the neighborhood were already asleep, I parked my car three houses down from Kasdeya's house. The dogs in the neighborhood had stopped howling at the moon and were sleeping.

There was no need to break down the front door. They always left their doors were open. There Kasdeya was on the couch with her back turned to the door. About twenty minutes before I arrived she had taken a sedative to relax for the night. Her boyfriend just sat on the other couch as I walked in. He then got up and closed the curtains. He nodded his head at me.

●●●

"Hey, what are you doing here?

"Have a seat! I have a few questions for you. Do remember what you did to me?"

"No"

"What did I do wrong? Was it my hair? Was it my smile? Was it my weight or was it the fact that I'm smaller than you are? Why did you hit me? Why did you laugh when I started to cry?

Why did you threaten to kill me? What did I do wrong? Why was it me you love to hurt, and treat like a piece of shit? How could you be so harsh and unfair? Why won't you leave me alone? Why did you keep on hurting me? Does it make you feel better?"

"What the fuck are you talking about?"

"Do you even know who I am?

"Oh look like a girl I went to school with…Maribeth Albertus?"

"No, bitch! It's Maribeth Stone from high school. I had worked done on me and changed my last name."

"Ohhhh...my fucking god! You are the fucking fat nigger we use to pick on. I can't believe you are with my brother. I have been dying to say something about you and my brother. I am still puzzled why my brother was with a fucking nigger.

Thank god, the boys are not as black as you are. I was only being nice to you because I was trying to do the sister thing but truly I can't stand you especially knowing who you are now. What a fucking joke!"

"Now I stand in your house..." She then cut me off and started to talk more trash. Her boyfriend jumped up from the couch and disappeared down the hallway.

"Fuck yeah... We loved messing with you. Just because you were prettier and smarter than we were, you made us look stupid."

Just before, she could say anything else. Her boyfriend Billy came up from behind her and hit Kasdeya across her head. This was a perfect time for us to tie her up and gag her. Her boyfriend helped me tied her down in the best torturing position we could get her in. I gaged the bitch with an old rag. He stripped her down to her tee shirt and panties.

●●●

May the fun begin

She woke up just in time for me to tell her a few things and for me to get even with her. Kasdeya started to beg for mercy but for her, her time had finally come. Fate has brought us together the victim and the mad criminal. Once her boyfriend was done, helping me out, he went outside and sat in his car to keep a close eye on the neighbors to make sure no one entered the house.

I have been a victim most of my life and now it was her turn. Say goodbye to that girl she bullied around. My mind thought about nothing else but her footsteps over the years. A whirlpool scoured my mind for some horrible memories about Kasdeya. Memories of her bulling replayed in my head as I looked at her. I was becoming sick. I felt like I was dying in life. An explosive adrenaline rush pulsed through my veins.

"I wish we could be friends. Why did you pick on me for so long?

"It was fun and won't change a single thing. Hell...everyone was always being picked on...get over it."

"Till this very day I can hear the voices of all the taunting, teasing that terrified me. Why...me? What the hell, did I ever do to you? Why didn't you just leave me alone?"

"You may think you are better because you called me names. You may think I'm hurting inside. You even decided to get violent. Do you really think I was going to hide from you after all these years? You may be a lot bigger than I may be and you may have won every fight. You may have even damaged so many people such as me but how do you sleep at night?

Especially knowing that so many people were running scared from your fist and when somebody decides to stand up to you. Hitting them was hard to resist and many people looked up to you because they were scared if they didn't you'll turn sour.

I bet half of them just thought you were just a bully who was a fat ugly bitch. When you find out what they thought of you, you say something to them, they just cower. Consequently, no one really idolized you and nobody wanted to follow your path.

They were just scared to open their mouths to you. Some of them won't even laugh as you sat there telling everyone your stupid jokes. You made sure that you had everybody below you. You made them obey your every demand as if they should give two shits about your needs. If somebody bigger and harder came along you always find a way to put the down.

You would bury people's head in the sand. You think it's good to pick on people while pointing out anything you can. So many children tried their best to challenge you while the majority of them just ran. These brave little soldiers were taught to stand up for their rights, but you are the bully you are.

You saw it as an excuse for a fight. You made others and I feel like we were nothing. At our expense you watched as went home crying all the way home. I didn't want to admit that you were a bully. I felt had to fight you alone, but you continued to bully me even into my adult life.

You knew I was to a shame to tell anyone and you knew I wouldn't tell anyone.

When, my parents asked me where the bruises came from. I always lied to them and anyone else who asked. I would tell them that I felt; but the truth was if I had told someone, you would have my life even worse. If I did tell someone what you did.

You always waited for school to end and you would come to the door I was supposed exit out, waiting for me to come out so you can put me back into my place. I would hide until you were gone and I would head home in the opposite direction of your house.

I wouldn't be where I am today, but your name would have been shamed and laughed at and you would not have won by far. Instead took the punches and I didn't say a word because I thought no matter how hard I screamed no one would listen to me.

Other peoples' voices will never be heard, like the two kids you bullied. You remember the two young bodies that were found and now they are nothing but bones. As they lie 6 feet under the ground and nothing anyone does will change their death. They obviously found it too hard to cope your bullying.

You made them wish they weren't born but to you it's just a joke. To me you are a murderer because you made those two kids kill themselves.

You robbed them of their happiness and you took away their lives. You may not have actually killed them but you killed them deep inside .You tore at their emotions and they knew they had nowhere to hide.

Consequently, they did what they thought they had to do. Their pain was too great to mend. They wanted to go somewhere you couldn't find them and they knew you couldn't hurt them again, but now think of both their families. How each day was another struggle. They can't hold their children's hands anymore.

They can't reach out to them for a cuddle.

You can live your life now. You can still target your dreams but for the families that have lost their kids.

Well their lives have been ripped at the seams. I hoped that one day someone bullies you and I hope you wish you were dead. I hope each day was a battle and you wish you'd stayed in bed. These children are dead because of you and you've left so many lives in a mess.

All because you're just a coward. Who bullied two children to death. I hate my life can't take it anymore just when it seems like it will be ok another door slam in my face. They pretend to be my friends in front of grownups putting on a good act when they leave; it's back to the chopping block.

I can't keep going through this one day feeling good and the next day like dirt just want to get away from all this but I don't know how. Wherever I go, torture followed me. I don't know whom to turn to anymore. It just feels like there was no one left in the world I could trust and talk to anymore. How would it feel to be you as the victim I as your bully? You are being quiet and scared having no place to run to maybe my experiences need to be shared.

●●●

Being the victim isn't much fun looking down the barrel of the proverbial smoking gun. If we were to switch places, you would see. It's not much fun being the victim. Just look at the scars it has left on me.

Some might think they can hit me if they do I might fight back. Sick and tired of being the target a victim of yet another attack. If they continue to push me, I really didn't want to fight with my thoughts about you anymore.

I am on the edge of losing control. I feel like I just might. The cops don't want to help me. I guess I knew they wouldn't at times I think I may have to do something I know I shouldn't. I have changed into someone I didn't want to be.

I was afraid I might not be able to change back to the person I used to see. I can't turn into a bully that's what I fear might come true. I hate these thoughts I'm having please tell me what I should do.

I have now officially crossed over that line. I was striving to keep my anger in tact but only God knows how hard I'm trying.

Hate has burned a gaping hole in my soul.

The rancid reek of charring flesh was dancing on my very soul and as the rising fumes enmesh my crumpled heart, I play the role of crabby fart, gassing off a diatribe, bleeding out a bitter part of me: an ugly twisted woman.

● ● ●

A bit of Heaven

I grabbed one of her cigarettes, lit it, and began to smoke it. The taste was disgusting. I put the cigarette onto her face. I was trying to scream. I punched her in the throat causing her to choke. Oh, my god the adrenaline was starting to rush through my body. I took a box cutter and made little cuts up and down her body, then poured rubbing alcohol.

Tears poured down her face. Just seeing the pain in her eyes was turning me on. I cut her off nasty ass hair just to piss her off. Just to make me feel better I scalped bitch and placed it in her lap so she could see her hair.

I then cut open her shirt, exposing her disgusting saggy breast. I went into the kitchen and grabbed a fileting knife from the butcher block. She started to jerk around the couch. I catch her in the face with a right hook. Her eyes started to roll to the back of her head back she did not pass out. Good because I wanted her feel, everything I was going to put her through. I commenced to filet the skin off her breast.

I removed off about five inches of skin off her breast. As she bleeds out, I ran into the kitchen grabbed the sea salt. Without any hesitating, I poured the salt onto her breast. The bitch tried to jump off the couch. She was begging under the gag. I didn't care to make what she was saying. I was having too much fun.

I took a pair of pillars and pulled off her fingernails one by one. Once I was done, I ripped the rag out of her mouth. I then wedged a long tube down into her stomach. I put a funnel on the end of the tube.

I went into her kitchen, got the bottle of bleach, and poured it down the funnel. Once I empty the entire bottle down the funnel. I pulled out the tube. There was blood in the tube. Before she could throw up the bleach, I stapled her fucking big mouth shut.

I sat back to enjoy my work but I wanted to do one more thing before I leave her forever. I went out to the car and grabbed my hot comb curling iron. I put it on the stovetop. I let it get nice and red hot. I let it stay on the stovetop while I went back and cut off her panties.

I snatched the hot curling. For a minute, I waved it in her face as she screamed as hard as she could. Within a wink of an eye, I jammed the hot curling iron up in her nauseating pussy. The smell of her burning pussy was sickening my stomach. It was time to end this torture.

●●●

Finally able to breathe

I was hoping that all the demons that live inside of me goes away from her and die. She may have taken my power then but now I've taken my power back. I pulled out my gun. The gun was loaded.

I'm ready to aim; this life just isn't the same. As I pulled the trigger, I notice something new. I must kill YOU! I raised the pistol, ready to fire.

"And now I'm going to enjoy the sound of you dying."

She started to scream but I couldn't hear her words. I pulled the trigger. She fell, her dull, lifeless eyes were glazed with awful terror, but she would say nothing at all. She just died without a struggle.

She was finally gone. I untied her and took the staples out of her mouth. I set the house on fire. Her boyfriend disappeared with a smile on his face. He was free and so was I. I smiled evilly, for years of abuse had changed me into a bitter, heartless monster, bent on murder.

I went home and fell asleep in my Mason's arms. I slept the first night like a baby. There was investigation but it ended up as a closed case. They ruled as a suicide.

Kismet Romance

**Last Will and Testament
In California**

Today was going to be my last day on this earth. I am dying. Death was lurking over my bed waiting to take me home. I had my oldest son come and seat by my bed to talk to him about a secret I have never told anyone. He seats by my bed with curious look on his face. As I began to talk to him about my past, I listen to the rain outside. Each raindrop holds the secrets of my past, as they splatter to the ground.

All the hurtful words of others and the things I have done. It's there a secret I hide deep within, because those words are masked with pain. For those abandoned mysteries of my secret. In my world has failed to notice two things I have done. My deepest secret hides with passion. I struggle to have any meaning in this world, which we all know I tried but I wonder where I should go with my hidden secrets, where they cannot find.

I hold the key to all the answers, which are hidden, deep inside my head and embedded in my soul. All of my secrets are hidden beneath the surface so it has ruined my life for the most part and the life I have taken. Those dark secrets and the memories will fade hidden in away in my head. The story and secrets will be left untold but today and only I will share them with you my son.

"Why...now?"

"I am dying and I need to get this off my chest. Just please listen I don't have much time left."

The things I didn't want people to know but once I tell you my son and make my feelings known you will know the truth about all my secrets and who I am. The struggle will be over and I will finally be home, so today I will tell you the real me. I have to tell everything from the beginning."

●●●

In California

In early 1943, I was 23 years old. I was a soldier at the Camp Cooke in Lompoc. I was a regular customer at a nearby diner, but today was different because there was a new waitress working there. Her name was Beth. I knew getting to know her was going to be hard because the way I traveled so much. I was in love.

She didn't stay long. Rumor had it that she left after a fight with her father. She ended up moving to Santa Barbara. It was here that the juvenile authorities arrested her for underage drinking. She had called one my friend's girlfriend to bail her out. She was sent back to Medford by the juvenile authorities in Santa Barbara. I have rarely seen her. She would come back into town here and there to see old friends or to look for work.

● ● ●

Ms. Beth

Beth was 5 feet 5 inches tall, weighed 115 pounds. She was the feminine ideal woman of my time. Her skin was like a porcelain doll with light blue eyes, brown hair, and badly decayed teeth, but you could barely see them. She was still perfect in my eyes. They would remind me of the sky on a clear and calm day. Her meaty legs and her full hips was such a turn-on. She had the cutest pig nose.

She had the softest raven black hair with blood red lips. She even took the time to put a white flower in her hair every day. She was never without doting admirers who would pay for her meals and buy her clothes and gifts. Beth was a courteous and soft-spoken. She didn't smoke, drink or swear. Her lust for life meant she frequented visited nightclubs, loved the music and was always surrounded by men.

At age 19, she moved from her hometown and went to live with her father in Vallejo, California. She was hoping to pursue her dream of being in the movies. She was a wannabe actress. Elizabeth was born in Boston, Massachusetts. She grew up and lived in Medford with respiratory problems that developed into asthma and bronchitis, over the years. That didn't slow her down.

● ● ●

My Obsession

She was so beautiful. We both had the same friends. Whenever she was around, I always find a way to hang out with my friends. She was so full of laughter and sunshine. I was enjoying the memories, the people, and Beth. They were all mine. Life was difficult sometimes, but my faith in God always kept me strong. I never knew that things in my life couldn't go so wrong.

I watched her everyday walk by me. She didn't even notice me waving at her. I finally got the nerve to walk up to her and commence to talk to her. Wow, I was so surprise when she actually turned around and started to talk to me.

I don't remember what the conversation was about. I just remember how beautiful she looked until very day. Her raven black hair was enough to stop traffic. Something about her made my heart stopped. Every day she stopped by my station on the base. We talked for hours until it was closing time. Then one night she asked me out for a nightcap.

● ● ●

There was a person named Joe. That she was talking too. She was writing to him. On the days that she would receive a letter, it would all depend on the contents of the letter she would be in a good or bad mood. Joe complained about her never ending flirting with other men. He believed that she loved him but sometimes I wonder about him. He was a sneaky of son of a bitch. Joe was hoping that she would stop flirting. She refused to do so.

●●●

January 8 Beth decided that she was moving to Chicago to be a fashion model. Hell…Joe couldn't even give her the things she wanted and needed because of his marriage. I knew that she had a defect with her vaginal area. The defect wouldn't allow her to have sex or have any children but I can overlook this problem. I loved her and that was all that matter.

●●●

On January 9, would be a day I would never forget. Today was the day I was going to propose to her. Despite that, she was still talking to Joe, maybe this will make her happy and get rid of Joe. I knew that was Joe was going to drive her to Los Angeles. He was helping her to check her luggage at the bus station and was planning to return to the hotel she was staying at.

She wanted to go to Berkeley to stay with her sister but her sister couldn't meet up with her. She was planning to meet her at the Biltmore hotel downtown. Joe accompanied her into the hotel lobby just to see her make inside okay. He talked to her for while then he left to return to his family in San Diego.

I watched her walk to the elevator. I followed her up the next elevator. I knew what room she as staying in. I had everything planned out. I got off the elevator and almost threw up I tried to collect my thoughts. I was so nervous. I arrived to her door and knocked on it. My nervousness, my anxiety, my feverous trembling all began when she opened the door. Beads of cold sweat appeared on my skin and my pale hands weakened and shook. This nervous made my soul quiver. I just want to cower and hide just to regain my control.

● ● ●

The Proposal

Fearing that I would be rejected. I tried not to think it. How could she not want to be with me? I always did what was expected; pleased, appeased, capitulated, and ensuring conflict was mitigated. I hoped it wasn't lust that was being confused with joy. Well anyway, I dropped to one knee and I asked her to marry me. Within a blink of an eye, she said, "NO".

All the while, with introspection, soul-searching and deep reflection, I realized people pleasing had a cost. My authentic self was all but lost. Surprisingly, to my delight, my ego put up quite a fight, assertiveness came over me, rejection set my spirit free but the pain quickly came back. What a hindrance, what a pain, to find myself in love with her.

My youthful heart was too easily won by her charms. I hated how this game to get her heart. For the outcome was always the same. She smiled when I tried to explain to her how much I loved her. I was alone in my feelings, nothing to gain but I was going to do something different about it.

Twice, this has happened before when I tried to talk to her and now but this time it hurts three times harder. I felt like I have climbed up to heaven and landed face first in the dirt. Her rejection was painful. My senses lose focus when I tried to look her in the face, as she said no. The way she said it was so cold. Therefore, I rein in my feelings, and pull back the tears. I tried to remind myself that I have many years to go to find true love.

My pride has been shattered as I tried to regroup myself. I am blaming, the hormones of what I call my youth. My imagination was started to spin into something demonic. I tried to listen to her terrible lies about she can't marry me. It was all lies. I knew the truth. As her rejection played repeatedly in my head, my heart was aching and it was crying inside. I told myself that I could get over it, but the thought of her moving on and seeing her on television... I don't know how I would live with this damn rejection.

All I could see was red. With tears in my eyes, I looked at her in the eyes. My heart cried out to God, let this be a dream, let this not be real but she looked at me with such hate and she was going on with her lies. That she wasn't "in love with me" but loved me as a brother and sister way.

How could she do this to me? How could she claim to love me? How could she look me straight in the eyes and not shed a tear, a heartbeat, a whisper, not even a thing towards me. She invited me in to talk some more. I looked up and down the hallway then I put the "DO NOT DISTURB" on the outside handle and closed and locked the door behind me.

● ● ●

My tears rolled down inside my heart. They soon became like blood dripping out of my heart. I struck her across her mouth. Blood began to pour out her mouth. Chucks of her teeth flew from her mouth. She tried to fight back. I was getting excited to see her fight back. She was no match for me.

She allowed every man to ride her. I will turn her into a horse that she was. I loved her for who she was but she didn't love me the same. She just wanted to string me around like a puppet. To silence her, I muted the Beth with a gag-bit contraption, which I anchored to a sturdy fixture at her back. I put Beth in my jury-rig bridle/headstall device. Part of the contraption dug two ugly indentations into the sides of her nose. I really fixed her pig nose.

After I haltered her, I branded her with my initials as if she was a horse. She fought the halter during the branding, but this wasn't going to stop me. She was in my device nice and tight. There was no escaping for her. I bite her. Her skin was warm and sweet, like a crisp fresh apple. There she laid there with tears in her eyes. I stopped to express to her how I was feeling about her and damn lies. For once, she was going to listen to me.

Screw your tears, today you will witness hell. Unlike any hell, you have seen before. You will beg for my love, but love was long gone. I loved you, more than you know, but lately Joe has been in the way. I don't want to need you like I thought I did. My world was based on what you put me through. I don't want to be in love with you, if you can't return it to me. I wanted to love you and marry you, but I guess I am not good enough for you.

Therefore, I will try to stop caring for you. I don't question you Beth; you made me question myself, because you act as if I wasn't as important as everyone else was. It makes me think you don't deserve me. You can't say anything to convince me that everything you did wasn't true.

I know you don't feel the same as I do. I've known it all along. I even tried to turn a blind eye, but it felt so incredibly wrong. I gave you everything I could give you. My hand, my soul, and my heart, but to me, you chose not to live or love me. Now I'm falling apart. I'm suffocating inside. I can't breathe; my tears blur my vision, as if someone died inside. I am going to start to grieve once you are out of my life for good.

My heart was broken and my world was dark. I see no future ahead, when you said no, you took my spark. Now inside I just feel dead. I just wanted you to fall in love with me, but you have fallen for someone new. You wanted start a new family and forget about me. I can't let go of you.

I've tried a million times, to forget and move on, but then I will remember you were mine, and it will start straight back to square one, all the feeling and thoughts of you . If I can't have you, no one can! I told you always and forever and meant it. I will love you for eternity. Even if we are not together, you're still everything to me. I wished you only happiness, in everything you do, but that was a lie. I don't give two shits about you or future.

This was the last time I'll express, how much I truly love you. Please don't ask me to be happy. You're the reason I'm not the person I should be. You may not have meant to hurt me so bad, but you did and I'm the one who has to deal with it. The hurt, the embarrassment, the unwanted love, and the impossibility of happiness will always haunt me. This will be the last time you hurt me!

● ● ●

My Final Gift

I took one last look at her and then I struck her several times in her head and face, knocking her unconscious. I ripped off her clothes. As I stood over her body, I stopped to have a cigar. It was time to make her feel the pain I was feeling inside. I put my cigar out on her. I need get on with it…time to go to work. I was going to have the time of my life with her, one way or another.

I marked up her forehead, to give her a horse credentials. I sliced her mouth from ear to ear, to give her a whopping wide horse mouth. I started to cut up her left nipple but I think I want the right one just for my trophy. Then I slashed her abdomen from pubis to the navel, to give her a bodacious horse vagina.

For the hell of it, I stretched her anus to a nice 1.25 inches in diameter. Too bad, I did not have anything bigger I would have ripped her ass apart. Since I wasn't good enough to be with. I sodomized her ass with the broken end of a table. She was now boasting a big old horse anus. Afterward I pulled out the Beth's pubic hair and rolled it into a tuft, then stuffed the tuft into her ass. She now sported a nicely tufted horsetail, "on" her tail end…ha-ha.

Since her reproduction wasn't good enough to bare any children, I cut up her organs with multiple X's. I removed a large section of her left thigh and insertion of it into the vagina. This heralded that she was now going to be coming out as a horse when everyone sees her. The public was going to get an eye on my amazing work I did. I strangled the *horse*. Her lifeless body looked better than ever. It was time to clean up her up and needed to make her up for all to see her true beauty.

● ● ●

Well Into the Early Morning

I took her lifeless body and placed in the tub. I completely drained her blood from her body. I washed and scrubbed her naked body down with coconut juice. Then I brushed her down with a fiber brush to get rid any traces of my hair on her. I then cut the bitch in half.

I dropped her mutilated body in the Leimert Park district of Los Angeles on January 15, 1947. I left her remains in a vacant lot on the west side of South Norton Avenue midway between Coliseum Street and West 39th Street. I posed her with her hands over her head and her elbows bent, like a model.

I watched in the distance in my car at the vacant lot. I watched as a woman walking by discovered her Beth's body. It was priceless to see the look on the woman's face. The crime scene quickly filled with police, bystanders and reporters. It was out of control. There were so many people trampling on any evidence the investigators could hope to find. I left the scene once more people kept showing up. I then dropped her black patent leather purse and her black open-toed pumps in a nearby dumpster at 1819ᵗʰ E. 25ᵗʰ Street.

• • •

Over the next few years

The cops spent all their manpower looking for me. I was right under their noses. The murder was never solved it was because of the reporters and the lack of evidence. The reporters and the people were all over the crime scene, the lack of evidence, the evidence did had was trampling on and useless, the reporters was withholding information from the police. No one would give the police anything to work with. The case just went cold.

It was ashamed that it took several days for the police to take control of the investigation.

During which the reporters roamed freely throughout the department's offices, sitting at officers' desks, and answered their phones.

• • •

A massive investigation into finding her murderer was launched. The brutality of the murder and Beth's somewhat sketchy lifestyle, the rumors and speculation were rampant. They were often incorrectly reported as a fact in the newspapers this made the investigation harder. She was buried at the Mountain View Cemetery in Oakland, California. I never tried to visit her grave.

• • •

Months and years later

Just for the hell of it. I called the editor of the *Los Angeles Examiner* claiming to be the killer. I wanted to express my concern that the news of the Beth's murder was tailing off in the newspapers. So I offered to mail items belonging to her. I sent them to the editor of the paper.

In the package, it contained her birth certificate, business cards, photographs, names written on pieces of paper, and an address book with the name Mark Hansen embossed on the cover. Hansen was an acquaintance of hers. He even became a suspect. I only did that to piss off the police. I put everything in the past and kept the secret with me.

● ● ●

Bensalem, Pennsylvania

I moved out and started a new family with the Pentons. That was how we came to be. The rest was history. That's the truth. Until this very day, I still see her face and smile playing in my memories. I had live with the idea that she didn't love me. I realized I still love Beth even after I met your mother. I had to learn how to deal with the thousand emotions I felt about her.

Every memory of her was conflicting with the next. Every day I cry, but the crying doesn't help. The crying makes it worse. Every day, it just gets worse. That's one more day she doesn't love me. I have counted each days hoping that what I did would disappear in my memories.

Every day hurts worse than the last. I miss her deeply! I miss her laugh, her life, her tears, her so-called innocence, and her fears. My heart aches for her. I pleaded and begged God to send her to back to me, but there was no answer. I would have loved to hear how much she cared and loved me but she didn't. I know that now. I knew that she couldn't return to me but I can dream. Right!

I thought little by little over time, I could let her go. What was once mine was not anymore. She was gone for good. I hoped that wherever she was, no one knows your name. No one knows her pain. Maybe when I let her free out of my heart, she could fly and be truly free. So there she goes, she will be gone for good. You need to get in touch with Raven. She was all you have left. Cherish every moment as if it was your last. I love my son…this was the end for me!

The 13ᵗʰ Floor

Camden New Jersey

As the years go by and time fades away, what used to be good days are now filled with dismay. Tomorrow comes, goes and here another day passes, it goes by and my ambition to become something more grows and grows. I hoped that around the corner, my future would get better but I have more miles to go. The life I wanted now gets closer each day.

All I ever wanted was something to live for. I don't want to be this little person anymore. I'm basing my life upon what others think. I wish I could go back and redo everything, every time at the blink of an eye.

Free from the rules I followed as a child. Now it was time for a change and I realized nothing was fair, and sometimes it seems like nobody even cares.

I've fought to become who I am and what I wanted to be. I have to remind myself that one day, I would be free. I wanted to know where I'm going.

It's as if no one pays attention to what I felt was best for me and what I thought about the way some things should be. I understood now, that I knew pretty much on my own and much of what I could do will never be known.

● ● ●

All the time, I think about everything I can't say, what I have to keep in, and by doing this, my thoughts only get more complicated and deepen. Soon I hope to find out who I am, and what I am meant to become.

I don't need to be reminded of where I came from. Don't get me wrong I love the coworkers and the customer. This job was putting a toll on me it was eating my soul and spirit alive. I don't know how much more I can take this job.

Just when I was ready to quit one of my regular customers comes in and offers me a job at his office at 1300 Admiral Wilson Boulevard. OH MY GOD, it's the old Sears building in Camden.

● ● ●

A New Door Opens

Wow, I'm so excited! Today was my first day of change. As I start on my new venture this brings a wish my way. Many happy moments to fill each coming day and as I face the future that's waiting just for me. I soon discover that my dreams have all come true, finally.

Not 100 percent sure what this job really wants me to do but I took the job offer. This could be my break away from the other job I work at now. I was trying to find something to base my life upon, something in this strange world that goes on and on that makes me feel complete.

It was easy money for me but when troubles a mess I was the first one they would blame.

Now everyone up the management tree can kiss my ass.

This job was secure but I'm surrounded by the hate of the other workers. I'm sure to endure because I'm dead weight to them. It's been a giggle and fun, just having this job was so disappointing that a new job has been found.

It was sad working day after day the same monotonous routines. Work and more work was all I did, while others fucked around doing half ass work.

● ● ●

From this moment onwards until I'm old, I will be at this new job. I'll be walking to work, in the rain, snow and cold, I hope I love this new job as I forget about the old one. Thinking, can it be any worse if I was dead, where there are no more worries or heartache. My new job stood on the edge of Camden, New Jersey.

Camden was best known for its struggles with urban dysfunction. It was sad when three Camden mayors have been jailed for corruption. Camden has been the highest crime rate in the U.S. Camden was lucky if only two-thirds of the students graduate from high school. Two out of every five residents are below the national poverty line. You can only imagine, why the hell I want this job and to move the hell out of Camden.

● ● ●

History Lesson

The Sears Building was one of very few major historic landmarks left standing in the city of Camden. This beautiful building was built in 1927 during the time when Camden was a thriving manufacturing center of the famous Admiral Wilson Boulevard that serves as the main entrance to Camden. This wonderful architectural style, intended to honor the city, was unique among Sears's stores. The Greek revival Sears building was to resemble an ancient Greek temple

The building was surrounded with a white Mediterranean style villa and plain green fields. The air was clean and fresh. There were a peace and beauty of this building, but still there was a certain sadness in the atmosphere.

● ● ●

My new job this job may not be the best kind of job, but it was a step up from wearing a pumpkin orange shirt with my special yellow nametag, marked with how many years I worked at. Now I get to wear my business attire look.

● ● ●

New Job Awaits

Today was my first day. I got my orientation, which only lasted an hour. I finally was getting a tour of this wonderful historical building. They transform this into a huge office building. They revive all the architectural details that once spread across the inside of the building that was once a department store. It was more beautiful now than it was in the 20's.

"This is your desk. If you have any questions talk to Beelzebub. You can find him the second door on the left."

I was the head receptionist. This job should be a piece of cake. All I had to do was answer phones, help direct the clients, answer their questions, schedule appointments, which was going to take me a while to get used all the different employees here. Thank god, I don't have in the mail I just call down to the mailroom to come it.

●●●

Six months later

Day after day, like many who have come and gone before me. This nine to five eats at me because I am so much better than this. The seating here registering all these people in and never seeing if they ever leave. I was curious about what else was going on in this building. I wrote up a note and walked out of Mr. Beelzebub's door.

I knocked on the door hoping he would ask so I could meet him. After a few knocks there was no answer. I slide the note under the door. The next door I came to work there was a letter from Beelzebub, telling me to come into work on Sunday so he can give me a complete tour of the building, but we were close. Oh well, I was excited that he was going to tell me more about this place.

● ● ●

Later that evening

I was so excited that I couldn't sleep that night. I was horny as hell. I decided to call up an old friend to come over. It's been about 5 months now, since my boyfriend dumped me. I only fuck my dildo nowadays. I really needed a sexual relief so; I freshen up and waited for him to arrive.

He took off his shirt; I looked at his body with pure unadulterated lust in my eyes. He told me to close my eyes and promise he would show me something that I would never forget. Intrigued, I went along with it. I did what he asked as he covered my eyes with a silk blindfold and started to undo my cream-colored button shirt.

While he unbuttoned them, both his thumbs gently skimmed over my skin, first over my collarbone, then above my chest. My breathing became rapid as I felt his touch but I couldn't see anything and it only enhanced my senses more.

He worked in the middle of my top where my cleavage was. I held my breath and waited for him caress and it came. His hands held my shirt open as he rubbed inside my bra and between my strained breasts that caused my nipples to harden. He bent over to touch my ear lightly and I sighed as he first licked around then darted it in.

Close to my face, I felt his warm breath on my lips as he brushed his full mouth over mine, back and forth. I wanted him to kiss me very badly but he refrained from it and I whimpered in protest. He traveled down my chin to the hollows of my neck, sucked on it and knew he would leave a mark as he licked the spot.

My pussy started to throb as he cupped my breasts over my bra and top and when he took the shirt and ripped it open, it made the rest of the buttons to pop off. I moaned loudly as he removed the fabric.

His hands grabbed my swollen mounts over my bra, stroked and rubbed my hard nipples and sensitive breasts. He knew I haven't kissed another man in a long time. I felt him kiss me while our tongues danced. It was very erotic, I was even more turned on that I was at that moment.

He took off my bra and when he continued to kiss me, I felt another pair of hands ran up my thighs, under my loose white mini skirt and opened my legs. I knew it wasn't his because his hands were still on my back. Confused, I was about to ask who else was there, when someone glided their finger over my soaked panties and rubbed my clit.

●●●

Ménage a Trio

The question left me as he broke our kiss and moved away as the finger pushed harder on my clit. Just then, another pair of hands tugged at my huge breast then my nipples and replaced it with a mouth that drew them in as much as it could hold. Someone behind me placed their hand around my neck, held my head up, stuck a wet finger between my ass cheeks and played with my asshole. Desire engulfed me, as I knew it was another man in my house.

My leg was held up and fingers spread my pussy lips as a mouth was placed on me. I groaned as they ate and licked my dripping pussy and two fingers slid in pass my pussy lips, they ate and sucked my clit harder and faster.

Just when I was about to bust, someone laid me down, held my arms above me and I lifted my body off the ground and hope to find anything to give me what I wanted. A chuckle rang out, all of a sudden, my legs were pulled back, spread wide, and my juices poured all over my pussy and ass.

Fingers pushed inside me again, I sighed in relief when it started to move, another finger went in my tight ass followed by another and I moaned out loud, as they glided in and out of both my holes.

Legs began to shake as my pussy and ass started to squeeze, I knew I was about to cum. The fingers stroked in a circular motion on my swollen clit, faster against the slippery wetness and I cum quickly as they processed the torture, I felt myself squirt out and it drenched me.

Still shaken from the aftermath, I was yanked up to my feet and parted my leg. Hands on my hips lowered me down and I felt a big, hard stiff cock pushed in my wet pussy. I gasped at the length and fullness, moaned as the stranger held me up and trusted his cock deep inside me.

He fucked and rammed his cock all the way in, as another part pair of hands massaged my breasts as they bounced up and down with his movements. Lips kissed my ear, neck, stomach, but when I felt a mouth and tongue between my open legs, lap up my soaked clit, I climaxed as the pace increased.

The cock was pulled out, then he flipped me over on all fours, I could feel him under me. He smeared my cum over my pussy and ass. His cock reentered my pussy again, soon after, the other cock rubbed between my butt cheeks, spread the wetness over my asshole then stretched it to its size as they pushed it in and fucked me from behind.

Fingers touched and moved in short strokes over my still sensitive clit, and I was overwhelmed by the sensations of two cocks thrust and fucked me hard. They picked up the tempo as multiple hands and mouths joined in, caressed and roamed over my body. I couldn't believe I was about to cum again so soon, the cocks fucked and fingers on my clit picked up their speed and I screamed out as my body shook and spasm, explosions of multiple orgasms washed through me, repeatedly.

Felt drained and well satisfied, everything stopped and I was drawn up and the blindfold was removed from my eyes. I saw the guy invited over and stranger I never seen before but he was so damn sexy too. There they stood in front of me, naked, and smiling at me. The stranger grabbed and feverishly kissed me, tongues played inside our mouths as I tasted myself in his mouth and when I moved back, I thanked him for that mind blowing experience.

He nipped my bottom lip; he told me he wanted me to meet his roommate Logan. I gave him a wicked grin of excitement washed over me and my cunt started to pulse at the thought. I trailed my hand down his throbbing cock, and began to jerk him off, as my friend come up from behind me and rammed his cum soak cock into my ass. We all cum one more last time.

I finally kicked both of the guys out of my house, jumped in the shower and washed off then went to sleep I had at least five more hours before I had to be in to work.

●●●

The Next Morning

It was a stormy day walking to work, eyeing the clouds, hoping I can make it before the sky opens up. So far, it's a dry storm, but I can feel the electricity in the air. I know it will be coming soon. The streets are completely empty, but that's to be expected with a storm moving in. The way the clouds block out the sun.

I pick up my pace, glancing nervously at the sky. Once in the building I take one last and noticed, the alley outside was empty and undisturbed. The sky above was still cloudy. The storm was brewing, but the rain hasn't fallen yet, good because I had two more blocks to go. I made to work, I took a deep breath and look at the sky.

At last, it begins to rain. The patter of gentle raindrops strikes my face, running down my cheeks and pooling in my eyes. I was glad I made it before the rain really poured down. The lobby was empty but the manager Mr. Beelzebub. I walked over to him.

When Beelzebub looked down, I noticed his face had cast a weird shadow, but I thought I saw a smile there. He was a tall and blond haired man, with a face that looked too innocent for his years. He starts to smile when he sees me, but his expression turns to one of concern when he sees the condition I am in. He says, "Alena, are you okay? Are you ready?"

"Ready for what?" you ask.

"You wanted to know what your job was really about. All the people you register in, while now you will see why you never see them leave. It was time that you know the truth."

● ● ●

The Tour Begins

I bite my lip; my heart was pounding with a different kind of fear I never felt in my life. Instead of the elevator going up, it went down. We stopped on the 13th floor into the ground. Now I was freaking out inside. I come up next to him while he carefully opens the door slightly to the elevator. Before my eyes, there in front of me was never-ending lake. I couldn't see past the fog. In the distance, I saw a boat coming into view ahead.

"Why are we here?"

"Charon is going to pick us up."

"Who is Charon?"

"He is the boatman of Hell who takes souls across the Styx."

The River Styx was the main river of Hell, usually identified as the River of Hate. The souls of the dead must cross the River Styx. The river was marshy, muddy, slimy, and disgusting. The grimy banks of the river are crowded with miserable shades shrieking, begging, and jostling one another, trying to get in line to go across. It was a noisy scene of confusion and anguish.

I couldn't believe it. Slowly through the fog an old boat, a coin to pay Charon for passage, usually an oblus was sometimes placed in or on the mouth of a dead person. Charon was an old man clad in foul garb, with haggard cheeks and an unkempt beard, his eyes glowing like flame, a fierce ferryman who guides his boat with a long pole. He wears a dirty red tunic and conical hat.

There are a 100 of souls who were begging and screaming to be let across, but only those souls who have enough cash money to pay the fare. He lets the paid souls on and us and he violently pushes back all the rest. Those who had not received due burial and were unable to pay his fee, would be left to wander the earthly side of the Acheron, haunting the upper world as ghosts.

If the newly dead couldn't pay, they would have to walk along the bank. This would take them over 100 years to get where they are going. As the boat arrived, we paid Charon and had a seat as he turned the boat around and started to head towards the destination.

● ● ●

"Let me tell about where are going. God as a place primarily created hell for Satan and his demons who are rebellious, fallen angels. Satan was originally created as God's most powerful angelic being.

However, Satan rebelled against God and convinced one third of the angels now referred to as demons to join him. Michael, an archangel of God, fought with God's angels against Satan and his angels, with Satan losing the battle and being cast from heaven down to earth."

"Are you serious? I blurt, "This is ridiculous."

"Let me finish telling you where you are going!"

I stopped to listen to this ridiculous story.

Hell as you may have heard it as a child it was descripted as a place with fire and brimstone. That there was a burning wind that swept through the different levels of hell. A fiery oven bakes the sinful souls. A flame of fire and a lake of surrounded hell but I could see there were flames of fire, about 10 miles away from me. I knew it was 10 miles.

● ● ●

There was a pit of fire, about 3 miles across, had flames that lit up the skyline enough to see the landscape of Hell just a little bit. There was enough to just see some of the skyline. It was all brown and desolate! I mean not even one green leaf, not anything of life of any kind, just stone, dirt and black sky, and smog in the skylight. The flames were high, so I could see it.

The type who was sent to hell are have committed the following greed, adultery, theft swindling, factions, envy, lying, fits of rage, impurity, witchcraft, sorcery, murder, have hatred, selfish ambition, lust, wrath, too much pride, gluttony, sloth, hate against God, fraud, and violence in any way.

The sinners live in an eternal fire. They will encounter eternal punishment. A person will be punished by fire or torment. Many souls will go through some type of punishment in hell smoke of their torment; there was no rest day and night.

As we approach a floating door in the middle of the sea, I could hear people weeping and gnashing of teeth. We both stepped off the boat. There to greet us was various monsters, such as Gorgons and Harpies.

"You don't actually expect me to believe all this, do you?"

He shrugs, "You asked. We must now orient ourselves to the hell and to the journey through its labyrinthine passages."

"Let me out. Let me out now! I don't want anything more to do with you and your crazy world!" As screamed at the top of my lungs. I turned to get back on the boat but it was gone. The smell in Hell was so atrocious; I can't even describe it even if I wanted to.

There was a smell of burning flesh, of sulfur. The smell of these demons was like an open sewer, putrid, rotten meat, bad eggs, sour milk and everything you can imagine. It was so toxic.

"I'm looking for the truth," he said

"What truth would you like to know?"

"All of it!" I was feeling strangely vulnerable. Therefore, I hurried onward, following him toward the door. Pain and rips in the very fabric of the universe appear all around you.

•••

Hell's Workers

The creatures crawl through, of all shapes and sizes, skinless horrors with wings or fangs or many pairs of legs, shrieking with delight. They were raging, smashing everything around, hissing, gnashing, and screeching, as the head towards me. Beelzebub snaps at the creatures "Stay back, demons. She was under my protection now, and you cannot harm her."

These rebellious or fallen angels are known as demons, they are evil spirits or unclean. These fallen angels with wicked hearts and poisonous tongues. The winged demons each more disgusting than the last. Their faces are eyeless sockets and shapeless noses, with little mouths that gape in a constant silent scream at the horror of their own existence. Their bodies are skinless, red sinew and white bone exposed to the air.

They were demons. He commences to tell me who they were. Demons are the one who torments the sinners in hell. They were seeking attention by stamping legs. Throwing objects making loud sounds with their eyes closed. Some were about 12 or 13 feet tall.

They flex large, bat like wings as they come into this world and then fly off their perches in the tears of reality to come hover around their prey. They now serve Satan and, like him, they are evil and hate God plus all people. They enjoy and want to cause pain, misery and suffering to people repeatedly.

Demons can be violent and unstable creatures and as spirits, they are parasites. Though they will sometimes completely possess a person, they mostly prefer to simply attach themselves like a leech, feeding on a person's energy, which in turn gives them, power. Symptoms of demonic attachment include energy loss, fatigue, paranoia, depression and irritability.

They are intelligent enough to know not to take so much energy that they kill they the individual, nevertheless their effect can be quite debilitating. Attachment can be hereditary or demons can be brought through from past incarnations and in these cases, symptoms can be seen during early infancy.

Demons may also attach during periods of extreme emotional, mental or physical trauma. Extreme measures are often required to remove these creatures since all methods of regular exorcism can at times be ineffective. They are the cause of physical and mental illnesses towards people on earth.

●●●

Lost Souls

Now for the people who dies and they are filled with sin. A person dies their soul will be tormented alone by the demons. When a person dies the body will join the soul, and each will suffer brimful of pain.

Some of the souls were sweating in its inmost pores, drops of blood, and the body from head to foot suffused with agony, conscience, judgment, memory, all tortured, but more the head are tormented with racking pains, their eyes starting from their sockets with sights of blood and woe. Their ears are always bleeding from the tormented sounds of sullen moans and hollow groans will all you will hear and shrieks of tortured souls.

Their heart was beating with a high fever. Their pulse was rattling at an enormous rate in agony. Their limbs crackling like the martyrs in the fire, and yet they are unblunt. Some are put in a vessel of hot oil, pained, yet when they are coming out undestroyed.

Their veins becoming a road for the hot feet of pain to travel on, as every nerve is a string on which the devil shall ever play his diabolical tune of Hell's Unutterable Lament. The souls will forever ache, and their body palpitating in unison with their soul.

I could see through the flames, just enough to see bodies, people in the fire screaming, screaming for mercy, burning in this place! There were people were begging to get out. There were other demons who were lined all around the edge of the pit, and as the people crawled up trying to get out, they would be shoved back into the fire and not allowed out.

•••

Lagneia Epipedo (Lust Level)

Chastity Lloyd was here for letting her appetites sway her reason. Lust was the desire to experience physical, sensual pleasures. Her desire for physical pleasures was considered sinful because it causes us to ignore more important spiritual needs or commandments.

Sexual desire was also sinful according to traditional Christianity because it leads to using sex for more than procreation. You have come to a place mute of all light, where the wind bellows as the sea does in a tempest. This was the realm where the lustful spend eternity. Here, sinners are blown around endlessly by the unforgiving winds of unquenchable desire as punishment for their transgressions.

The infernal hurricane that never rests hurtles the spirits onward in its rapine, whirling them round, and smiting, it molests them. She has betrayed reason at the behest of her appetite for pleasure, and so here, she was doomed to remain. There she stood there fully exposed. Her long flowing hair was burnt off not even a residue of hair was visible to the naked eye.

She had burned patches up and down her fragile body. Her caramel complexion was now a reflection of inner side. She one of the first ones who was truly punished in a very mild way.

Her soul and other souls are blown back and forth by the terrible winds of a violent storm, without any rest. Then she was smothered in fire and brimstone. This symbolizes the power of lust to blow one about needlessly and aimlessly.

We moved onto the next level, that there was a person. This person was unfamiliar to me meaning I don't remember signing this person. This person was fading in and out. First, it was a light brown skin woman then a white older male. Apparently, this person was posed by two souls. Therefore, when she died they both came to hell.

● ● ●

Laimargia Epipedo (Gluttony Level)

Raven Penton aka Jack the Ripper, their crime was gluttony. Gluttony was normally associated with eating too much, but it has a broader connotation that includes trying to consume more of anything than you actually need, food included.

This puts a completely different meaning to the phrase "glutton for punishment" isn't as metaphorical as one might imagine. In addition to committing the deadly sin of gluttony by eating too much, one can do so by consuming too many resources overall water, food, energy, by spending inordinately to have especially rich foods, by spending inordinately to have too much of something cars, games, houses, music, etc., and so forth.

In their case, his guilty pleasure was eating the organs of his victims. The souls of the Gluttons who failed to utilize the gifts given to them by God in a meaningful and higher way, and wasted their lives in consuming excess and giving back nothing but garbage in their lives, are the ones who reside in the third level of hell.

The great dog Cerberus guards the gluttons such as Raven/Jack, forced to lie in a vile slush produced by ceaseless foul, icy rain and then to be nice we warm her/him in fire bath and then repeat. Cerberus was a ferocious, monstrous guard dog with three heads that bristle with snakes. The horrific beasts howl with excitement as we draw closer, leaping past the damned souls in their eagerness to get to me.

The three head dog runs and leaps, out-pacing. Its skin seems to have been flayed off of them, leaving nothing but bone and bloody sinew. Their teeth gleam in the darkness, great threads of saliva hanging off of its lips.

Cerberus's heads lends over to me and started to lick my face, they are almost on top of me. His heavy weight slams into me, knocking the breath out of me. They fall upon me, I slam demon-dog, it squeals, flying backwards, and makes a painful crack as it hits the far wall. Gathering my rage and stand back next to Beelzebub. Beelzebub threw some honey-cakes to the hungry dog to distract him.

"What did you do to them? Never mind. This was Naburus was a Marquis of Hell who has connections to Cerberus. He sometimes jumps in on the fun forcing the souls to feed on the rats, toads, and snakes, while they're filling their bellies until it burst.

● ● ●

Okniria Epipedo (Sloth Level)

Despite all the people who I checked in, here interesting person because, I remember reading about Andre. I never put the two together I thought it was two different kinds of people. They never put his picture in the newspaper. It looked like half of boys in Camden with a pick in his hair.

His fucking pants were hanging underneath his ass with his butt just hanging out for all to see. He reminded me of some of the men who live a life of drugs. There was always a bunch of black guys that hung on the corner on Line Street by my house. You could see all the track marks on his fucking arm. Here he was in hell.

Andre Keyshawn represents sloth was the avoidance of physical or spiritual work. Sloth was the most misunderstood of the Seven Deadly Sins. Often regarded as laziness, it was more accurately translated as apathy: when a person was apathetic, they no longer care about their duty to God and ignore their spiritual well-being.

Condemning sloth was a way to keep people active in the church in case they start to realize how useless religion and theism really are. He was shiftless, lazy, and good for nothing, price of shit. He was being thrown into snake pits.

● ● ●

After, his painful trip in the snake pit. The former are forever lashing out at each other in anger, furious and naked, tearing each other piecemeal with their teeth. The latter are gurgling in the black mud, slothful and sullen, withdrawn from the world. He whipped with a cat o' nine, which have sharp metal teeth bitten viciously through and shredded his skin. We just make sure we show him love with hot lava that was poured in his cuts.

A demon watched over the punishment from his little throne. He was laughing. This one had scales all over its body, giant jaws with huge teeth, and claws sticking out, along with sunken-in eyes. He was just enormous but it had razor sharp fins all over with one long arm and out of proportion feet.

Everything was deformed and twisted and out of proportion, out of symmetry, no symmetry, one arm longer and one shorter and just odd looking creatures, horrible looking things.

I was really starting to understand what was going with all these people. I still needed Beelzebub to tell more about was going on. This was the shit I was working for, great just what I wanted to do. I was beginning to wish wasn't so nosy.

● ● ●

Aplistia Epipedo (Greed Level)

Here was another black woman I checked in. She was a quiet and well-dressed woman when I first meet her. Her skin was flawless. Not even a piece of hair out of place. The beautiful woman I once was amazed to see when she came in now had bruises and cuts up and down her body.

Beelzebub then expressed to me about how Giana was abused throughout her marriage and how she killed her husband. I could understand why she was in hell but she was here for her greediness.

Giana Jennings, she was ruled by her greed. She was doomed by greed. She keeps the poor in their place, though, and prevents them from wanting to have more. Greed was a desire for material gain. Those whose attitude toward material goods deviated from the appropriate mean are punished by carrying a heavy boulder like weights on their back, which represents the wealth that they accumulated in their life. Then they were boiled alive in oil.

●●●

Zilevo Epipedo (Envy Level)

Now, we persistent to the fifth level of hell. I can't believe how many people were down here. So, many souls that fueled the fire in hell. I never felt so surprise and scared to see all the people I checked in I felt like I personally sent them here. I was wondering if I didn't check them in what would happen to them or to me if I didn't do my job. There stood in front of me was Edwin. He was a creepy white man.

Edwin Brawford, his love for another man's woman. Envy was the desire for others' traits, status, abilities, or situation. His envy was manifested in the individual who spurns love and opts instead for fury.

His punishment in hell will be put in freezing water. Then his eyes are sewn shut with wire. He was very lucky he has a potluck event day for the rest of his life.

"What is a potluck event?" I asked puzzled.

"Well a potluck is buried alive, flaying, disembowelment, impalement, abacination, human branding, castration, Chinese water torture, crushing, denailing, garrote, and strappado."

"Wow that is a lot of different types of torturement. Can you describe each one for me, please?"

"Sure."

He continued to tell me about each one as Edwin started to get his potluck for today. Buried alive, Premature burial leads to death through one or more of the following: asphyxiation, dehydration, starvation, or in cold climates hypothermia.

Although the human survival may be briefly extended in some environments as body metabolism slows, in the absence of oxygen, which was likely to be within 1-2 hours from burial time based on the consumption level, loss of consciousness will take place within 2 to 4 minutes and death by asphyxia within 5 to 15 minutes. Permanent brain damage through oxygen starvation was likely after a few minutes, even if the person was rescued before death.

If fresh air was accessible in some way, survival was more likely to be in the order of days in the absence of serious injury. Something he doesn't have to worry about because once everything was done he was back to normal and we repeated do anything we like him.

●●●

Envy was a desire to possess what others have, whether material objects, such as cars, or character traits, like a positive outlook or patience. Envious people, those guilty of committing the deadly sin of envy, will be punished in hell by being immersed in freezing water for all eternity.

Another one was flaying was the removal of skin from the body. Generally, an attempt was made to keep the removed portion of skin intact. At times, it gets messy if the skin falls off into pieces.

"Oh mine that sounds very painful!"

"Yes, it is but it so much fun to watch!"

Disembowelment was the removal of some or all of the organs of the gastrointestinal tract usually through a horizontal incision made across the abdominal area.

An old one but a good one was impalement was the traumatic penetration of an organism by an elongated foreign object such as a stake, pole, or spear, and this usually implies complete perforation of the central mass of the impaled body.

Abacination was a form of corporal punishment or torture, in which the victim was blinded by having a red-hot metal plate held before their eyes.

Human branding was the process in which a mark, usually a symbol or ornamental pattern, was burned into the skin of a living person, with the intention that the resulting scar makes it permanent. This was performed using a hot or very cold branding iron.

It therefore uses the physical techniques of livestock branding on a human, either with consent as a form of body modification; or under coercion, as a punishment or imposing masterly rights over an enslaved or otherwise oppressed person. It may also be practiced as a rite of passage such as within a tribe, or to signify membership in an organization such as a college fraternity or sorority.

Castration was any action, surgical, chemical, or otherwise, by which a male loses the functions of the testicles or a female loses the functions of the ovaries.

Chinese water torture was a process in which water was slowly dripped onto a person's forehead, allegedly driving the restrained victim insane. This form of torture was first described under a different name by Hippolytus de Marsalis in Italy in the 15th or 16th century.

Death by crushing or pressing was a method of execution that has a history during which the techniques used varied greatly from place to place. Any governing body no longer sanctions this form of execution.

De-nailing was the forcible extraction of the fingernails or toenails. This was a favorite method of medieval torture that retains its popularity in the 21st century. It was both efficient and extremely effective as a form of torture and, in modern use, causes limited physical injury: while brute-force tearing out can and does damage the cuticles, surgical extraction without anesthesia does not.

In its simplest form, the torture was conducted by spread-eagling the prisoner to a tabletop. They will secure the hands by chains around the wrists and the bare feet by chains around the ankles.

Then using a metal forceps or pliers often heated red-hot to individually grasp each nail in turn and slowly pry it from the nail bed before tearing it off the finger or toe. A crueler variant used in medieval Spain was performed by introducing a sharp wedge of wood or metal between the flesh and each nail and slowly hammering the wedge under the nail until it was torn free.

A garrote was a weapon, most often referring to a handheld ligature of chain, rope, scarf, and wire or fishing line used to strangle a person.

Strappado was a form of torture in which the victim's hands are first tied behind his or her back and suspended in the air by means of a rope attached to the wrists, which most likely dislocates both arms. Weights may be added to the body to intensify the effect and increase the pain.

● ● ●

Punishment for Edwin

"Today we are going to watch Edwin get the disembowelment as his potluck torture."

"Can we just move on?"

"Ok"

●●●

Yerifaneia Epipedo (Pride Level)

Here we have Dante Demarcus his pleasure was pride. Dante desired to be more important or attractive than others, failing to acknowledge the good work of others, and excessive love of self especially holding self out of proper position toward God.

The demons cut Dante leaving an open wound on him. The entrance wound was surrounded by a reddish-brown area of abraded skin, known as the abrasion ring, and small amounts of blood escape through.

An exit wound, on the other hand, was larger and more irregular, with extruding tissue and no abrasion ring. There was far bloodier that escapes an exit wound, and it can possibly be profuse.

Pride was excessive belief in one's abilities, such that you don't give credit to God. Pride was also failure to give others credit due them. Therefore, if someone's Pride bothers you, then you are also guilty of Pride.

It was defined that if one has nothing but love of self-perverted to hatred and contempt for one's neighbor. He was placed at this level in hell. Dante's skin was boiled off and slowly sliced off.

Then he put on a broken wheel. The breaking wheel a large wooden wagon wheel with many radial spokes. He was lashed to the wheel and their limbs were beaten with a club with the gaps in the wheel allowing the limbs to give way.

● ● ●

Orgi Epipedo (Wrath Level)

This level was where wrathful, the gloomy and depressed souls reside at this level of hell. These souls are filled with anger and wrath due to which they constantly keep on attacking other souls and at times bite themselves too. Nalia Franklin was anger and a wrathful person who was the sin of rejecting the love and patience.

Hell has no fury like a woman scorned; she should feel for others and opting instead for violent or hateful interaction. Instead, when the opportunity was given to her she turned away.

Her heart filled with so much anger. If she couldn't have Ridley, no one could. Therefore, she thought her wrath would be the interim solution. Ridley and his whole family are dead and she thinks she has won.

Condemnation of anger as a sin was thus useful to suppress efforts to correct injustice, especially the injustices of religious authorities. Although it was true that anger can quickly lead a person to an extremism, which was itself an injustice, that doesn't necessarily justify condemning anger entirely. It certainly doesn't justify focusing on anger but not on the harm which people cause in the name of love.

So angry people, especially those who are guilty of committing the deadly sin of anger or wrath, will be punished in hell by being dismembered of alive. Nalia and many others will fight each other on the surface.

The sullen lie gurgling beneath the water, withdrawn into a black sulkiness, which can find no joy in God or man or the universe. In the swamp-like water of the river, Zaebos a demon that was part human, part crocodile watches over her and the others just to make sure each person gets a turn to be dismembered.

Nalia tries to hide in the corner, but then was snatched up and ribbed apart from limb by limb by other demons, who laugh as they threw her body into the swamp.

"Who is that in the corner?"

"It is Nalia's son, he watches in the distance. You will meet him later but right now I will continue your walk through."

We continue to the next level. I really didn't know these people, just from when they first arrived.

●●●

Airesi Epipedo (Hersey Level)

Drusilla De Rais was on this level because of her belief or theory that was strongly at variance with established beliefs or customs about God. Her sin was known as Hersey.

Heresy was distinct from both apostasy, which was the explicit renunciation of one's religion, principles or a cause, and blasphemy, which was irreverence toward religion.

She was trapped in flaming tombs. Drusilla and other souls of the blasphemers, sodomites, and usurers are forever in a box that always on fire.

You can hear Drusilla screaming inside the tomb. Some demons are dancing around her as others are throwing more gasoline on her tomb. There are many tombs lined up and each of them was on fire. The smell of their flesh being burnt off them.

The violent blasphemies against God, they are stretched out naked with their face upward on the ground, as the burning rain pouring over them. I fletched back as if I was getting burnt, I remembered the days when hot oil popped out of the pan onto my skin how much it hurt, but the idea of lying there and raindrops of fire fell down I wasn't the pain I would enjoy. They also shout and curse God. The sodomites wander in the hot sand for eternity, naked, and squatting with their arms.

● ● ●

Via Epipedo (Violence Level)

Wow, even Damien was here. He was a cute white man. He was so nice. I was even surprised when he first came in a little toddler boy was standing in the lobby. The little boy was crying Damien was kind enough to talk to the boy and took him back into the daycare that near my desk.

Damien Grimsom well he will not be corporeally resurrected after this final judgment since he gave away his body through suicide. Instead, he will maintain his bushy form, with his own corpses hanging from the thorny limbs.

The suicides who have committed violence against them self are stunted and gnarled trees with twisting branches and poisoned fruit. At the time of final judgment, his bodies and others will hang from their branches thorny trees with black leaves. In those branches the Harpies, foul birdlike creatures with human faces, make their nests the overseers of these damned souls.

Beyond the wood was scorching sand where those who committed violence against God and nature are showered with flakes of fire that rain down against their naked bodies. Blasphemers and sodomites writhe in pain, their tongues more loosed to lamentation, and out of their eyes gushes forth their woe.

The Minotaur who snarls in fury and encircled within the river guards this. Phlegethon was filled with boiling blood, while centaurs armed with bows and arrows shoot those who try to escape their punishment. The stench here was overpowering.

●●●

Apati Epipedo (Fraud Level)

Now in these circles can be reached only by descending a vast cliff. We get on the back of

Geryon, a winged monster traditionally represented as having three heads or three conjoined bodies.

They are an image of fraud, having the face of an honest man on the body of a beautifully colored wyvern, with the furry paws of a lion and a poisonous sting in the pointy scorpion-like tail. The Geryon was our ride to travel through hell.

Hell even a doctor walked into my job and here he was. He was a fucking cocky motherfucker when he came in. He keeps talking about himself in the third person. Larry this and Larry that, that was all I heard until he left my desk.

● ● ●

Larry Williams has vowed conscious fraud. This was the level where Larry lived. This ring consists of river Phlegethon that consists of boiling blood and smells of strong fresh and clotted blood. As these people played with blood when they were alive, this level punishes them to be immersed in the boiling blood forever. The depth of immersion depends upon the degree of sin from ankle length to over the head.

● ● ●

Prodotes Epipedo (Traitors Level)

We moved onto the next level. It was starting to feel like we have been traveling through for hours. I was getting so tired. Beelzebub looked over at me and started asking me about another person I checked in.

"You remember Adolf Crawford from yesterday?"

"Yeah…he kept thanking me when I signed him in. Why you ask?

"Well, this is where traitors to those around him are punished here. Then he was lying supine on the ice, which covers him, except for his faces. He was punished more severely than the previous traitors were, since the relationship to those around him was an entirely voluntary one.

The frozen pool of Coytus was like a sheet of glass and the freezing breeze kills all the warmth present in the atmosphere. The winds are from the wings of Satan flapping eternally to freeze Adolf and the other souls by chilling the ice as their heads are facing upward to him and their eyes frozen with tears.

●●●

Here was the last person I checked in this week. It was Mrs. Maribeth. She was smiling even after I check her in. Maribeth Stone was filled with nothing but lust wrath, greed, pride, envy, gluttony person. She hops from each level of hell.

Each day she indoors different kinds of torment that feels never-ending. Despite she was being tortured in here in hell. She was always smiling. That was so weird. We finally reached our final stop. There stood in front of me was the tallest crimson red door ever did see.

●●●

Spiti (Home)

"Welcome Home...... Beelzebub said with a diabolic smile.

"What are you talking about?" I ask.

He looks at me and quietly says, "I'm sorry." His face was an impassive wall of stone as he turns to block to my path.

"You fucking bastard..." I whisper. Then a voice rings out, "Not so fast!" I was confused, a creature stood up and holds his hand out to gesture you toward a seat, saying, "Where are my manners?

Please, sit down. I will make you some tea. Beelzebub that will be all, Thank you!"

I am your boss...your husband. I was in shock. I stared at him. He was hideous to look at in his true form. He had four faces, each facing a different direction. One was like a man. To the right side of the man's face was a lion's face. The face of an ox was on the left side. An eagle's face was in the rear. He had horns on his head and was completely bald.

He had six pitch black eyes that all blinked at once and sunken in. He was beating his six jet-black wings in the wind. He was fat for one, like extremely obese. His body was covered tightly with sharp, pointed scales. When shed, the scales are dangerous to encounter

He smiles at me I could see rows of sharp shark-like teeth but his damn flaming breath. His skin was red like blood. He also had hooves for feet, with the appearance of polished brass.

Before I knew it, he turned into a man the man from last night......oh my god the ménage a trio I enjoyed so much. Wow, I think I would prefer this man instead the hideous fucker that stood in front of me.

Beelzebub vanishes in a puff of smoke and brimstone. I take a seat, feeling more confused than when I arrived. Soon, he returns with a small, steaming cup of tea.

"Thank you," I said. He looks a little uncomfortable and says gruffly, "Don't mention it."

"What's going on? Why is this happening to me?" "Who are you?" I asked.

"Since birth, it has to be the joining of a human and angelic soul. You are someone who sits on the divide of both worlds. You've had the power all along; you just don't know how to use it yet. You are very special, more than you know. You are the one who has the keys to the Gates of Hell.

You have a power unique to you in all of history, the power to change history. So, welcome to this hell you have forded from your own manipulate hands, welcome to the death and destruction only rage and malice conceive... Welcome Miss Alena Chadwick, welcome to a place where no one ever leaves.

"I don't understand. What does it mean?" I ask.

He was just a whisper in my ear but now he was real I thought he was just a joke until he said.

"Do you remember? Logan, the guy you fucked the other night. Well that was me! I am also your father, Ryder."

"My father was Ryder Franklin." I really didn't know what to say about that.

I had fun with Logan don't get me wrong I had nothing to say about what he said. The thought that I fucked my father sickened my stomach.

"Oh…what I have another surprise for you."

"No more surprises! I can't take anymore."

"Well, you know how your mother takes very little of her mother?"

"Yeah…well what about it?"

"Your grandmom was Nalia. The woman that was being dismembered."

"No way……you are fucking lying!"

"No I'm not! She really is Lilith who was reincarnated and doesn't even know it."

I was speechless. I really didn't know what to say. All I could do was think about the things I saw and the things I now knew. Into the pit of hell, we all have fallen in the empty grave that awaits us. Internal burns from the fire, cold rain, ice, with a never-ending torture; we are devoured by our own darkest desires.

● ● ●

My New Life

My chains are ever binding as it holds me back. There was no escape for my savage. As, I lay in his bed he rips, tears, and claws around my flesh walls. The driving pain thru to madness, my mind was here no more. He was indefatigable. He takes me by the hand leads to our throne; he looks at me and says, "You're one of us now. We watch out for our own!"

All around you, the stream of demons thickens and rushes past, the beating of their wings filling the world. They spread out across the earth, bringing darkness and flame wherever they go, each waving and grinning at me as they pass.

Day after day after day, I will be here in this hell. My demon fights for freedom while I wage the holy war to keep my soul. Finally, it all made sense it was not by luck; it was by destiny for me to get this job.

This was not the everlasting peace I wish to live eternally in heaven I dreamed that I would be able to live see my mother again instead I live with my sin and see my deadbeat dad. My father wasn't meant to stay in my life, because his home was here.

Now I know the truth he was my father and my husband now, all in one.

•••

I am now the queen of the realm of the forces of evil. I am the sin of my father. The sins of my father have caused me so much pain when I was young. I couldn't help but believe the lies that rolled so off his tongue when he told me I was worthless and get out of their sight.

It all echoed. The hurt and humiliation familiar it was all I ever knew I have caused. I knew that my father loved me so it was worth the pain from him, each wound and word my father marked me with.

•••

My Husband, My One Night Stand

Satan aka, Lucifer was impotent, ignorant, and full of hate, in contrast to the all-powerful, all-knowing, and loving nature of God. His personality was just a big ball of anger, yet he hides it extremely well with a sadistic and usually perverted sense of humor. He enjoys torture, violence, sex, and evil in all kinds of ways.

I don't even bother speaking to him because odds are he'll lie to me. He's a pathological liar to the point where I don't think he can help himself. He always wants more than what he deserves and if he doesn't get what he wants he throws a tantrum and then still plots to get what he wants anyway.

His karma was so horrible that it's amazing. He's found a way to deflect all his bad karma onto people that are nearby him so that would explain why shitty things always happens around him even when he doesn't mean to, but nothing bad normally happens to him. This was my husband what else can I say.

I knew that I deserved for being less than human waste. I must be punished. My twisted lies and anger was right and true so unworthy of anyone's time. The trials I put my friends and family through each bitter word he said to me has surely taken its toll each time he strike and beat me down leaving scars upon my soul.

• • •

My Revelation

The Sins of the Father made this choice near impossible. Now everything made sense. I decided to continue down this trail of pain. Darkness covers me like a blanket and the eerie mist surrounding me as the damned soul float around me to keep company.

I feel like there was no way to flee me, I run, stumble and try to break free. My heart becomes black with other people's hatred. I have nowhere to hide from this hatred. Happiness was now fleeing and I feel all hope was gone. Darkness embraces me like a child. The darkness surrounds me. I am all alone in this place.

My new world was so empty. All what that was left was the pain and no sunshine to light my way. I drown in tears, my heart was crying. There was no one to notice must less anyone who may care.

My soul doesn't belong to me, it was now his to have forever or until he lets me go. This darkness has swallowed me, and now I am trapped in this sad world but the sad part was I have felt more at home than I ever thought.

This was my home. This was mine......
HELL.